MW01125426

EXTINCTION

HELL ON EARTH BOOK 3

IAIN ROB WRIGHT

SALGAD PUBLISHING GROUP

For Molly,
welcome to this wonderful world.

With love to my Patrons!

*Hallsworth, Andre Nieuwland, Tracy Guinther, Michael
Archambault, Kristie Stailey, Deborah Ross, Christine Brown, Ricky
Davey, Deirdre Stuart, Dinshaw Dotivala, Elizabeth Bryson, T. M.
Bilderback*

"I know not with what weapons World War III will be fought, but World War IV will be fought with sticks and stones."
   Albert Einstein

"Death is not extinction. Neither the soul nor the body is extinguished or put out of existence."
   Oliver Joseph Lodge

"I ain't heard no fat lady!"
   Captain Hiller, Independence Day (1996), 20th Century Fox

1

MARCY

"Max, come back here! It's not safe."

"There's food, mummy."

Marcy crouched beside the flat-tyred Volkswagen and waved at her son. At four years old, Max hadn't yet developed an adequate danger-radar, which meant he ran off wildly at every opportunity, and trying to control him during the apocalypse was no easier than it had been before. The key difference was the severe shortage of alcohol to help recover mummy's senses once evening came.

Christ, I'd kill for a G & T.

Marcy's bond with her enthusiastic son had only galvanised since a demon invasion had driven them from their home. There were no more rushed shopping trips or stress-filled play dates with bitchy mum-friends. Now, she and Max gave each other their absolute attention and had become inseparable—an apocalyptic team, scrounging through bins and hiding out in burnt buildings. It was a simpler life, having only to worry about food and shelter, instead of mortgage payments and cheating husbands, yet being terrified constantly did eventually take its toll. Marcy's hands shook endlessly, and she started most mornings by anxiously vomiting. Damn her husband for not being here with them.

"Max, be careful," she snapped. "We don't know if we're alone out here."

Max peered at her from behind the wheelie bin he leant against and frowned in the way only inquisitive four-year-olds can. "I don't like the monsters."

Marcy looked left and right, and then scurried from her hiding spot. She crossed the road and made it over to the bins. "We haven't seen any today, but we still have to be careful."

"Okay, mummy." He gave her a hug, and she winced as she felt his ribs poking her. "Look though."

She eased her son away. "What have you got there?"

Max yanked a crumpled pizza box from the bin and held it out like a prize. He lifted the lid with an excited smile, but his expression turned to a frown when all that greeted him was an unravelled condom—Max had taken to calling them 'wet worms'. Now he groaned.

"I want pizza."

"I know, honey, but I think all the pizza is gone. I still have a couple of chocolate bars in the backpack. You want one?"

He shook his head and pouted. "I want pizza."

"One day, there'll be pizza again, sweetheart, I promise."

It wasn't easy lying to her son. Food was becoming an issue. The supermarkets were full of stray dogs and other scavengers. Anything not in a can was either spoiled or devoured. Searching through bins was becoming a waste of time. They survived the last couple of weeks by rummaging through cupboards in empty houses. Sometimes they found bodies. Max knew to close his eyes and call to her whenever that happened.

Six weeks now since the gates had opened.

Six weeks since those first horrifying reports on the news.

Six weeks since Max had last seen his father.

Marcy's sweet little boy didn't deserve this. No child did.

But at least hers was still alive. I'm the luckiest mother in the world. Maybe the only mother…

"Come on, Max. It's getting dark. We should find somewhere to sleep tonight."

"Can we find somewhere with a boy's bedroom? I want toys."

She smiled, buoyed that colourful trinkets could still distract her child. Max's innocence protected him in ways she envied—he looked neither forward nor back, only at the reality of the moment. For Marcy, their inescapable fate created an endless maelstrom in her tummy. Humanity's future had become ticking seconds on a rusty clock. She couldn't protect Max forever. Not in this world.

A noise.

Marcy pulled Max closer to keep him quiet, and then tilted her head, sure she had heard something.

No, not heard—she had felt something. Vibrations beneath the worn soles of her shoes.

Thwump.

There it was again. Something distant. Something big. Big enough that the ground shook.

"Oh no..." Marcy felt the ligature around her guts tighten. "Max, we need to get inside."

Max had learned his mother's body language well enough that he didn't argue. Sticking close together, the two of them took off across the road heading for a row of shops further along the pavement. Marcy had made a mental note of a ransacked charity shop with a broken door they had passed by earlier. That was where she headed now.

Max's short legs had to hop to keep up with his mother's frantic strides. "The monsters are coming, aren't they?"

"Yes, sweetheart. We need to get indoors."

The charity shop lay just ahead—a dead cat fouling the gutter marked its location. Funny, the methods she used to navigate this new, horrifying world. No more sat navs. No more directions. Just dead cats and burnt out cars.

Marcy yanked Max into the broken doorway. The shop's interior smelt damp—rank and rotten. A pile of moulding paperbacks littered the entryway rug. Muddy footprints marked their pages. The broken door was irreparable, but the plate glass window still stood intact. Looters had put through the windows of most shops, but charity shops were not prize pickings.

Max released his mother's hand and went running deeper into

the shop, picking through the detritus of abandoned knickknacks. The first thing he grabbed was a grungy bunny rabbit. He clutched it by his side. "I like it here."

She shushed him. "Just keep moving towards the back."

The demons acted more as roaming gangs than fastidious searchers, and if you kept off the streets, they usually passed right by. The early days of the apocalypse had seen mass slaughters, but human beings were now so rare that the demons seemed uninterested in picking off stragglers. Marcy assumed they were focused on something greater—perhaps murdering a last bastion of humanity somewhere. Maybe people were fighting back.

She hoped.

If there was someplace safe—truly safe—then Marcy had to get her son there. She couldn't protect him on her own. Not forever.

"Mum, can I have this?"

Marcy looked over and saw that her son had obtained a hobbyhorse. Its brown and black fur was still plush and upright, and both beady eyes were in place. Such a rudimentary toy would have held no interest to her son two months ago, but now, in the absence of electronic entertainment, it was what leapt out at him.

"Sure, you can have it, but no more talking."

"No, you cannot have that!" someone shouted from the back. "How dare you come in here and take things that don't belong to you? This is a charity. You are stealing from a charity!"

Marcy stumbled in fright and collided with the cash register, which slid across the desk on rubber feet and made a screeching sound. "I-I-I was… we were… we are just looking for somewhere safe to hide. I'm sorry, sir."

"Don't you sir me, you thief. Get out of here before I call the police!"

"The police? Are you crazy?"

"Mummy says the police have all gone away," said Max gravely to the shadow at the back.

An old man stepped out of the gloom and entered the dim shaft of sunlight filtering in from outside. His eyes were red and swollen, cheeks blotchy. A feral look about him—a crazed look.

Marcy threw out her hand. "Come here, Max! We should leave this gentleman in peace."

"But the monsters, mummy. You said the monsters were coming."

She sighed. Max was right. Something was coming. But this old man made her feel more threatened than being exposed outside. "We'll hide somewhere else," she said. "Let's go."

Max moved towards her, but the old man struck like a snake and caught the boy by the wrist. "Hold it right there, sonny."

"Mum!"

Marcy's hands curled into fists. "Don't touch him, you crazy old fuck!"

The old man shot her a bug-eyed glance, while still clutching her son. Max struggled, the grungy bunny in his free hand flopping like it was having a seizure. "What did you call me, miss?"

"Let my son go, right now. We're leaving."

"He's trying to steal this horse. This horse was donated to charity. Your boy is trying to steal from charity."

Marcy strode towards the old imbecile. "No, he just forgot he was holding it. Let him go."

"You people disgust me."

Strangely, the comment offended Marcy. Perhaps because it sounded as though he meant it so vehemently—that she truly disgusted him. "What do you mean, *you people*?"

"I mean, mothers letting their kids run amok. Whoring about and smoking drugs while their kids get up to who knows what. I see it on that Jez Karl show every morning. Scum, the lot of you."

The Jez Karl show? This guy had lost the plot. There had been no television for weeks. "I'm sorry, sir, but you're mistaken. I'm a married woman, and Max is a well brought-up boy. We made a mistake coming in here, that's all. Let him go, and we'll leave."

"No. I'm calling the police."

"You're mad."

Max struggled and the old man yanked his arm, making him cry out. "Mum, he's hurting me."

Marcy reacted. She closed the short distance between the two of them and lashed out, shoving the old man under the chin and knocking his head back. He cried out in surprise and released Max. The boy scurried over to Marcy's side and she gathered him close. Pointing a finger in the old man's face, she spat with anger. "Maybe you've got Alzheimer's or something, I don't know, but my son and I are leaving, and you will back the Hell away."

The old man did the opposite. He lunged at her.

A jolt of pain shot through the back of Marcy's hand, and when she looked, she saw blood.

"Mummy, the man has a knife."

"Stay back. Just…"

The old man lunged again, his delusion evolving to full-blown mania—feral expression twisting and distorting like his face was made of maggots. His snarling mouth lacked teeth. His grey tongue darted in and out of crusted lips. "Bloody whores and thieves. Ruining the country." He slashed a small penknife and missed Marcy's face by an inch. If it had been a longer blade, she would have had a hole through her nose. "I'll kill you, bitch!"

"Mummy!"

"Run, Max. Run!"

Marcy shoved her son towards the broken doorway. The old man's aged joints popped as he pursued her, and he turned the air blue with his furious heckle.

Max made it outside onto the pavement ahead of Marcy who was a step behind him. He was crying out loud—the chase summoning panic. "It's okay," she told him, pulling him along the pavement. "It's okay, sweetheart."

"Mummy, he's behind us."

Marcy shielded her son and faced the old lunatic. He stalked towards her with that pathetic yet deadly little blade out in front of him. "I'm going to do the world a favour, you dirty whore."

Marcy covered her son's ears. "Fuck you, you crazy old fuck!"

"How dare you?" In the grey glow of the waning sun, the old man unveiled his true madness: shit and piss caked his trousers; bruises blotted the tissue-paper skin of his forearms.

Marcy kept Max behind her and threw her arms out in front of her. "Stay bac-"

Suddenly the old man went airborne. One minute he was

there, about to strike her, the next he was launching into the sky like a rocket. He didn't make a sound. Marcy's vision blurred. Her hearing buzzed.

She heard her son's terrified screams.

Marcy turned her head to see what stood over her shoulder.

Max dropped the grungy bunny on the floor and clung to Marcy's thigh. "Mummy, it's a big monster."

Marcy froze. She'd known this moment would eventually come, but now it had, and she could do nothing except yield to its inevitability. The suffering was about to end. Her son's life was about to end. It was a relief in some ways. But in others, she was a mother failing her son.

She muttered one word.

"Please."

The twenty-foot angel glared at Marcy, the same disgusted expression on its face that the old man had worn before being launched into oblivion. The angel had saved her, but it had been no noble deed. With its perfect, beautiful, snarling face, this giant abomination wanted her death for itself. "Bugs," said the angel in a booming voice. "Insects and bugs."

Marcy pulled Max into her bosom. The boy trembled, and it hurt her heart. "Be brave," she said. "Mummy's got you."

The angel reared back, massive hand outstretched and ready to swat her like the bug it deemed her to be.

Just let it be quick.

Bang! Clatter-tatter.

Marcy flinched. The angel tottered back, reaching out and catching its balance against the roof of the charity shop. It let out an angered roar and spun around, ripping out a section of roof tiles, which shattered against the pavement like giant hailstones.

Bang-bang! Clatter-tatter.

Marcy clutched her son tighter, stifling his terrified screams.

Someone was shooting.

In the early days of the apocalypse, gunfire had been as common as bird song. Marcy had not realised Britain possessed so much firepower, but in the first days of war, it seemed every family heirloom—antique revolvers and dusty shotguns—came out of the cupboard to join the modern equipment of the nation's armed services. Then, a week or two later, the gunfire had stopped and only silence remained.

The gunfire had returned in anthem.

Bang bang! Clatter-clatter-tatter.

The angel swatted its arms like a swarm of bees was attacking it. To Marcy's surprise, the angel bled. Bloody holes pockmarked its body—bullets finding their mark—but that was impossible. Angels couldn't be harmed. The news reports declared it with absolute certainty before going off air.

"Take that, you big piece of stank!" someone shouted.

The angel spotted its attackers and stomped across the road. Marcy saw three men—one black, one white, and one Middle-Eastern with baggy trousers and shirt. Each of them sported guns and were firing at the approaching angel.

No, thought Marcy. *It's they who are the angels.*

Marcy wanted to make good use of the distraction by running for cover, yet she was rooted in place. The men had injured the angel, but it was undeterred, picking up speed as it stamped across the road. One man legged it across the street, getting the angel's attention. It was the white man—a massively muscled guy wearing a tight black t-shirt. He dodged between two parked cars, using them as obstacles to keep the angel at bay.

What was he doing? He would be a sitting duck.

One of the other men emerged from a side street. It was the black man, a lad with a bright green baseball cap. He held what looked like a bottle of whiskey in his hand and lit it on fire.

Marcy watched the flaming whiskey bottle arc through the sky before coming down and shattering against the distracted angel's back. Flames engulfed it and sent it into a panicked spin.

"Take that, you lanky asshole!"

The angel's deep bellow became an animalistic screech. The flames grew higher, singeing the air. Trapped in agony, the angel fled, disappearing down the road and slipping behind the row of shops.

Several moments passed while the three men let the dust settle, then they came racing across the road towards Marcy and

Max. Marcy cowered, having no reason to trust these men any more than she had the crazy old man or angel. Everything living had the potential to kill you in this new world—and probably would.

"You okay, luv?" asked the lad in the green baseball cap. When he spoke, she glimpsed metal in his mouth.

"W-Who are you?"

"I'm Vamps. These are my bros, Mass and Aymun."

"It is a joy to see a female soul," said the Middle-Eastern gentleman in a thick accent. He gave a little bow.

"You'll have to excuse him," said Vamps. "He's from the desert or summin'. Got here by way of Hell Gate. Are you okay, luv? Your little boy okay?"

Marcy moved Max away from her slightly so that she could examine him. His eyes were wet, his nose snotty, but he was no longer crying. She turned him to face the three men. "It's okay. This is Vamps, Mass, and... I'm sorry..."

"Aymun, my dear. My name is Aymun."

Max waved a hand coyly, but did not speak.

Vamps grinned at the boy, exposing two gold fangs. "You must be a right gangster, little man, looking after your ma out here. What's your name?"

"M-Max."

"Good to meet you, Max. Hey, you know what, I think I have something for you." Vamps nodded to his muscly white friend who turned around to expose a backpack. Unzipping it and fumbling inside, Vamps pulled out a colourful packet and handed it to Max. "Here ya go, bud. You like these?"

"Haribo! They're my favourite."

Vamps smiled again, flashing those teeth. "Good thing it's a family pack, huh? Should last you all day."

"I think you'll be surprised," said Marcy, giggling with joy at a stranger showing kindness to her son. Those days had seemed long gone. "Thank you for saving us. I... I have a few things in my pack you can have but—"

Vamps waved a hand and cut her off. "We don't want your

stuff, luv. We do just fine. The streets ain't so bad once you know how things go down."

"I'm afraid I spent most of my life as an accountant."

The big guy—Mass, apparently—shrugged his wide shoulders. "S'okay. Aymun here used to be a terrorist. Past's the past, innit?"

"Are you… are you comparing accountants to terrorists?"

Mass shrugged again.

"I was no terrorist," said Aymun. "Just a soldier born to one side fighting against those on another. Now there are no sides. We all must be as one."

Vamps gave Marcy a sly smirk. "What Aymun is try'na say is we all need to look out for each other. It's us against them."

"Really?" asked Marcy, trusting the situation enough now to relax her tense shoulders. "Because that would make you the first good guys we've met in weeks."

Vamps nodded as if he understood. "You fancy tagging along with us? I'm sure we can rustle up some more sweeties for your boy."

Marcy attempted to reply, but wavered. "You're…. really what you say you are? You won't hurt us?"

All three men shook their heads.

"Only things we hurt are demons," said Vamps. "So, tagging along or not?"

Marcy grinned. "Hmm? Stay here waiting to get attacked again, or go with three heavily armed men who just saved my life. Hell yes we're tagging along! Thank you, thank you, thank you."

Vamps laughed and patted her on the back. It was a friendly gesture, not lascivious in any way. Ironic, because in her earlier life, this street-wise kid would have frightened the life out of her. Today, in this moment, she was eager to trust the lad with her life. *Please just let him be what he claims to be.*

"Thanks for being our friends," said Max, already chomping on his sweets. "I miss having friends."

Vamps put an arm around the boy as if he were a big brother. "Let's go find you some more then, bud. We could all use more friends."

2

GUY GRANGER

"It's beautiful," said Lieutenant Tosco on the bridge.

Gazing out through the same long glass window Captain Guy Granger was inclined to agree. The sight greeting them most certainly was beautiful. As perfect and as sublime as a mirage —but real.

Skip stroked his wiry, grey beard and grinned from ear to ear. "Well done, you stubborn Brits!"

Guy tried to count the number of ships amassed in the waters outside Portsmouth but gave up after ninety. More than a hundred warships huddled together in the Channel, large and small, from many nations. Most were British, but Guy also spotted French, German, Belgian, and Spanish flags painted on hulls. Tosco had done what he could over the past weeks to discover the situation in Western Europe. What spotty reports he'd gathered hinted human resistance was inland around the capitals. That left naval forces of little use to nations like France and Germany with their capitals Paris and Berlin. Britain, however, being an island, was an obvious rallying point for rudderless sailors. This was a place a seafaring man could go to wage war against his enemy—and it was glorious.

Ships everywhere.

"I think I even see a pair of Yankee ships," said Tosco. "And look, that's a goddamn German nuclear sub. You could flatten a city with what they have on board."

The mention of nuclear capabilities turned Guy's stomach. A miracle no country had let loose its sparrows of death during the moment the world fell. When the direst of times had arrived, no world leader had pressed that big red button. There was something comforting about that. Perhaps mankind wasn't so bad.

Guy cleared his throat and let the crew hear him. For those not present in the bridge, he switched on the ship-wide intercom. "Men and women of the USCG Hatchet, this is your captain speaking. As you all see from the railings, humanity is alive and well in the United Kingdom." He chuckled as a cheer rang out from the decks. "We are low on food, thick with injury, and many of us have contemplated the future with bleak souls and heavy hearts. None of us knew where our fates would lead us. Yet, today, we have arrived to greet our fellow man and add our might to this great beast of defiance you see amassed before you. We are about to enter the port of Portsmouth. Anglophiles amongst you might already know this port goes back to Roman times, but we will help ensure it survives even longer." Another cheer. "We have radioed ahead, and our arrival is welcomed. We are among friends, and so must act as appreciative guests, ambassadors for our respective nations. The world has not ended. Captain Granger out."

Those in the bridge beamed so widely Guy worried they might get lockjaw. The old chief, Skip, looked like he might cry, but he kept it together long enough to take Guy aside briefly. "You think things are better than we thought? Have the Brits fought back?"

"Let's not get ahead of ourselves, Chief. There's a lot of manpower here, granted, but until we speak with whoever's in charge, we shouldn't assume anything. The last thing we need is to give the people aboard the Hatchet false hope. It's been a long journey."

Skip nodded. "Aye, that it has."

In the last week, people had reached their tipping points. Men and woman threw themselves over the railings with alarming regularity, and the Hatchet had lost more than a dozen souls—including three sailors. There had also been a spate of violence, no doubt stemming from the cramped confines and strict rations. The ship had bordered on anarchy.

But today was a new day.

Guy turned to Tosco. "Lieutenant, spread word that no one is to disembark until arrangements are made. I do not want an unruly stampede onto allied soil."

"Yes sir. Will I be coming ashore with the landing party?"

Guy nodded. "I shall take you and Skip." Then he turned to his petty officer, Bentley, sitting at the Hatchet's main console. He placed a hand on her shoulder. "Bentley, let British Command know we're requesting a berth."

Bentley did as commanded, and Guy left the bridge to oversee the rest of his people. The passengers and crew would be excited. That was dangerous. Excited people struggled to contain themselves, and the glorious sight of land might push some of them into a frenzy. So Guy spent the next hour moving between the Hatchet's decks and speaking with civilians, assuring them they would be taken care of. He also reminded his crew of their duty. By the time he finished his rounds, Guy was only slightly more confident that order would remain.

He stood stiffly on the foredeck as the Hatchet drifted into an allocated berth. Off the Portside bow, HMS Ocean towered over their smaller Coast Guard cutter and reminded Guy how few resources he actually wielded. The massive Royal Navy vessel was a helicopter carrier, and Guy spotted half-a-dozen Apache attack choppers lined up on its main deck. It gave him a warm glow to imagine a downpour of Hellfire missiles streaking down on the enemy from the clouds—like the wrath of God himself.

Were things truly as good as they looked here? Compared to what Guy had witnessed at Norfolk base all those weeks ago, Portsmouth was a well-oiled machine. The drizzly sky buzzed with small recon choppers, and masses of riflemen patrolled the docks. It would take a whole lot of demons to overrun this place.

That didn't mean they couldn't though.

Tosco and Skip joined Guy at the railings. Tosco handed him a radio. "Lieutenant-Colonel Spencer on the wire for you, sir."

"Thank you, Lieutenant." Guy took the radio and put it to his lips. "Lieutenant-Colonel Spencer, this is Captain Guy Granger of the United States Coast Guard. Thank you for allowing us to dock, Portsmouth. Over."

"You're more than welcome, Captain," came a voice from a mouth that sounded like it was sucking plums. "We're having ourselves quite the tea party here, as you can see. Can't let our enemy have all the fun, can we? Over."

"Never a truer word spoken, Lieutenant-Colonel. Are you in command of operations here?"

"Oh no, old boy. That privilege falls to General Wickstaff, but the good general is otherwise engaged. You'll have to settle for a lowly lieutenant-colonel for now."

Guy chuckled. Maybe it was just being so long at sea, but he liked the stuffy old lieutenant-colonel (pronounced 'left-tenant' in these foreign lands). "Meeting any superior officer is a welcomed comfort," he admitted.

"Had it tough out there on the big blue, old boy?"

"You might say that. You're not a sea dog yourself?"

"British Army, man and boy. Spent most my stretch with 202 Signal Squadron, but spent the last few years as head of recruitment. Some fine young lads I've seen come and go. Pains me to think about them now. Anyway, enough jawing, I suspect you would like to come ashore?"

Guy shivered at the thought of being on solid ground. "That would be most welcome, sir. The sea is my mother, but no man wants to spend every day with his old lady."

A bark of chesty laughter on the other end, then: "I can't argue with that, old boy. You and your people are free to disembark, but I'm afraid they can't pass through the main checkpoint until they've had the once over."

"Understandable. Where should I direct my landing party? I would very much like to lend aid where needed, but I have injured civilians on board that need attending to first."

"Head to the Customs building, Captain Granger, and someone will be with you shortly. It's been a pleasure meeting you. Ta-ta, for now. Over"

"Likewise, Lieutenant-Colonel. Over and out." Guy handed

the radio back to Tosco and took a deep breath. The stuffy old officer had seemed as laid back as can be, a good sign. No hint of being under threat here.

"What the Hell does 'ta-ta' mean?" asked Tosco.

"Think it means goodbye," explained Skip.

Guy wasn't listening. The Hatchet clunked into place beside the cement pier, and the catwalk lowered. Guy had all his remaining officers beside Tosco lined up to block the walkway and prevent people spilling out in a mad rush. Already the civilians on board were bunching together and shoving one another. Some of them waved excitedly at the crewman working high up on the decks of the massive HMS Ocean.

Guy climbed the railing and turned to address his people. "Men and women of the Hatchet, settle down, please. We have permission to disembark, but I will remind you we are visitors here. The United Kingdom has long been our ally, and today it welcomes us with open arms, but behave yourselves or face my consequences. My officers will disembark you in groups, and if anyone tries to jump the queue or disobey instructions, they will spend the rest of the day in a holding cell. You want to stretch your legs, I understand, so don't sabotage yourselves. Act like civilised human beings. Our enemy cannot take that away from us."

With that, Guy slipped behind his officers and trotted down the ramp. That same ramp had seen him flee Norfolk only weeks before. It felt surreal to still be alive after so much death, but here he was.

Skip and Tosco followed him in silence, glancing around with awe. The double-impact of stepping onto *terra firma*, twinned with the sight of the largest modern naval force—possibly ever—assembled was unsettling. For weeks, they had lived an isolated existence aboard the Hatchet, and now they were ants stepping into a colossal nest not their own. Guy felt insignificant, which was liberating. Maybe he could stop being responsible for the lives of so many. Someone else could give the orders. He could hang up his hat and go find his children at last. Kyle and Alice, that's all he cared about.

He needed to see them.

A small party of British naval officials met Guy on the pier. The fact they sported clipboards made him grin. Such a thing was absurd, yet endearingly representative of man's fastidious nature and love of creating order from chaos. The British officials directed Guy to the customs building that Lieutenant-Colonel Spencer had told him about. There they were left alone to settle in. Tosco was quick to spot a tea urn filled with hot water, alongside UHT milk, tea bags, and—

"Coffee," he shouted. "Oh my sweet Lord, they have coffee. Who wants a cup?"

"I'll take two," said Skip. "I've been having shameful dreams about coffee, son."

Guy chuckled. "I'll take a tea, please, Lieutenant. My nerves are enough on edge as it is."

"You know," said Tosco. "I've gone my whole life and never tasted tea. I think I'll join you, sir. When in Rome, right?"

"Good point," said Skip. "Maybe we should do as the natives do."

Guy shook his head, still smiling. "That they have coffee leads me to believe that the English don't turn murderous when someone refuses tea."

"Still," muttered Skip. "Why risk it? I'll have a mug of tea, please, Tosco."

Tosco chewed his lip and looked sheepish. "Great, um, who knows how to make it?"

Guy sighed and had to tell him. Tosco had many talents, but making hot beverages was apparently beyond him. Eventually he got it though, and a few moments later they were all sipping gloriously hot liquid. A petite woman stomped into the customs building, cursing under her breath and wiping her hands against herself. Late thirties, fit and attractive, she wore stained khaki trousers over a plain white t-shirt. Oil streaked her hands and arms. She spotted them and smiled.

"Greetings, men!"

"Hi," said Tosco. "We're waiting to speak with someone in

charge. General Wickstaff ideally. Do you know where he is? We've been waiting here a while."

The woman raised a black eyebrow. "And you might be?"

"Lieutenant Tosco, ma'am, United States Coast Guard. We're here to parlay, so we'd appreciate you getting your superior."

"Ah, so you're not the Captain of the Hatchet, despite acting like it?"

Tosco frowned. "Well, no, th—"

"And to my reckoning you've been waiting here, safely in the warmth, with fresh tea, for all of twenty minutes, so let's not be dramatic, ay? You chaps are aware we have coffee, right?"

"We wanted to try the tea," explained Skip sheepishly.

The woman smirked and chuckled to herself. "We're not simple tribesman, you know? You don't have to savour our local delicacies lest you offend us. Now, which one of you two remaining gentlemen is Captain Granger?"

Guy had already stood, although he didn't remember when. Despite the woman's dishevelled appearance, she possessed a commanding aura that had brought him to attention. "I'm Captain Granger, ma'am. Pleased to meet you…?"

The woman offered her hand to shake. "General Wickstaff. Pleased to have you in my home, Captain."

Guy almost choked and shook the woman's hand vigorously. Afterwards, he wiped oily residue off on his trousers.

Wickstaff examined her soiled palms and wiped them off on her shirt. "Ah, sorry about that. You must forgive my appearance; I've been tinkering with a Challenger 2 we have on base. Poor thing got scuppered in Afghanistan and was brought here as a display piece. Could use the bugger right now, so I've been trying to get it working."

"You know how to fix tanks?" said Skip, bushy eyebrows dancing.

The woman shrugged as if it was no big deal. "I spent my career with the Royal Armoured Corp, you pick up a few things."

Guy cleared his throat. "Thank you for receiving us, General. We feared there'd be nothing here when we set off, but it appears you have quite the operation."

"I inherited command from Field Marshal Mackay. The blighter dropped dead of a heart attack two weeks ago now. He was eighty-two, so I suppose I can't begrudge the fellow. Field Marshal duties typically fall to the head of the Armed Forces, currently Prince Charles, but who needs a soddin' blue blood coming and messing things up? I hear there's a bunker under Buckingham Palace, so I suspect he's down there now, growing plants under a UV light—mad sod."

Guy was a little lost by all this, so he just smiled and nodded. "We're happy to add our forces to your own, General."

"Temporarily," added Tosco. "In all likelihood, we will resupply and return home."

"Ah, at my expense, I presume?" Wickstaff made herself a cup of coffee from the urn. "Never could stand tea," she explained, sipping at the hot drink.

"If you don't wish to resupply us," said Tosco, "then I am sure we can move further down the coast and find someone else willing to."

"Oh, do be quiet, lad. You're giving my arse quite the headache. Lieutenant," she eyeballed him coolly, "anyone not here in Portsmouth is, I assure you, on their way here to Portsmouth. We are the only scrap of unsoiled paper left on the roll. We have patrols bringing survivors in almost daily, and none of them report anything being out there but demons and filth. This is humanity's last beachhead, at least in this neck of the woods. By all means, move on if you want to discover that for yourselves."

"There are other last stands going on," argued Tosco. "I've spoken to resistance in France, Belgium—"

"Not for us," she interrupted. "This is Alpha and Omega for us. The radio lines are almost silent, and no other military force exists that could be of any use to us in the battles ahead. We are on our own, and so I'm rather uninterested in resupplying you folks just to send you on your merry way. Stay and help, or don't, but don't make demands of me, gentlemen. Your cocks aren't big enough. Why are you even here in the first place?"

"My children are here," said Guy. "My... my kids are somewhere here."

Wickstaff raised an eyebrow. "And you appropriated a vessel and crew from your homeland to come get them? How very treasonous of you."

Guy swallowed. "It wasn't that simple."

"I suspect not. Look, I don't have kids, so I can't say I understand why people love the grubby little blighters so much, but I realise it would take quite the leader to gain the loyalty of a crew enough to make them desert their homes. I also see many civilians aboard your ship. Rescued?"

"Every one of them," said Skip. "Captain Granger is the reason any of us are alive."

"Part of the reason," amended Tosco with a sniff.

Wickstaff looked at Guy and nodded her head sideways at Tosco. "He always like this?"

"Pretty much. He's good in a fight though."

Tosco grunted.

Wickstaff smiled. "What do you chaps think of the tea?"

Tosco glanced down at the steaming mug in his hands. "It, um, lacks something."

"Sugar, lad. You can't make a good cuppa without plenty of sugar. Anyway, you'll have plenty of time to learn how to make a proper brew. You chaps are welcome to stay as long as you like—if you help out and pull your weight. I may opt to resupply you and send you home, but I won't do it for free. That's not how things work."

"My children…" started Guy.

"Are most likely gone, Captain, but I shall make enquires. If fate has kept them alive, they're as likely here as any place else. I'll have a clerk come take details from you. For now, I'd like to get the Hatchet and its personnel vetted and your wounded seen to. The civilians may come aboard and stay in the barracks, but the crew must bed down on the ship, I'm afraid."

"They'll be dying to come on land," said Guy.

"And they are most welcome to come and go as they please, Captain. They only need lay their heads aboard your ship. Last thing I want is a bunch of ships dead in the water because everyone is asleep on land. The Hatchet needs to be battle-ready, so keep your shift patterns in place, chaps."

Guy nodded. It was something he would've done anyway. If the shit hit the fan, he wanted to make a quick getaway. "I will do as you ask, General."

"Good'o! We're in an enviable position here, chaps. Things have gone poorly for us all so far, but that's only because the bastards got the drop on us. Now it's our turn. We're getting our shit together, and I plan on taking the fight to the enemy very soon. See how they like it up 'em. You gentlemen can be part of it. I would like you to be a part of it."

"We'll consider it," Guy allowed, "but…"

Wickstaff nodded. "Your children, I know. Give me the day and I'll see what I can do for you. In the meantime, make sure your people behave and tell them they're safe. I'm about to give the afternoon briefing if you'd like to attend. There'll be more tea —if you chaps are getting a taste for it."

Skip cleared his throat and put his mug down on a side table. "Any coffee?"

THERE THEY STOOD ten minutes later, gathered around a large mahogany table in a polished conference room. Most of the assembly was male, but they all paid close attention to Wickstaff's every word. Guy didn't know the history of this group, but the female general had clearly earned their greatest respect. Lieutenant-Colonel Spencer introduced himself briefly, showing himself to be the ageing, well-cut career officer Guy had imagined him to be. The man looked to be pushing seventy, but was square-shouldered and stiff-backed. After seeing them, he left before the meeting began.

Skip and Tosco were both standing to one side, drinking hot coffee and sighing after each sip. There had been coffee on the Hatchet during the early days, but after picking up so many refugees, it had dried up in a week. Guy had gone without its heady scent for too long. Skip and Tosco too, apparently.

Now well into the meeting, Wickstaff turned to a young Navy officer at the back of the room and asked for an ammunition report. The barrel-chested sailor put a fist to his mouth and cleared his throat.

"Yes, we're doing well—all things considered. We're limiting the choppers to small arms fire for their patrols, and we have a decent supply of the belt-fed 30mils. I counted twenty-four CRV7 rockets and sixty-six Hellfire missiles, but they are not hugely effective against the enemy infantry. They may come in handier against the big game, if we find a way to hurt them, but for the small fry, we are better off using other tactics."

"Our liaison in Istanbul," began a black officer with pock-marked cheeks, "Sergeant Cross, says the UN forces operating in Turkey have had luck with napalm. The Turks shouldn't have been stockpiling the stuff, of course, but it turns out that burning the enemy to a crisp works rather well. Surprising, seeing as half of them are already oven-baked. No success fighting the angels yet though."

"I've received a report that an angel around London was injured," someone else said in the room.

Wickstaff nodded as if she already knew. Guy suspected she knew everything and that this entire meeting was really to ensure everyone else was up to speed. "The Slough Echo gathered the Intel?"

The speaker nodded. "They said the explosion was a gate on Oxford Street. There have been sporadic reports that a nearby angel was hurt. A witness hiding out in a nearby department store sent out a last-gasp email before the grid went down saying they saw the giant bleeding. The Slough Echo has lost power too now, but we have a line open via sat phone with Corporal Martin, a survivor from the Hyde Park engagement."

"Yes, I've spoken to the man myself," said Wickstaff. "A good man, and a useful asset. In fact, I sent a detachment out yesterday to help the people there secure their position. They have children to protect, I've been informed."

That got Guy's attention, and for the next ten minutes he fidgeted at the back of the room, dying to talk to the general one-on-one to find out more. She took the last of her reports from her assembled officers, and then came straight over to Guy, seemingly having noticed his desperation.

She waved a hand before he could speak. "Yes, yes, I know what you're going to say. Before you get your hopes up, the Echo has only two children under its care—a boy and a girl."

Guy nodded. "Kyle and Alice!"

"Does your son have Downs Syndrome?"

"What? No! Kyle is normal."

Wickstaff winced. "I assure you that a child with Downs Syndrome is quite normal."

"Sorry, I meant nothing by it. Kyle doesn't have the condition."

"Then the Echo doesn't have your son. The boy under their supervision has Downs, and his father is also present."

Guy almost hit the floor. For a moment, he'd been so naively hopeful—so excited.

"What about the girl?" asked Skip. "Could she be Alice?"

Wickstaff sighed. "It seems unlikely, doesn't it? I can't rule it out though."

"Then I need to go there," urged Guy. "How do I get to Slough?"

"Hold your horses. Slough is an hour away by car, and that was before the roads teemed with monsters. You heard it yourself; we have an open line with them. Come to my office, and I will put you through."

Guy felt his hands shaking as he walked, which was why he appreciated it when Skip reached out a hand and steadied him. "Settle down, Captain. Everything will work out."

In silence, Guy followed the general into her office. Skip and Tosco remained outside. They understood this was a private moment.

Wickstaff motioned to her desk. "Take a seat, Captain."

"No, thank you, I'd rather stand."

"Right'o. I'll just tap in the coordinates. It's a satellite phone they have there, so reception is spotty. Seeing as the normal exchanges are barely working though, it's the best we have."

Guy said nothing, just swallowed and waited.

It took several minutes of Wickstaff fiddling with the bulky receiver in her office, and several times it looked like the whole thing might end up being a complete bust. Guy felt like vomiting, but then Wickstaff's face lit up along with a blinking green light on the receiver. "Ah! Yes! Hello, whom am I speaking with?"

"...poral Martin, who's this?"

Crackle.

"General Wickstaff."

"Oh, apolo... ma'am, I didn't ...cognise the voice. There's ...terference."

"No need to apologise. Sorry for the unannounced contact, Corporal, but I need to ask you a few things about your companions."

Crackle. "...ing bad, I hope?"

"Not at all. May I ask the name of the young girl you have there with you? Is she well?"

"Yes, ...ry well. Her name is-"

Crackle.

There was an odd sound, like banging on a window.

"Corporal Martin, are you there? Come in Corporal Martin!"

"I'm here. Sorr... line is ba..."

"The young girl you have with you, Corporal. I need her name."

"Alice. Her na... is Al..."

Guy almost leapt across the room. Wickstaff dodged back against the wall and put her hand up to say, *I'm bloody doing it, man. Calm down.* She spoke her next words rapidly.

"Okay, Corporal. I need you to get Alice right now and put her on the line. There's a possibility I have her father standing here in my office."

Silence for a moment. *Crackle.* Bang bang. "Impossible. ... father is a Coast Guard Captain in ...United States."

Guy almost fainted.

Wickstaff cleared her throat and looked a little faint herself. "Get the girl now, please, Corporal."

"Roger that."

There was more crackling while the Corporal did as commanded.

Guy squirmed. "I'm going to be sick."

"Then be sick, man, but do it quick because I think you just found your daughter. Christ, I didn't think there were any miracles left in the world. Guy, you need—"

"Hello?" The voice was American. The voice was Alice.

Guy hyperventilated.

Wickstaff steadied herself with a hand on her desk. "Yes, hello there, sweetheart. Is your name Alice...?"

"Granger," said Guy.

"Alice Granger?"

"Yes, do ...know you?"

"No, you don't, sweetheart, but I know your dad. He's here with me."

Silence.

Wickstaff filled it. "I know that's a lot to take in, Alice. Your father, Guy, came all the way from home to come and get you. He's here with me. Do you want to speak to him?"

"Yes." More crackling.

Guy struggled upright, and then wobbled across the room. He put his hand on the receiver Wickstaff offered him, but before he snatched it, he paused and made eye contact with the general. She was grinning.

"I'll leave you two alone," she said, and exited the room.

Guy spoke into the receiver. "Alice, it's daddy."

"...DADDY! Daddy, oh my, oh my. Daddy, that's really you, isn't it?" His little girl exploded in a shower of emotions—all of them high-volume. The line had become crystal clear, almost as if their very yearning was powering the communication. The strange banging continued in the background, faint.

"Yes, honey, it's really me. Where's your brother?"

Alice stopped chattering and went deathly silent.

She breathed into the receiver.

"Alice, honey, where's Kyle?"

More banging. It seemed a little louder.

"Kyle's gone, dad. The monsters got him."

Guy almost dropped the receiver. It felt so heavy in his hand. The saliva in his mouth turned to half-set cement, and his words came out garbled. "Alice, tell me... Alice, are you... what?"

"Kyle was trying to help, and the monsters got him. I'm sorry, dad. I should have..."

"I'm coming to get you, sweetheart, that's all you need to be thinking about."

"Daddy, I miss you."

"I miss you too, honey."

Crackle.

The banging started again. This time it was closer, louder.

"Honey, what's that?"

"I... I don't—"

Shouting in the background, people panicking.

Gunfire.

Screaming.

"Dad! Dad, the monsters are here. Dad, come and—"

The line decayed with static. Guy shouted into the receiver. "Alice! Alice! Alice! Alice!"

3

VAMPS

"**B**ack there when you saved me, the angel was hurt. It was bleeding."

Vamps stared at the woman, but it was Aymun who answered her. "The angels are only invulnerable so long as the gates they came through are intact. The one you saw came from a gate in London that no longer exists. Its tether to whatever force empowers it has been broken. The angel can be killed."

"We been tracking that prick for weeks," said Vamps, "ever since we closed that gate."

Marcy balked. "You three closed a gate?"

Vamps cracked his knuckles and grinned. "Yeah... sorta... kinda."

What had actually closed the gate was Vamps shoving a lowlife called Pusher into it, but that much Marcy didn't need to know. She seemed a nice lady. Max, her kid, rode on Mass's wide shoulders, but Marcy always stayed close to him—she clearly didn't trust them yet, and that was understandable. After her initial surge of relief at being found, Marcy hadn't spoken much. Yet, Vamps sensed her gradually opening up.

"We're fighting back," said Vamps, nodding to the MP5 on his hip he'd plucked from the corpse of a black-clad police officer. The SMG was down to its last magazine, but he'd put the previous one to good use. "We closed a gate by ourselves, and I bet there are other people taking it to the demons too. This is war, and it ain't over. Not by a long shot."

"Wow!" said Marcy. "I never thought Max and I would see anyone again who wasn't crazy or dangerous—or both."

Vamps tapped the woman on the back playfully, but realised it was a gesture to which she was unaccustomed. He folded his arms so they could do no further harm. "Never said we ain't crazy, luv. Aymun, especially, has a few screws loose. It was him what told us about the angels being tethered to their gates."

Marcy turned to Aymun, her eyebrows curious. "How did you find that out?"

Aymun blinked slowly like a holy man imparting great wisdom. The guy cracked Vamps up. "I know because I came out of a gate."

Marcy's eyes widened. "You're one of them?"

"No, my sister. I am as human as you. I came out of a gate because I stepped through one first."

"In Syria," Vamps added. He still loved hearing the story of how Aymun leapt into a gate in the desert and popped out of another in the paved heartland of London, like some inter-dimensional version of taking the Tube.

"The gates are all connected," said Aymun. "They lead to the enemy's realm."

Marcy frowned. "Hell?"

"Yes, my dear, Hell—or something akin to it. The reality of what I saw on the other side is hard to describe. It is a place devoid of feeling. Numb, dark, and lacking anything other than despair. Those I met were not tortured of the flesh. Instead, they were abandoned to an eternity of nothingness. Nothingness forever. That is why the demons want out. They want to feel again —to exist again. Just moments in Hell were enough to make me start to lose a grip on myself. Hell makes you forget who you were and become something else. Something empty."

Marcy covered her mouth. "So, Hell really is invading earth? There were rumours, at the beginning."

Aymun blinked slowly and sighed. "It is an invasion from a

place so twisted and malformed that the creatures who live there lack anything resembling compassion. Yet there is a small contingent that fights to cling onto what they were. There are souls in Hell that still possess a spark of humanity. I met one such being named Daniel."

"Wait for it," said Vamps, grinning. "Shit's about to get real."

Marcy frowned but kept her attention on Aymun, even as they walked side by side. Further on, Max giggled on Mass's shoulders as he began doing squats. Aymun took a deep breath and continued.

"Daniel is a fallen angel, one of Lucifer's kin. He wishes to aid humanity against the forces of darkness."

"Lucifer? As in the devil? Why would anyone associated with the devil want to help humanity?"

"Because the forces behind this invasion threaten more than merely us. I was not beyond the gates long enough to fully understand, but the fallen angel, Daniel, told me help is coming, and that the angels can be hurt if we destroy the gates they came through. You have witnessed this for yourself."

Marcy nodded, completely enraptured. "The angel caught fire."

Vamps flicked his wrist and made a *snapping* sound. "Because we're badass motherfu—"

"Vamps!" Mass barked from up front. "Not in front of the kid, man."

Vamps cringed. "Sorry about that, little man. How you doin' up there?"

Max turned around, losing his balance and forcing Mass to grab a hold of his small thighs. "My butt hurts. Mass has hard shoulders. My dad's shoulders were comfier."

"Want me to put you down, kid?" asked Mass, looking up.

"No, it's safe up here, and I can see far."

"Okay then. Get ready for the crocodiles!" Mass hopped around and started leaping. Max squealed hysterically, the most beautiful sound Vamps had ever heard. Who knew Mass was so good with kids? Dumbbells, barbells, and the ladies, yes, but kids, no.

Vamps kicked a dead fox out of the road so Marcy didn't have to step over it, then turned to the woman and spoke quietly. "Max's dad…?"

"We weren't together when the end came."

"Divorced?"

Marcy sighed. "Not exactly. He… He cheated on me with his secretary. I found out a few days before the gates opened. Last I heard of him, he was off to see his brother in Crapstone. Tell you the truth, I've been heading south hoping to get there and find him. For Max, more than anything."

Vamps covered his mouth and tried not to laugh. "Crapstone? That's a place?"

Marcy ended up chuckling too. "Yes, it's on the south-east coast. I went there once; it's pretty."

"Well, me and Mass are from Brixton, so we don't really know pretty. Before all this we were… well, we weren't much of anything."

"And now you're wandering heroes, saving women and children from certain death." She looked up, forced herself to make eye contact. "I don't care what you were, Vamps. You and your friends are good people. Look at my son; he's laughing. You have no idea what that means to me."

Vamps shifted uncomfortably. "Hey, it's no problem. We just keeping shit real, you feel me?"

Marcy reached out and squeezed his arm. "Thank you."

"Hey," Mass barked again. "We got a petrol station up ahead. Worth checking out."

Vamps sidestepped so he could see around his friend's wide back. Sure enough, a brand-name petrol station with an adjacent mini-mart lay ahead. The place was shuttered.

"Must be a rough part of town to have shutters," said Mass. "Might mean no one's been inside though."

Aymun pointed to a white van parked by the pumps. Someone lay dead inside, rotting in the driver's seat. Mass skirted around it to keep Max from seeing the grisly scene. Vamps was once again impressed by his friend's paternal instincts.

"There's no way in," said Marcy. "We've tried to get through shutters before; it's impossible."

"Nah," said Vamps. "You just got to know the way in."

Mass dropped Max to the ground and took off his backpack, then tossed it to Vamps who quickly unzipped it. From inside, he pulled out a heavy copper mallet. "Here's our key."

"You've been carrying that around in your pack?" Marcy asked Mass, incredulous.

Mass shrugged his boulder-shoulders. "It's a workout, innit?"

Vamps turned to his friend and grinned. "Boost?"

"Yeah, man."

Vamps trotted up to the front of the petrol station and waited for Mass to link his fingers. Once he did, Vamps stepped up and allowed his friend to launch him upwards like a child. Ten feet in the air, he wrapped his fingers around the lip of the low roof and hung on. It wasn't difficult to hoist himself—he'd lost at least a stone in the last few weeks, so he was soon standing up on the roof.

"Be careful," Marcy shouted.

"And watch out for bird poop," added Max.

Vamps looked down and saluted. A strange gesture, but one he thought the little boy would appreciate. "I'll be done in a jiffy, little man."

The roof of the petrol station was flat and lined with sticky felt. A large air conditioning unit took up the centre of the space, but that wasn't the way in. The way in was anywhere on the long flat roof not close to an edge. Vamps got to work. Picking a spot at random, he raised the mallet over his shoulder and brought it down as hard as he could.

The roof cracked.

But it would be some time until it yielded completely, so he struck at the same spot again and again, several times, before stopping and tearing up a section of felt. Underneath lay wooden planks. He struck at the timbers one at a time, causing them to split. Nails jutted out of the splintering wood, but Vamps worked around them and got to the plasterwork beneath.

"Almost in," he shouted after twenty or so minutes.

"Cool," shouted Mass from the forecourt. "I'm getting hungry down here, man. Reckon they'll have Pot Noodles? Gunna boil me some water and wreck a couple tubs of Chicken Chow Mein."

"What's that?" asked Max.

"You never had a green Pot Noodle, kid?"

"No."

"Then prepare to become a man."

Vamps chuckled and allowed the voices to fade. He still had work to do.

It took another thirty minutes before he was finally through the roof. There wasn't much that could go wrong breaking into a building when it didn't matter about noise or visibility. No one was around to call the pigs, so burglary had become extremely easy —a way of life in this new world.

Vamps lowered himself carefully, swinging his feet until he located a shelving unit underneath him, which he then descended like a ladder. At the bottom, he found himself inside a dimly lit store resembling a thousand others that existed up and down the country. As he'd suspected, the place was unlooted. Half the stock lay rotting and spoiled, still on the shelves, but the other half…

Gallons and gallons of soft drinks and water lined the unlit refrigerators. A year's supply of booze too. Canned foods of all varieties piled the centre aisles and made Vamps' mouth water. Having done this many times before, he hurried behind the counter and grabbed a handful of plastic carrier bags. He filled them with sports drinks first, and then moved on to chocolate, crisps, peanuts and biscuits. The high calorie snacks were handy because they were small and easy to stock up on.

Once he had filled a dozen bags, he climbed the shelves again and tossed the bags up through the hole and onto the roof. Finally, he filled a dozen more with the lightest stuff he could find, along with one other thing he didn't want to forget. By the time Vamps climbed back onto the roof, the sky had dimmed, and the temperature had dropped by a couple degrees.

Mass and the others stared up at him from the forecourt.

"Your search yielded well?" said Aymun.

Vamps nodded. "Yeah, man. It yielded very well. Here!" He tossed down the bags. "Make sure you catch this shit, yo!"

Mass and Aymun caught most of it, and Max and Marcy stood there as if they couldn't believe their luck. When a bag of chocolate hit the pavement and split open, Max squealed with delight. It was another sound that Vamps loved. He was getting soft.

With the final bag tossed, Vamps clambered off the roof and landed with a heavy splat that sent shock waves up his heels. "*Shit*, why does that always have to hurt!"

"Are you okay?" asked Marcy, hurrying over.

He put up a hand. "Just need to learn how to land. I got flat feet, but don't you tell nobody. If you're hungry, dig in. We have enough to last us a few days."

"Did you get everything? I can't believe our luck."

"There's still loads left inside, but we can't carry more. Besides, we've been on the road long enough to know there'll be other places."

Marcy closed her eyes and looked off into the distance. "It's so insane..."

Aymun stood nearby and begun to nod. "That world ended so suddenly? Yes, it is insane. Places like these are echoes of the past."

Marcy laughed, an edgy noise that sounded fraught with anxiety.

Vamps folded his arms. "What's funny?"

"Oh nothing. It's only that I've been struggling to provide for Max for weeks now, and in a few hours, you manage to provide more food than I could in a month. I've been fleeing in terror at any demon that comes within a mile of me, while you come along and chase off an angel. Ha!"

"Why is that funny?"

"It's not. In fact, it makes me feel rather useless, like the apocalypse is only as hard as I've been making it."

Vamps let his arms hang by his sides. "We struggled at first too, but once we stopped being victims, things eased up. You'll be okay now, Marcy. You and Max will be okay."

"Yeah," said Mass. "We look after each other, don't worry."

"But for how long?" Marcy ran a hand through her frizzy brown hair. "We can't wander the earth forever."

Vamps glanced sideways and saw Max tucking into a *Freddo* bar. He grabbed a sports drink from the line of shopping bags and took a decent swig. Then he went back to Marcy and looked her in the eye. "We're heading down to the coast. Three days at most if we walk."

"The coast? Why?"

"Get on a boat or something, innit?" said Mass. "Or maybe find a place on the beach and fish. The Navy might have things under control. All we know is that there's nothing around here. London was a ghost town by the time we left."

"I wanna go on a boat," said Max, unwrapping another Freddo bar. Chocolate stained his mouth. "Daddy has a boat. Maybe he'll be there."

Marcy huffed. "Daddy has a tiny little motor boat that rocks in bad weather. But fair enough, it sounds like a good plan. Would be good to have a destination, wherever it is."

"Then let's make the most of what sunlight we have left, my friends," said Aymun, fastening the lid on a bottle of water from which he'd been swigging. "A traveller must keep moving until the moon meets his back."

Vamps rolled his eyes. "Yeah, okay, Aymun. Let me take a slash first."

Mass glared at Vamps. "Language, dude!"

"What? That's not even swearing! Fine!" He knelt to face Max. "I'm just going for a *weewee*, little man, okay?"

"Me too! I need a weewee."

Vamps glanced at Marcy who wavered for a moment before nodding. So Vamps found himself holding hands with a child and leading him around the back of the building to make weewee. Something he never would have imagined himself doing at one time.

Life has turned bizarre.

When he pulled out his python to commence peeing, Vamps found himself unable to go. Perhaps it was because Max was staring right at him. "You're black," the little boy said.

"Um, yeah. That okay with you, little man?"

"I've never had a black friend before. I don't think my daddy likes black people because he never talks to any."

"That doesn't mean he doesn't like us. Some folks... some folks don't have much of a comfort zone beyond what they're used to."

"What's that mean?"

Vamps strained, tried to push his urine out. The boy continued looking at him. "It means your daddy probably just didn't have a chance to make any black friends."

"I'm lucky then."

"Yeah, I guess you is. I'm glad we friends, little man."

"Me too, Vamps. I hope I can help you kill lots of demons." With that, the kid finished peeing up the wall and trotted off to re-join his mother.

Vamps sighed as his own stream began. "That kid is gunna be some badass."

From the other side of the petrol station, Mass yelled at the top of his lungs, making Vamps spill piss down his jeans. "Green Pot Noodle, baby! Oh, hell yes! You the man, Vamps!"

Vamps smiled and put his dick away.

4

RICHARD HONEYWELL

R ichard stared out the window at the setting sun. From the high elevation of the Slough Echo's upper floor, he studied the city's ghosts. The nearby office blocks and car parks resembled scenes from a dull painting, grey and lifeless. Nothing moved.

But that didn't mean nothing lived.

Skullface.

The abomination that butchered Richard's wife—and Dillon's mother—was still out there somewhere in the ruins. Maybe it was watching them right now—waiting, biding its time—preparing to finish what it started.

Along with Portsmouth, the Slough Echo was the only haven in the South. A detachment of soldiers arrived a week ago, with more on the way thanks to General Wickstaff. Everyone at the office had a rifle or gun, and the soldiers possessed grenades and tools for building defences. Barbed wire and sandbags cluttered the lower floors and stairwells. Soldiers kept watch day and night. Wickstaff wanted the Echo to continue the intelligence gathering started in the early days of the invasion.

Except that intelligence gathering had stopped now.

Three days ago, the newspaper's emergency generator packed up. The main grid had been up and down for weeks, but gave up the ghost permanently a few days ago. Several power stations, such as Coryton in Essex, caught fire or exploded early on, but ironically, none of the nation's nuclear plants caused harm—they merely wound down quietly. This, and more, Richard knew because he had been a part of the news team for three weeks now. A part of a family he neither loved nor wanted, yet the family who kept him safe—kept Dillon safe.

But was this a life worth living?

No.

David appeared at Richard's side with a cup of tea. His melted face glistened with tender healing flesh. He battled infection for a while, but finally seemed to be recuperating. A thin-lipped smile stretched his face as he passed over a second steaming mug. "Freshly heated by a military engineer's blow torch. Drink up."

Richard took it. "Thank you, David."

"You're welcome. Anything out there tonight?"

"No, all's quiet, as usual. They're out there though. I can feel it."

David swigged his tea. "Doesn't make sense they would just forget about us. I'm not sure if they want to wipe out every last one of us, or if a few stragglers are insignificant enough to ignore."

"What did you learn from Andras? Any idea what the demons want?"

"The key to winning this war is closing the gates. The demons, the angels, they all rely on them staying open. Corporal Martin thinks we should change our objective."

Richard frowned. "To what?"

"Establishing a battle line. Most of the enemy has moved south through London towards the coast—most likely heading for Portsmouth. Martin thinks we can gain ourselves some breathing room if we fortify a wider area. He has men looking for iron scrap. It's the only thing that keeps the buggers at bay."

Richard turned his head and watched his son, Dillon. He played beside Alice at one of the computers. With the power off, they only pretended by tapping away at the keys, playing some imaginary videogame. Would there ever be places for a child to play again? There had to be more than this.

"I don't think we have any chance," said Richard, sipping his tea and allowing it to burn his mouth. "We're finished."

David sighed. His ruined face made it impossible to decode his expression accurately. "You've been through a lot, Richard—losing your wife the way you did and having to care for your boy. I've witnessed you fading into yourself ever since you arrived here. You've forgotten how hard you fought to stay alive. If everyone did what you did, the demons wouldn't have a chance. Weeks ago, you said you had a plan. You said you were going to—"

Both men frowned as a high-pitched trilling filled the office behind them.

Richard wasn't sure, but he thought he heard banging too.

Corporal Martin leapt up from a desk and hurried across the room. "Sat phone. Must be Portsmouth."

"Well answer it then, lad," urged Carol, still the de facto leader of the group. She stood beside Aaron, the young lad who proved his bravery helping Richard during the early days of the invasion.

The soldiers in the room stood to attention as if whoever was calling might see them.

"Hopefully it's good news," said David to Richard. "Wouldn't that be nice? The war is over chaps, come on down for fish supper."

Richard grunted. He used to have a sense of humour, but hadn't smiled since he saw his wife's head reduced to pulp. There were no more reasons to laugh.

"So anyway," said David, realising his joke had gone down like a lead helicopter. "That plan of yours?"

"I have no plan. My plan was to throw myself through the nearest gate, but then someone did it for me."

"There's a gate in South Downs, I hear. Directly between Portsmouth and us. If you would be so kind as to toss yourself through that one, we could all mosey on down to the coast in relative safety."

Richard blinked. For a moment, he thought he sensed something—a vibration. More banging, perhaps. "What was that?"

"That was a joke, Richard. How would you ever reach the gate, anyway?"

"I'd wrap myself in iron."

David chuckled, distorting his burnt face. "I suppose you could cover yourself in old pots and pans or something. It just might work."

"It's a stupid idea, but all the good ideas have failed us. We're just existing here, David. All we're doing is praying Portsmouth somehow obliterates an army ten times its size. There's no point in us being here."

"Where else would we go?"

"North. Some place secluded where we might eek out a few years of peace. I can't stay here anymore with no hope, no... anything."

There was a commotion at the back of the room.

Corporal Martin was gathering Alice to his side and thrusting the sat phone at her. What was going on? Who at Portsmouth would want to speak to Alice?

Richard sensed movement in the corner of his eye. Dillon smiled at him. "Alice is talking to her daddy."

"What?"

"Alice's daddy has come all the way from... um... her house."

"Her daddy's come from America?"

Dillon nodded.

"It's true," said Carol rushing over. She had aged five years in the last three weeks, but her wide grin now made her look like a giddy child. "Our little Alice still has a daddy."

David chimed in. "How wonderful. Could it really be? Alice's father made it all the way across the Atlantic to get to her? Oh, how I wish there were still news to report. This would make a wonderful human-interest piece." He turned to Richard and put a hand on his shoulder. "There's your hope, Richard. There's your hope."

Richard swallowed a lump in his throat as he watched Alice explode with excitement. Was it true? Had a Coast Guard Captain sailed the Atlantic to reach his daughter? Were people still walking through fire to protect their loved ones?

I have. I've faced monsters to keep Dillon alive.

If Alice's father had survived such a journey, then perhaps David was right. Maybe there was hope.

Maybe it was still worth surviving.

The office windows shattered.

Richard gathered Dillon into his arms and shielded him. He turned and glanced at where the windowpanes had been.

Andras stared back at him.

Now in his natural form, the angel rose three-stories. A squad of demons scurried behind him.

Skullface was there, staring up at the building like a dark sentinel.

Despite the obscene threat, Richard couldn't help but glare right back at the beast.

The monster that took Jen from him.

One second later, all hell broke loose.

5

GUY GRANGER

"I need to get to her!" Guy screamed in Wickstaff's face. To her credit, she didn't blink. She did, however, look mortified.

"If the Slough Echo has been attacked," she said. "We will just have to pray they pull through. I sent them a detachment weeks ago, and another is on its way. We can't help them any more."

"My daughter is with them. She's in danger!"

Skip and Tosco hurried into the room attracted by the commotion. Skip asked what was wrong.

"Alice is alive," said Guy, waving his hands madly and clenching his fists. "I spoke to her."

"That's wonderful," said Tosco. "A miracle actually."

Guy paced the room, a caged bear at the zoo. He wanted to claw at something. "She's in danger, Lieutenant. The people she's with were just attacked, right while I was talking to her. The line went dead."

Tosco looked at Wickstaff. "Can we patch back through?"

"I tried. There's no response."

"Oh hell," said Skip, and took Guy into his arms. Guy surprised himself by allowing the gesture. Madness still beckoned, but his breathing at least began to return to normal.

"I'll keep trying to make contact," said Wickstaff, folding her arms, but what Guy read in her tone scared him. This was not the only time the general had lost contact with a group of survivors. She thought Alice and the others were dead.

Like my son. Is Kyle really dead? It doesn't feel real?

If Alice is gone too, what is left?

"I need to know what happened," said Guy, pulling away from Skip and pleading with Wickstaff. "Help me find out."

Wickstaff perched on the edge of her desk and pinched the bridge of her nose. "I'm afraid I can't. The enemy is amassing outside Portsmouth, and I intend to meet them on the battlefield in one massive assault designed to wipe them out en masse. I cannot afford to spare a single man. Do you understand? This might be our one and only chance of victory, and that must be my sole focus. I mourn for your daughter, Captain, and for the others at the Slough Echo—they are amongst the bravest people I know —but I mourn more for the future of the eighteen thousand people under my care here. I mourn that this time last year, Britain's population numbered in the tens of millions, but now barely exists. The best you can do, Captain, is remain here and fight for humanity's future."

"You can't win," said Guy, hating himself for saying it. "You would need three times as many soldiers to have half-a-chance."

Tosco wrinkled his nose at Guy and turned away in disgust. Skip seemed disappointed too.

Wickstaff, again to her credit, did not waver. She stared hard at Guy, waiting until he shifted awkwardly. "We lack manpower, certainly, but our forces have teeth, I assure you. There are over a hundred warships in that harbour, with enough firepower to flatten Hell itself. I have heavily armed choppers, two Tornado attack jets, and six Eurofighters launching from a French carrier. You might also have noticed a German submarine docked. It has eight warheads onboard that can decimate a square mile if deployed. Trust me, Captain, if the enemy continue grouping together the way they are, we will annihilate them."

Guy couldn't deny it was impressive. The general might have enough hardware at her disposal to wage war, yet... "We've had firepower since the beginning, General—a hundred armies all over the globe wasn't enough to stop the invasion."

"It wasn't an invasion. It was an ambush. Now humanity fights a guerrilla war, and guerrilla wars invariably go to the incumbent forces. But forget all that, because it's mere window dressing. The reason I will win the battles ahead is that I have a secret weapon."

Guy turned his back. "If you're talking about nukes then—"

"I'm not talking about nuclear missiles, Guy!" The use of his first name made him turn back. Was it a lack of respect, or an attempt to be more intimate? Before he could figure out which, she went on. "What's the point of winning if you spoil the prize? No, I will not launch a nuclear assault. My secret weapon will do no harm except to the enemy. It will allow us to close the gates."

"You need to find someone dumb enough to jump through."

Wickstaff rolled her eyes. "You can do it that way, yes, but getting close enough is a tough task. I have something that can close gates from five hundred yards away."

Guy frowned. Skip and Tosco were paying close attention too.

Wickstaff moved from the corner of her desk. "Want me to show you?"

All three men said yes.

THE GENERAL LED them out of her office. Guy grew confused when she headed towards the barracks. Whatever weapon she had at her disposal, he'd not expected to find it housed in a place where people slept. Indeed, once inside the building, Guy saw families and civilians. No soldiers—or weapons—in sight.

"I house as many as I can in the barracks," Wickstaff explained, "but the rest have to make do in the nearby town-houses. I pushed our defensive perimeter out as far as I could without spreading ourselves thin."

"What are we doing in here, General? I don't understand."

Wickstaff had been forging ahead, but now she slowed so Guy could catch up. "Look, Captain, I would not usually be so accommodating to a Coast Guard with a relatively useless vessel."

"The Hatchet is not useless," muttered Skip at the back.

"But," Wickstaff continued, "you all showed great bravery

getting across the Atlantic, and it would be useful to have an American here with some authority. I have a few groups of your people scattered here and there, including a detachment of Marines who were over here on a training exercise. You could be most useful in taking charge of them."

"I'm only interested in finding my daughter."

"We shall see. Come this way." She opened a door on her right and stepped aside so that the men could enter. Guy exchanged glances with Tosco and Skip, but decided there was nothing to fear, so he stepped inside. He found himself inside a dormitory with six beds separated via concrete dwarf-walls. Most of the beds looked in use, but the people inside huddled around only one of the berths.

A paunch-bellied stranger with a modest bald patch spotted them standing there and narrowed his eyes. Guy felt like an intruder, so he waved a hand and nodded. "Hello."

The man grunted. "Who might you be?"

"This is Captain Guy Granger from the United States Coast Guard," said Wickstaff. "He is here to speak with Rick."

Guy frowned. *Rick? Who the hell is Rick?*

The man blocking their way shrugged. "You best come in then."

The room's inhabitants were playing cards on top of a crisply made bed at the back. Two women sat side-by-side, one a decade older than the other who looked barely past her teens. The older woman had short brown hair, the younger long and blonde. There was another man here too. He stood to greet them, and when he smiled at Guy he looked familiar.

He also looked ill.

"Hi, I'm Rick. You wanted to speak with me?"

Guy looked at Wickstaff and raised an eyebrow. "I don't know. Do I?"

Wickstaff shook Rick's hand. "I was hoping you could give the Captain a demonstration. He needs a little convincing that we have a chance of winning here."

"We have more than a chance," said the irritable balding man. "Those bastards won't know what's hit them."

"Look," said Guy, tapping his foot. "What am I here for? In fact, screw it, just point me toward Slough. I will get to my daughter on my own."

Rick frowned. The corners of his eyes were cracked and peeling. "What is he talking about, General?"

"His daughter is at the Slough Echo. They were just attacked."

"Then God help them," said the balding man.

Rick nodded to Guy. "I'm not a military man, so may I call you Guy?"

Guy nodded.

"Thank you. I'm Rick, and this is my brother Keith. These gorgeous girls are Maddy and Diane. We are survivors of the original gate in Crapstone."

Guy shrugged. "Not heard of it, sorry. I came from New York. My children were here on school vacation. My daughter might still be alive. I'm going to find her."

"I'll help you," said Rick.

"You only just met me."

"Yes," said Wickstaff. "Rick, you're needed here."

Rick wiped at his nose, and Guy saw a hint of blood on the back of his hand. "I'm needed to help win this war, General. I'm not doing that playing cards. My place is out there. I can do some good by going north with Guy."

Guy was tapping his foot faster. "What are you talking about? How can you help me find my daughter?"

Rick gave Guy a warm smile, then placed a hand on his shoulder.

Guy gasped, and reeled backwards, pawing at his eyes.

Tosco whipped out a gun and pointed it at Rick. "The fuck did you do to him?"

"Put that away, Lieutenant," warned Wickstaff, "Before I make you eat it."

Guy slumped forward, putting a hand out and clutching Tosco's arm. "It's okay, it's... okay. Put the gun away."

Tosco slipped the gun back inside its holster, but he remained tense and ready to pull it back out.

"What are you?" Guy aimed the question at Rick. What had he experienced? His entire body fizzed. "You... you're what?"

"I showed you Hell," said Rick flatly. "I'm connected to it. Whatever higher power the angels draw upon, I have the same hook up."

Skip backed towards the wall, his eyes wide. The old man looked frail. "You're one of them?"

Rick shook his head. "No, I am one of us. But an angel passed some of his power to me—to help us. Each day I get stronger. The demons can no longer harm me, and more importantly, I can close the gates."

"You can close them at a distance?" asked Guy, remembering what Wickstaff said earlier.

Rick turned and lowered himself back onto the bed. He sat like a stiff eighty-year-old. "At first, I had to get right up and touch them, but before stumbling into Portsmouth, I closed one while standing on top of a nearby hill. The demons never even saw me. The explosion took out hundreds of them. They seem to go down if the blast catches them."

"It greatly cemented our position here," said Wickstaff. "The Rick-closed gate was less than a mile away from the city's outskirts —we were fighting constant skirmishes and losing men every day. When Rick closed it, it gave us the breathing room we needed to dig in and get our heads together."

"He's closed five gates," said Maddy, gazing at Rick with pride. Guy wondered if something was going on there.

"But I need to close more," Rick let out a whistling sigh and rubbed at his sides. "I came here because I thought it would be safe for the people I care about. Now I need to get back out there. If you're heading out, Guy, I want to come with you. You're heading to Slough, right? There's a very important gate between here and there. South Downs."

Guy was sweating, and still short of breath since the soul-itching vision Rick forced into him. What had he seen? Walls of bleeding flesh... Legions of foul creatures... And beyond it all, something malevolent—something ancient.

"Why is this gate important?" asked Tosco, always one to

focus on parameters over emotion. "There are thousands across the world, so what makes this one more important than the rest?"

Wickstaff answered. "It's a nexus."

"A what?"

"A nexus," said Rick. "Some gates are larger and more powerful. They draw power from Hell itself and pass it on to other smaller gates. Almost like an exchange on a power grid. I never knew this until I closed the first gate. When I touched it, I felt connected to all the others on the same network. I saw the nexus gate. It's about fifty miles from here—on the way to Slough."

"So... so..." Guy rubbed at his forehead, trying to remove the cobwebs. "If you close this gate, what happens?"

"About two-dozen more in the South of England get closed right along with it," said Wickstaff. "And any angels that came through it will be rendered vulnerable."

"You'll be able to hurt the angels?" Guy nodded. It was making sense.

Wickstaff nodded. "We've already seen it. Someone closed a gate in London, and an angel got hurt. We have survivors from London here on base who claim they saw an angel come out of that same gate during the first days of the invasion."

Rick wiped a smidgen of blood on his lip. "Similar reports claim another angel came out of a gate in Haslemere. Lord Amon."

Guy huffed. "Who the hell is Lord Amon?"

"A leader," said Wickstaff. "At least of the army that threatens us here in Portsmouth. We take out that gate; we get our chance to take out Lord Amon too. The demons are congregating at his command, and if he were removed, they might lose direction—one can only hope."

"Look, I don't care about any of that. I just want to find my daughter. You've already said you won't help me, General, so I will take a crew from the Hatchet and go myself."

"No," said Tosco. "The men have done as you asked, Captain —they got you here—but now they should do as they wish. You said you would relinquish command of the Hatchet once we arrived in England. The crew and I want to travel back to the United States. This is not our fight."

Wickstaff turned on the Lieutenant. "Wake up, Tosco, you fool. This isn't about national identity anymore. We're fighting as a species. You travel back home and it will take you weeks. The fighting is happening right now. Here. Stand beside your fellow man."

Tosco stood unconvinced. "I'm sorry," he said, shaking his head, "but my crew members have homes... families..."

Guy folded his arms. "It's still my crew, Lieutenant."

"Not if you ask them to do this, Captain. You don't own their lives. Not anymore."

"He's right, Guy," said Skip of all people.

Guy raised an eyebrow. "You agree with the Lieutenant?"

"On this I do, aye. You can't claim dominion over the men and women on board the Hatchet anymore. They're not your own private army. They came here because they believed in you, not because they had to. You try to order them to come with you to Slough, now that they've found safety here, I'd say more than half would refuse, either to stay here and fight or return home with Tosco. They earned the right to choose."

Tosco nodded a silent thanks to the old chief, but Skip ignored it. He wasn't siding with the Lieutenant, just speaking what he thought to be true.

Guy sighed, took a look at the people standing around him. "Okay. Come with me by any means, Rick, but it looks like I might be travelling alone, so on your head be it."

Rick peered up from the bed. "You won't be alone, Guy. General Wickstaff will give us an escort."

The general shook her head. "I can't spare it."

"Yes, you can. Defending this place is priority number one, I get that, but you can spare a dozen men to get me to the nexus."

"We discussed this Rick. We will get you there by chopper. It's safer."

"No, it's not. The demons can use weapons. One of them gets something big enough to take out a helicopter and I'm at the mercy of fate. I don't like fate. Least on my own two feet I can run if I have to. I want to go with Guy. I want to see him rescue his daughter while she's alive."

Guy swallowed. "Do you know something?"

"I know your daughter is alive until proven otherwise. What's the point of going after her if not?"

Guy chewed his lip for a moment, and then he looked at Wickstaff. "Help me get my daughter, and I promise I'll get Rick to the gate."

Wickstaff unfolded her arms and let them fall to her side. "Fine! You can have a dozen men, plus whomever you can get from your own crew. Lieutenant, if you want supplies to get back to the States, I'll give them to you, but you leave me the civilians. I need bodies."

"I won't make anyone stay against their will," said Tosco, "but I imagine most would be glad to stay."

Rick smiled. His eyes flashed with inky blackness. "Great, then we'll leave in the morning. Until then, who's in for Poker?"

Guy turned around and headed back to his ship.

6

VAMPS

"Shite!" Mass kicked a detached headlight against the curb. "Ain't no way we're getting across here."

Vamps stood at the edge of the broken road and stared into the rushing water below. Somehow, the entire bridge had crumbled into the river. The scorch marks on the far-side embankment, along with the various shards of metal jutting up out of the mud, made it look like an aircraft had come down on top of the road and taken the river crossing with it. It was not a wide expanse, but the river looked deep and powerful. Raging. The pitter-patter of rain on its surface only made it seem more alive.

"We'll have to go around," said Marcy, arms laden with carrier bags. "There's nowhere to cross."

"Nah," said Vamps. "We just got to use our heads. I like a challenge."

"There's no way," said Mass. "I'm not a good swimmer."

"That's 'cus you're so heavy you'd sink like a stone, bruv. We can do this. Look, over there—it's narrower."

"I like swimming," said Max. He picked up a stone and tossed it into the water. "I reckon we can get across easy."

Vamps gave Max a fist bump. "That's my man!"

"I don't think this is a good idea," said Marcy. "Max we'll find somewhere else to swim, okay? The water is moving a bit fast."

Vamps knew they were just scared. He needed to be brave for them all, like always. He studied the narrow point in the river and became surer they could cross. All they needed was… "There. Right there is how we cross."

Mass frowned. "What?"

"That lamppost over there with the banged-up Merc crashed against it." The lamppost was bent and leaning at a forty-five-degree angle. It had ripped free of the ground, a chunk of concrete anchoring its base like a root bulb. "Together, we can lift that over the water where it's narrowest. We'll be able to walk right over."

Mass put his hands on his hips and licked his lip. "I dunno, man."

"Come on! After all we've been through, you're going to shit your pants at this?"

Mass winced and looked at Max who was giggling.

Vamps waved a hand at Marcy. "Sorry. Look, we can cross here. We're heading south and we're making good time, but if we have to walk around this river until we find another bridge we could end up going backwards. It's about to get dark and the village is that side of the river. Let's just get this done and then find somewhere to bed down for the night. It will be fine, I swear down."

Mass cleared his throat then exhaled. "Okay, let's do it."

"You sure we'll be okay?" Marcy looked at the river like it was a fire-breathing dragon. "What if we slip?"

"Nobody will slip," said Vamps. "Trust me."

"I trust you," said Max. "You're a gangster."

"Damn straight, little man." Vamps ruffled the kid's hair and got to work. Mass and Aymun followed him over to the skewed lamppost. It wobbled when they pushed on it, but the chunk of concrete was wedged beneath the bashed-up Merc.

"Hold on," said Vamps. He rattled the car's door handle and yanked open the crumpled panel. Reaching inside, he released the handbrake, and the car rolled backwards, almost dragging Vamps along with it. He pulled himself away just in time to avoid the tyres crunching over his foot. There was a loud clatter as the car's front bumper cracked and came away, hooked around the chunk of concrete at the base of the lamppost.

Vamps kicked away the shattered remnants of the car's front bumper and prodded the concrete with his toe. "There, it's free. Come help me get this up Mass. You too, Aymun."

Together, the three men wrapped their arms around the lamppost and hoisted it toward their shoulders. There was a moment where they nearly dropped the weight and injured themselves, but Mass grunted like an angry bear and redoubled his efforts. Like an Olympic power-lifter, he raised the post almost on his own. Once settled across the three men's shoulders, the weight became bearable.

"You sure this is a good idea?" asked Mass, his jaw locking with exertion.

"Yeah, bruv. It'll be a piece of piss. Aymun, you're at the front so you need to lower your end down into the mud at the edge of the river. Then me and Mass will shove the whole thing up and over."

Aymun consented to the plan, and once they reached the edge of the rushing water, he lowered the heavy pole to the ground. It was a struggle, which meant he more or less dropped it, but the swan neck with the broken bulb housing slid into the mud and wedged against the buried rocks.

"Okay," said Vamps. "Mass, heave this thing up."

Vamps was at the back, which meant he had to duck around the thick lump of concrete with the electrical wiring spilling out like worms as it rose. From the middle, Mass did most of the lifting, which was for the best as the final two feet were beyond Vamps's reach, even on tiptoes. Mass roared as he shoved the lamppost through the apex of its arc and balanced it upright. Mass was a monster.

The upside-down lamppost teetered for a moment, then tilted toward the river. Once it tipped, it fell fast, and smashed against the opposite bank with enough force to obliterate a skull. The lump of concrete embedded itself into the wet mud like a hook.

They had themselves a bridge.

"It worked," said Aymun, wiping sweat and drizzling rain from his forehead.

"You doubted me?" said Vamps.

Aymun shrugged and spoke gently as always. "A wise man doubts everything."

"Well you should never doubt me, man. I'm the real deal."

"It would appear so. Will you be the first to cross?"

Vamps considered what would be the smart thing to do. "I'll go first, make sure it's safe on the other bank, then Mass. Aymun you go last, make sure the kid gets across okay."

Aymun nodded.

Max was jumping up and down excitedly, tugging his mother around by her arm. "This is like P.E. I miss school."

Marcy laughed. "You hate school."

"Not anymore. I miss my friends."

That brought silence to the group. They had lost so much— the world had lost so much—but the absence of children playing was something no one realised how much they missed until it was taken away.

"Okay, I'm heading over." Vamps trod down the muddy bank until he was at the lamppost. He explored its stability with his foot and was pleased when it barely moved an inch. He hopped up and started across, one foot placed in front of the other. The surface was narrow, and curved too, so progress was slow and careful. But it was easy enough.

"Be careful," shouted Marcy. "The water is really moving."

Vamps watched the river rushing inches below his feet. It lapped at the bottom of the lamppost, and the occasional tide rose up and over the top. The steel finish of the lamppost might become slippery if they took too long crossing. The feel of his sodden socks inside his trainers made him shudder. He picked up speed.

Mass shouted. "Careful!"

Vamps turned back. "I got this."

Then he slipped.

Marcy and her son cried out. So did Vamps, although he snipped it short before it had chance to become a scream.

Screaming was not gangster.

His left trainer dipped into the river. His arms waved like tentacles.

Then his body stilled. He was okay.

His balance came back.

"Shit! Almost took a swim there."

Another six steps and he successfully crossed the river, hopping onto the opposite bank, leaping in victory. On the opposite side, the others looked relieved, except for Marcy who still seemed anxious. Vamps considered what being a mother must be like: constant worrying.

"Okay!" Mass pumped his fist against his palm. "I'm coming over, bro"

"Be careful, man. You weigh ten times what I do."

Mass looked funny as he crept up onto the lamppost, like an elephant balancing on a stool. His big shoulders bunched up, and he shuffled his feet humorously. Every time he peered down at the river, he swallowed like a cartoon cat watching a dog. It amused Vamps to see his manly friend so afraid of water.

Now was Marcy and Max's turn to cross. Marcy stepped up to the post, clutching Max's hand. The little boy was beaming, even as he faced the tumultuous waters that could carry him away in a second—he had not yet reached sufficient age to appreciate danger, that was still his mother's burden. Marcy visibly shook as she inched her way across the steel bridge. Max stayed close to her, obedient if nothing else.

"You are doing well," said Aymun, remaining on the bank. He held his palms together beneath his chin, engrossed by the situation. "That's it. Slowly, slowly, monkey catching."

"This is easy," yelled Max. "Easy peas-"

The ground shook. The river leapt up like a tiger's paw.

Marcy cried out, wobbling back and forth while trying to keep hold of her son.

Vamps spotted something on the other bank behind Aymun. Something large slid out from behind a roadside billboard advertising BMW electric cars. It was the wounded angel, now horribly burnt. They thought they'd been hunting it, but today, it had been hunting them.

The angel stomped towards Aymun, and Aymun must have sensed the vibrations from its footsteps because he spun around in horror.

Marcy and Max half-turned to see what was happening. When they saw the angel, they screamed and froze in place in the middle of the bridge. Fright almost knocked them both into the river, but Marcy held on and kept her son out of the water.

"Be gone!" Aymun shouted on the opposite bank. "I know why you are here, and you will fail, so be gone."

The angel said nothing. It always said nothing. It only scowled. A blackened scorch mark covered its upper chest where Vamps had burnt it, and weeping bullet holes riddled its torso. But there was no denying the ferocity of the creature.

Aymun leapt aside as the angel stomped the mud as though aiming to squash a bug. Aymun wore a pistol on his hip, and aimed it now, pulling the trigger over and over again. The loud report of gunfire mingled with Marcy and Max's screams.

"Come on," said Mass, budging Vamps into action. "We gotta do something."

Vamps pulled his MP5 from his belt and fired across the river. His shots went wild at such a distance, but he zeroed in on the angel trying to stamp on Aymun.

Aymun, who ran around on the muddy bank like a yapping terrier, fired bullets and dodged instant death. Mass opened fire too, striking the target several times.

The angel roared.

"Help us," shouted Marcy.

Max cried in terror.

Vamps was focused on the angel, bleeding from a host of new bullet wounds. He moved down the bank towards the edge of the river, yanking on his trigger three more times and landing two hits. "You better run, bitch, before we cook what's left of you. We Brixton boys, you get me!?"

Vamp's wet trainer slid in the mud. His leg buckled beneath him. The slip wasn't catastrophic, but he had to struggle to keep from tumbling down the slope. As he fought to stay upright, his finger clenched around the trigger and expended the last of his rounds, making the MP5 click irritably once empty.

Mass continued firing until his own weapon was empty too, but Aymun was able to reload and fire his pistol several more times, but he was growing tired. Eventually, the angel swiped out with a long left arm and clipped Aymun in the back, sending him tumbling into wet mud beside the river.

Marcy continued to scream.

Scream.

Scream.

Vamps regained his balance in the mud and patted his pockets for more bullets. He had to have something on him somewhere...

His jaw dropped when his eyes fell upon the bridge.

Marcy dangled in the water, clinging to the lamppost by one arm while the hungry waters tried to carry her away. In her other arm, she held Max, but the boy was silent and still, moving only with the water.

"You shot him," Marcy wailed. "You fucking shot him."

Vamps stared at the smoking sub-machine gun in his hand and realised what he'd done. God, please no. *I slipped. My finger squeezed the trigger. Oh, please, fuck no!*

"Fuck," said Mass. "We need to get her."

Vamps didn't move. He kept trying to say something, or to move, but nothing his brain commanded went through to his body. Mass shoved past him and got back onto the lamppost. After several steps towards Marcy though, he stopped. Something on the far bank caught his eye.

The angel stood beside the water's edge and grinned. The gesture was aimed right at Vamps. Then, slowly, the angel looked down, down at the spot where the lamppost lay secured against the bank.

Vamps swallowed. "No, don't!"

Marcy was too busy screaming to notice the angel. Her attention was only on Max whom she tried hysterically to wake up.

He wasn't waking up.

Mass hurried back towards the bank, moving away from Marcy rather than towards her. "Oh shit, oh shit, oh shit!"

The angel kicked the end of the lamppost and launched it into the river as if it were a twig. The other end—the end with the concrete base—remained embedded in the bank, which caused the whole thing to pivot. Marcy hung on in the middle, clutching her son. Barely.

"Move!" Vamps finally got control of his body. He shoved Mass aside and hurried towards the lamppost.

"There's nothing you can do," cried Mass, grabbing him. "Vamps!"

Vamps shrugged free of his friend's grasp and struck him with a right hook. Mass grabbed him again, and this time threw him to the ground where he was forced to watch the lamppost slip away from the bank and sink into the water.

Marcy's grip finally failed her. She and her dead child slipped beneath the water. The river carried them away like offerings.

Vamps struggled to get to his feet, but Mass held him. "Let me go. I can save her. I can save her!"

On the opposite bank, the wounded angel glared. Then it slipped away into the shadows.

Night had fallen.

7

RICHARD HONEYWELL

"They're trying to come inside," shouted David. "Daddy. The monsters are coming."

A huge car wheel came flying through the broken office windows and collided with Aaron. It hit the lad so hard it destroyed his face completely.

This is it, thought Richard. *This is the end.*

Corporal Martin jumped up on a desk and started barking orders. "Everyone into the second-floor stairwell. To the fire escape."

Richard grabbed Dillon by the hand and raced out of the office. People stepped on his heels in the rush, but he didn't look back—didn't care who was with him. All that mattered was that he was first, which meant he and Dillon had the best chance.

Then he saw the demons piling up the stairwell from below, and he wasn't so sure anybody had a chance.

Dillon cried out.

David from somewhere said, "Shit."

Richard tried to turn back up the stairs, but the huddled masses bore down on him and forced him lower. The burnt creatures surging upwards howled with eagerness, their love of slaughter undiminished since the last time he had encountered them.

"Daddy, they're going to get us."

A burnt man made it up to the balcony six feet below where the stairs twisted back on themselves. He glared up at Richard with hungry eyes, gnashing his teeth. Richard shoved Dillon behind him, but could not retreat. The panicked bodies on the stairs formed a wall. The burnt creature raced up the steps, half-a-dozen of its vile brethren following. Richard prepared to fight with feet and fists.

He prepared to die.

Part of him welcomed it.

Except for Dillon. He had to fight for Dillon.

The burnt man leapt up the final few steps, reaching out for Richard, but then broke apart in mid-air amidst an ear-piercing explosion. Wet vileness spattered Richard's face. He blinked in surprise.

Over the din of screaming people, Corporal Martin yelled like a tribal war chief. He held a shotgun in his arms and cocked it for another shot. "Let them have it, lads."

There was an almighty clatter of gunfire, and the demons on the stairwell tumbled backwards, limbs tearing, torsos splitting. Blackened blood ran down the steps like tar.

"Move, move, move," the Corporal ordered.

Richard realised he was now holding up the pack and in danger of being knocked down the stairs. Grabbing Dillon, he continued retreating, descending the stairwell, feet slipping in demon blood. Sporadic gunfire followed as the soldiers behind leant over the landing rails and took pot shots at the enemy reinforcements flooding into the downstairs lobby.

The survivors reached the second-floor stairwell and spread out. The soldiers moved up and took point, allowing Richard to fall back and keep Dillon out of harm's way.

"Everyone, stay behind me," said Corporal Martin. "Out the fire escape and down the ramp. David will unlock the bus and then we all file in."

"There's too many of them down there, we'll never make it," someone said, even though they'd all discussed this escape plan for weeks.

"Man up," said Carol. "Don't quit before we've even started. You have a dozen strapping young soldiers looking after you. You'll be fine."

"I need to get to my dad," said Alice. "He's at Portsmouth. I need to go."

David patted her back. "We'll get you there, lass. I promise you."

"Let's get moving," David barked. "We have more than demons to worry about. There's a goddamn angel out there, and a..." he couldn't complete the sentence. Richard glared at him.

"The monster that killed my mummy," Dillon finished.

Corporal Martin kicked open the fire escape and poked his shotgun out, scanning left and right. "All clear. Let's move our arses."

The soldiers filed out onto the metal catwalk that flanked the east side of the old building. Parked directly at the bottom of the ramp was a city bus long enough to hold seventy or eighty squashed up bodies. Best-case scenario, they might fill it with sixty. If anybody died in the next two minutes, it might be much less.

They needed to get on that bus quick.

Richard moved Dillon onto the ramp, and other survivors spilled out onto the catwalk around them. They started moving as a group, trying to stay quiet, but unable to stifle their cries of terror. A surge of demons appeared from around the front of the building, and the cries turned to screams. As if they somehow knew what the survivors were planning, the demons immediately surrounded the bus, severing their escape route. Part of the horde broke away, heading up the ramp towards the survivors.

The soldiers fired, cut the demons to pieces before they even got near, but already men were having to reload. They couldn't stay here out in the open for long. But what options did they have? Richard shook his head. They were screwed.

"Grab the chain," said Corporal Martin. "Somebody, grab that bloody chain."

Richard remembered the contingency plan and couldn't believe that he'd almost forgotten it. There was a chain, a relic the soldiers had gathered from a nearby museum during one of their scavenger hunts. It was made of iron. The chain had been set up as part of their escape plan.

Richard leapt towards the railings of the fire escape to grab it now. It hung from several curtain hooks secured against the steel railing with thick tape. More demons ran up the ramp. More bullets kept them at bay. The ammunition wouldn't last forever.

This has to work...

Richard wrapped both hands around the iron chain and yanked. The other end was attached to the rear bumper of the parked bus, and the chain leapt into the air. The demons unlucky enough to get in the way caught fire—incinerated in seconds. Those able to, backed off rapidly, leaving a gulf between two separate sections of the enemy army. One section—the smaller section —was squashed up against the news office building. It was these demons that presented the biggest threat, for they lay in the survivor's path between the brick wall and the iron chain.

Corporal Martin and his men focused their fire on this group and thinned their numbers quickly. The massive majority of the enemy remained on the other side of the chain, yet were unable to pass—roped off like a crowd outside a nightclub. Richard's days as a police officer, dealing with drunken revellers fighting and shagging in alleyways suddenly came back to him. Contrasted with what he was doing now, it was almost something he missed.

"Okay," Carol shouted amongst the huddled bodies. "Get to that sodding bus, and get there now!"

The soldiers led the way, smashing their rifle butts against any demon brave enough to peel away from the wall. On the other side of the chain, a hundred demons spat and hissed, but were unable to attack. The smell of burnt flesh and faeces fouled the air when a burnt creature with sliced open breasts was dumb enough to try to grab one of the soldiers. Its arm crossed over the chain and burned to dust.

"They can't hurt us," said David. "Just keep moving."

The group of frightened humans moved along the channel towards the bus, like sheep scurrying between pens. Muffled screams escaped some of the survivors, because even though they were safe, they were not fearless. Richard felt the sweat pouring from Dillon's palm as he led him through Hell. Even if they reached the bus, what then?

The vehicle's back door—a fire escape—had been left ajar, but secured with a padlock. David produced the key, and once the door was open, the survivors began to push and shove and panic.

"Stop," shouted Corporal Martin. "Stop pushing."

A woman in the crowd tripped and fell beneath the iron chain. A burnt man fell on her and started carving open her chest. Blood gargled in her throat. Carol grabbed the frightened man who had caused the women to trip and slapped him hard across his shocked face. "Wait your turn, or I swear we'll leave you behind."

Corporal Martin gathered people onto the bus—the crowd more orderly after having seen a woman fall to her death. Richard pushed Dillon ahead of him and shoved him up the back step, then squeezed in after him.

"Out the way!" David shoved his way through the bodies in the aisle. "I'm the one with the keys, so let me to the front or we aren't going anywhere."

"Last person in," said Corporal Martin from the back. The bus was so packed people could barely move, but at least now they had walls and glass between them and the demons.

The engine rumbled to life as David turned the key.

Outside, the demons moved away from the iron chain and started throwing themselves at the sides of the bus. The soldiers threw open the narrow top windows and poked out their rifles, firing into the crowd.

The bus began to rock on its springs.

They needed to make their getaway now, or they wouldn't be going anywhere.

David shifted into gear. "Hold onto your butts."

The bus jolted forwards, and those in the aisle staggered and fell. Richard held onto Dillon, but he himself fell onto Carol's lap.

"I knew you'd been eyeing me, Richard," she said, "but now is not the time. Come on, Dillon. You can sit on Auntie Carol's lap. Your dad's too heavy."

Dillon did as he was told, a dazed expression on his face.

"I'll be right back," Richard said to Carol, then waddled up to the front of the bus, stepping on toes and bumping elbows with passengers on either side. A soldier glared at him, but he kept going. He wanted to see what was happening.

In the driver's seat, David gripped the steering wheel tightly. He didn't blink, even as he careened into a pack of demons—the bus lurching and crunching their bodies beneath its large tyres. Richard clutched the back of David's seat to hold on, and it made the man flinch.

"Richard! You bugger."

"Sorry."

"It's okay." The bus lurched again, crushing yet more bodies. "If we don't get out of here soon, we're going to bust an axle. There's too many of them."

Richard wished it wasn't true, but the demons filled the street like swarming insects. Where had they all come from?

"Just try to avoid them if you can."

"Yes, thank you for that, Richard. What wonderful advi—" More bodies beneath the wheels. "God's sake. What? Oh, please, no."

Richard glanced through the cracked windscreen that was one or two more impacts away from shattering. Standing in the middle of the road, Skullface stood impassively. Behind him, the massive angel who wanted to see them all dead: Andras. A pile of fresh human corpses lay at the angel's feet—survivors dragged out of their hiding places and butchered. Their corpses were being displayed like trophies—and as a threat.

Even without a face, Skullface was clearly laughing at them.

Richard put his hand on David's shoulder and squeezed hard. "Floor it!"

David winced. "What?"

"Put your fucking foot down, David."

"We're doomed either way, so what the Hell. Hold on to your hat." He stomped on the accelerator and pushed back in his seat as the engine roared. He up-shifted and picked up speed—the bus's engine beefier than either of them had probably expected. Skullface remained standing in the road. The angel moved behind him, ready to meet the bus's charge.

David glanced back over his shoulder. "Richard, are you sure about this? I don't fancy ending up as a human pizza slice."

"Go faster."

"Oh, bugger it."

The bus lurched.

Skullface raised his arms on either side. At his feet, the human corpse pile began to move. Arms and legs straightened. Bloody jaws gnashed. Then, all at once, the human cadavers leapt up and wailed in agony.

"Zombies," said David. "Bloody zombies."

Richard cursed. "Our dead are being used against us. Our enemy gets stronger as we get weaker. There really is no hope."

"Fuck that," said David. "Our bacon's not burnt yet."

The bus neared eighty and began to complain. The engine whined. The bolted seats, struts, and fixtures groaned. The vehicle had reached its limit. Skullface, Andras, and a squad of newly raised corpses stood in the middle of the road, defiant and unafraid.

David growled, in fear or anger, Richard didn't know, but it was time to put his plan into action. He grabbed the wheel.

"What are you soddin' doing, Richard?"

"Just keep your foot on that pedal."

David removed his hands from the wheel and allowed Richard to take control. The bus kept its speed. Skullface and Andras stood their ground.

They would not move.

This was a game.

David closed his eyes. "Nice knowing you, chap."

Richard squeezed the steering wheel, eyes wide open and glued to the merciless beasts ahead.

"Richard!"

"Hold on!" He yanked the wheel hard to the right and the bus whipped sideways, throwing everyone inside against the windows or into the aisle. Screams filled the cabin, and grew louder as the wheels on the right left the road. The view through the windscreen tilted forty-five degrees. Skullface and the angel disappeared from view as the bus turned sharply and began to tip.

"Foot off the accelerator," Richard shouted. "Get your feet up!"

The bus skidded on its two remaining wheels, teetering at the point of catastrophe.

The screams grew louder, escaping even the soldiers now.

Richard shouted, "Step on it again, David. Hit the accelerator."

The back of the bus swung around, striking Skullface like a giant baseball bat and clipping the angel's knees. Both demons bellowed in a glorious mixture of pain and surprise. Richard chanced a quick look to his left and saw Andras crashing to the ground like a falling oak.

The bus's tyres squealed as they bit the road. The interior rocked back and forth.

The engine squealed.

Then the view through the windscreen stopped tilting and the world fell back into a horizontal frame. All four wheels gripped the road, and the bus's springs bounced hard enough that they risked snapping.

Gradually, like a calming ocean, the bus reacquainted itself with gravity. The vehicle had lost half its speed but was once again heading along the road, this time without any obstacles ahead.

The screams inside the bus stopped, replaced by shocked silence.

Richard let go of the wheel and slumped against David's chair. "Get us out of here."

"Where on earth did you learn to drive like that, old boy?"

"Advanced Driving for Police. Never tried it in a bus before though."

8

GUY GRANGER

Guy waited for dawn, as the birds were still sleeping when he first opened his eyes. Inside the Captain's cabin on the Hatchet, he switched on the light and got dressed, but before he left, he picked up a picture that lived on his desk. The photograph had been taken at the Lewiston Fair when Alice was 3 and Kyle a few years older. Guy and Nancy stood on either side of their kids with bright beaming smiles. The happy American family. Now Kyle was dead, Nancy most likely too, and home was just a memory. No more fairs. No more beaming smiles.

But Alice was alive. He had spoken to her, heard her voice.

I'm coming to get you, baby.

There was a knock on the door as Guy had been about to open it. He found Skip waiting for him in the passageway. The old chief gave him a thin-lipped smile. "You ready to get going, Captain?"

Guy frowned. "Are you intending on joining me?"

"Of course. I signed on to serve you, not the ship. Besides, I don't think I could take orders from Tosco."

"But what about the things you said yesterday? You said the men deserved to stay and fight or go back home."

"Aye, and I still believe that. My choice is to help you find little Alice."

Guy felt warmth fill his tummy. "It will be dangerous out there."

"Aye, but anything willing to eat my leathery old hide is welcome to it."

Guy laughed and patted the old man on the back, but then changed his mind and decided on a hug. "Thank you, Chief. At least I'll have one person with me I can trust."

"Let's get out on that deck and meet the sun. Might be our last chance. Looks like the morning might bring a storm with it."

The two men strolled out onto the rain-soaked aft deck in time to catch the sun rising beyond the stern. The silent ships filling the harbour cast long shadows across the shimmering water, but Guy's attention was taken by something even more beautiful. Standing to attention on deck were two-dozen men and women. Most were sailors, but a few were civilians.

"These are the folks with no one left to fight for," said Skip. "Except for little Alice. Finding out she's still alive after having travelled so far to find her... well, for some of us, it makes it all the more important to see things through to the end. We're coming with you to save your little girl, Captain."

At that, the small assembly saluted in agreement with Skip's assertions.

Guy had tears in his eyes as he stepped forward. "I thought Alice was the only family I had left, but I was wrong. Let's go and find our baby girl."

The sun rose fully to the sound of cheering.

RICK WATCHED the sun rise from the small all-hour coffee shop that operated in Portsmouth's main barracks. There he sat nursing a hot chocolate. He'd never had much of a sweet tooth, but ever since Daniel... *changed him*... he'd developed a raging appetite for sugar. He felt like Jeff Goldblum in The Fly. Maybe it was a part of Daniel's personality.

Am I even me anymore?

Rick knew he was dying—and had been dying ever since the

moment he came back from death. Daniel hadn't saved his life that day his skull had cracked open, only postponed its end. The angelic power inside of Rick was too much for his human body to contain, and every morning he woke with another small piece of him rotting away. Even his fingers, now grasping the hot chocolate, had grown twisted and gnarled. He could barely feel the scalding heat through the plastic cup. He was cursed. Cursed to die piece by piece.

But that curse was also a gift.

Daniel had given Rick the power to do something important before his time came—a chance to hit back at the demons spilling forth from the gates. The closer he got to death, the more this strange inner strength grew. That last gate he had closed had been like flicking a switch—so easy. One brief moment of focus and he had reduced the demonic portal to ash, and he had done it from a distance. A hundred demons had vanished in the ensuing shock wave. Rick was a weapon, and with one last chance, he could tip the scales in humanity's favour. If he succeeded, Lord Amon would be rendered vulnerable. The rest would be down to General Wickstaff.

Keith strode into the empty seating area and nodded to Rick. Maddy and Diane followed behind him.

"I've got you all a drink," said Rick, motioning to the hot coffees in plastic cups on the circular table.

Keith rubbed his hands together and sat down. "Just the thing. I hate early mornings. Only thing about my old life I don't miss."

Rick laughed. "One of the rare things we have in common."

"Rare is the word, what with you being a demon now, little brother."

"He's not a demon," Maddy chided as she took a seat beside Keith. She handed one coffee to Diane who took the final chair and then took one for herself. Diane was still the quiet type, but the apocalypse had drained the fear from her like pus from a boil. Although she didn't look like it, she was a warrior—still alive when most were not.

"I've always liked mornings," she said. "I used to like the

sounds of the birds. Anyone else noticed they don't seem to sing as much anymore?"

"I guess," Maddy admitted. "Maybe the gates affect them."

"Or maybe they're too busy feasting on carrion," Keith muttered. "Can't say I much care."

"Are we still leaving to help the American?" asked Diane, ignoring Keith's grumpiness and sipping demurely at her coffee.

Rick thought she might have muttered arsehole under her breath. He smiled.

"Yes, I still intend to help Captain Granger," he said. "I'm not asking any of you to come. It's suicide, leaving Portsmouth, but I don't have a choice. It's why Daniel brought me back. Lord Amon has destroyed every human outpost between here and London, and soon he'll make a move here and try to wipe out what's left of us. I have to destroy that gate, or the people here will have no hope of winning."

"Ha!" Keith barked. "They're all fucked, whatever you do. Even if you weaken Lord Amon, he has the numbers."

"Cut off the chicken's head," said Rick, "The demons are selfish, aimless souls—that's what got them sent to Hell in the first place. The only thing that galvanises them is the angels. If we take out Lord Amon and the other angels, the demons will fall to disarray. I'm certain."

Maddy nodded at every word. "Then we go out there and close that gate. Just like you said, Rick. We can do this."

Rick shook his head. His next words were going to hurt. "You're staying here."

Maddy flopped back in her chair like a punch had hit her.

"I'm going with you," said Diane. "You can't leave us here."

"I'm not talking about you, Diane. Only Maddy."

Maddy leant forwards again, placing her hands on the table. "What are you talking about, Rick?"

"I'm talking about you staying here where you're needed most. You're a medic. The people here need all the medics they can get."

"You're going to need me out there. What if you need help?"

"If I get injured, I'm done for. You can't help me out there amongst the demons. There's no point trying to patch up a wound too big to heal on its own out in the field. You need to stay and help those who can live to fight another day."

"I'm coming with you Rick."

Rick shook his head firmly. He'd already made up his mind after much wakeful thinking last night. "You're staying here. I'll have Wickstaff restrain you if I have to."

"Rick!"

"Listen to me!" Rick felt his eyes flash with something inhuman. His voice crackled like scrunched-up tinfoil. Everyone at the table recoiled. Diane spilled her coffee. Rick took a slow breath and calmed himself. Slowly the strange sensation retreated, and he felt like himself again. "You three around this table are the only things left I care about. I need to know at least one of you is back here relying on me to succeed. It will keep me going knowing my success will help at least one of you to survive to live out a future. Those who come with me probably won't get that chance. Maddy, you are most useful to the people at Portsmouth. Wickstaff needs good people by her. And if you come along..." He blinked, keeping back tears. "I won't be able to do what I need to do."

Silence hung in the air.

Maddy seemed to understand what he was trying to say because she picked up her coffee and sipped it without further argument. She avoided making eye contact with him.

Keith placed an elbow on the table making it rock slightly. "I'm coming with you, brother. Who knows, maybe I'll find Marcy and Max out there. You can grab a demon by the balls and make him talk."

Rick had known his brother would come, but feigned surprise. "You're sure? It might be a one-way trip."

"Truth is, I feel safer with you than I do here. We survived two weeks out there on our own because of your abilities. Your powers are getting stronger too. I trust you to keep my arse out of the fire, but if not, I'd rather just get it over with and die. I can't wait around here wondering which day will be my last."

"I can't promise to keep you safe, Keith."

"That's okay. I've never known you to keep your word anyhow."

Rick sighed. The world may have ended, but his older brother's subtle contempt was still very much alive. "What about you, Diane? Stay or go?"

"I'm staying."

That, Rick had not expected. Her decision saddened him, but he didn't show it. That would not be fair on her. But was this to be his final goodbye to both Maddy and Diane? It raised a sticky lump in his throat.

"I want to come with you, Rick, but if Maddy is staying, then so am I. I won't leave her alone. You'll have your brother on the road. Maddy will have me."

Maddy reached out and touched Diane's hand. "You don't have to."

"I know I don't." She smiled sadly at Rick. "I'm staying here, and when you get back, we'll sit down like this and compare stories. This isn't a suicide mission, Rick. You're coming back. I'm ordering you to."

A chuckle escaped Rick's mouth, but it wasn't mocking. "Maybe when I come back, you will have usurped General Wickstaff and taken charge of this place. You have a deal—I'll do everything in my power to obey your orders."

Keith glanced at the expensive, now cracked watch on his beefy forearm. "Day's about to start. Longer I sit around talking about it, more likely I am to back out, so we should get going."

Rick stood, felt an odd sensation in his spine but ignored it. "You're right. The sooner we go, the more light we will have. Wickstaff will be in her office by now—the woman barely sleeps."

"Probably because she's got the job of being humanity's saviour," said Maddy. "That would keep me awake at night."

"Ha!" Keith barked. "Thought that was my little brother's job."

"More saviours we can get, the better," said Maddy. "Um, guys, could I speak to Rick alone for a second, please?"

Keith raised an eyebrow, but nodded. He and Diane left the coffee shop and went back out into the frigid morning. Rick stood facing Maddy, wondering if she was going to try to convince him to stay. He hoped not. She might succeed.

"You sure you don't want me to come along?" she asked.

"Do I want you to come along? Yes. Of course. But…"

"Don't have to repeat it. You might do the scary eye thing again."

Rick turned and cupped a hand over his eyes. "I'm sorry. My emotions seem to manifest a little more forcefully lately."

Maddy pulled his hand away from his face and made him look at her. "I love my husband," she said, somewhat unexpectedly. "I think about him every day."

"I-I know you do."

"But when you leave, I will be thinking about you too. You're not my husband, Rick, but I love you. You saved my life, and I saved yours. That means something."

"It means a lot," he admitted.

Maddy surprised him again. She kissed him on the mouth and placed a hand against his cheek. He sensed the blood running through her palm, like a faint echo.

"What Diane said goes for me too, Rick," she said, pulling away. "This is not a suicide mission. If things get too hard, you come back, and we'll find another way."

"I have to do whatever's necessary."

"I'm not talking about what's necessary. I'm talking about you staying alive. Come back to me, Rick. You hear me?"

He nodded. "I hear you, Maddy."

The two of them shared a moment just staring at each other, and then Maddy headed for the door. Rick went after her, legs shaking. From the kiss or from the changes going on inside of him, he wasn't sure.

Outside, the sun had risen high enough to cast a weak, grey light over everything. Rick had expected to see yawning sentries awaiting replacement, but instead, he witnessed a group of two-dozen soldiers bunched together around the parade square. Something was happening.

"What's got their knickers in a twist?" Keith appeared out of Rick's blind spot with Diane. He was frowning and trying to get a clear look ahead,

Rick felt that strange tingling sensation in his spine again. "Do you know what's going on?"

"We wanted to wait for you first," said Diane.

"Okay, let's go find out."

Rick hurried, and the others kept pace. The closer he got to the soldiers ahead, the odder he felt. His flesh tingled. His teeth ached. The air felt charged like those tense moments before a thunderstorm. To add to the sensation, it had begun to rain. A light drizzle that threatened more.

"I see General Wickstaff," said Maddy, pointing to the centre of the crowd. Rick saw the woman too. Portsmouth's no-nonsense leader was wearing silk pyjamas and slippers. It wasn't the first time she'd strode around camp in less than authoritative fashion. Perhaps the days of respecting a uniform were over. The woman led by example, not appearances. Even so, an aide was hurrying towards her with a pair of overalls to put on.

The general was worried. Rick could read it in the way she folded her arms tightly and couldn't keep still. Something on the ground had her attention, but it was unclear what. Too many soldiers in the way.

Rick picked up his pace, merging with the crowd. "What's going on? Let me see."

When the soldiers noticed Rick, they parted. Everyone on base knew who Rick was—the demon-blooded survivor who could close gates with a look. He was Portsmouth's resident VIP. And he hated it. Just like he'd hated it in his earlier life. Now that his pop career was behind him, irrelevant in this new world, he finally realised how much it had ruined him. He had become a pop star for his love of music. Everything else soured his passion.

General Wickstaff spotted Rick's arrival and sagged with relief. "Rick! Just the chap! Please tell me you can deal with this."

Rick moved past the last two soldiers standing in his way and glanced towards the object at Wickstaff's feet. He almost collapsed at what he saw.

"No," he moaned. "No, how could this happen?"

Wickstaff glared at the glowing black stone like it was her worst enemy. "Who cares how it happened. Can you get rid of it?

If this thing opens... Jesus Christ, there'll be a bloody gate right in our midst."

"Shitting hell," said Keith. "Now I'm even more determined to come with you, Rick. This place is fucked."

"C-can you deactivate it?" asked Maddy, looking at Rick like a child asking her daddy to crush a spider.

Rick shook his head. "I-I don't know. Let me try."

General Wickstaff hiked up her pyjamas and turned to the crowd. "Okay, you lot, let the dog sniff the rabbit. Move back and give Rick some space."

The crowd stepped back as one, the circle of bodies expanding.

Rick took one step towards the black stone, as close as he dared get. His vision blurred, as if the stone emitted a blinding light that only he could see; yet it seemed to do the opposite. All light died within the obsidian rock.

Rick reached out his hand.

The stone began to throb, vibrate.

"It's working," said Wickstaff. "You're doing it."

Rick focused on the stone. He imagined his fingertips were lengthening, stretching out towards it. He gritted his teeth. His entire body tensed, spine creaking, threatening to break.

"Rick, are you okay?" asked Maddy. "You're sweating."

"Maddy, I... I can't."

"You must," shouted Wickstaff. "We're doomed if you don't."

"I can't," Rick repeated, he felt pressure in his eyes, like they were about to burst. "I..."

The black rock screeched, and an invisible force swatted Rick with enough force to launch him six feet in the air. He landed hard on his aching back twenty feet away on the parade square. The back of his skull struck the concrete like a soft melon.

Maddy rushed over to him. "Rick? Rick, are you okay?"

"I can't... I can't stop it. It's coming."

"What's coming?" General Wickstaff demanded.

Rick's vision was curling in at the edges. When he spoke his last words, his tongue felt sluggish and fat. "The biggest gate of them all."

GUY WALKED the docks in the rain.

"Well, that's not a good omen," said Tosco, looking up at the dark grey clouds. The lieutenant wouldn't be accompanying Guy on his journey, but had insisted on seeing him off. The Hatchet had finally become his. Good luck to the man. While the lieutenant was wretchedly ambitious, he was also brave and honourable. He had helped Guy reach England, as promised, and had not developed into the thorn in his side Guy had been anticipating—a mild pain in the ass at best.

"Nothing wrong with a bit of rain," said Skip. "It'll remind us all of the sea."

Guy smiled. "Indeed. It will also mask the sound of our travels. It's a good omen, Lieutenant, not a bad one."

The expedition's headcount had reached twenty-six, a number less than Guy had hoped, but it would have to do. He was on his way now to collect the men Wickstaff had promised him. He needed to find Rick too. The man gave Guy the creeps, but his help was appreciated.

When he came across the parade square, Guy found Wickstaff in her pyjamas and Rick unconscious on the floor. Most disturbing of all, was the cold black stone embedded in the concrete nearby.

"I think the omens just got worse," said Tosco.

Guy stared into the black stone and saw nothing but darkness.

9

VAMPS

Vamps raced towards the group of burnt men with the alluminium baseball bat he had found in the garden of a crumbling maisonette. His MP5 had run out of bullets, so it would be melee from here on in. That suited him fine. The sun had risen on a brand-new day, and Vamps was there to meet it, arms swinging.

The bat connected with the skull of a first burnt man and caved in fragile bone like *papier mâché*. Blackened pulp spilled from the creature's brainpan even as it remained standing for another three seconds. Vamps turned his attention to the next in line and used his foot to trip the demon to the ground before swinging the bat and caving in its skull too. That left three more burnt men.

Each creature had been a person once. Vamps saw green eyes and blue, plump, womanly lips, and thin elderly ones. Who had these monsters been? When?

Vamps and his crew had spotted the disbanded group of demons at dawn, travelling south along the side of the road. Vamps had wasted no time in attacking them. Aymun and Mass tried to stop him, but he wasn't listening. No stopping what he needed to do: kill as many of the bastards as he could. They all deserved to die. Every last one.

"Be careful, man," shouted Mass.

Vamps ducked a swipe of a sharpened finger-bone and sprang back up, ramming his head under the chin of the demon that had tried to slash him. The creature staggered back, giving him enough room to swing his bat and take the thing's head off. The decapitated skull hit the road and rolled against the curb.

"Vamps, calm down!" Mass came to help, but it was unnecessary. Vamps dropped his baseball bat and grabbed the two remaining demons by the back of their rotting heads. With a strength he didn't know he had, he smashed their faces together again and again until all that remained was maggot-filled mush.

Vamps let the corpses fall to the ground and spat on them. Then he turned with a wide grin on his face. He straightened the peak of his bright-green baseball cap. "You see that shit? Five of 'em on by myself—bare handed. Beat that, boys."

Mass stared at him. "Vamps, man. You got to be careful. You can't just run off and fight these things on your own."

"Think you might be wrong there, bruv. See these dead bodies? I'm taking it to the motherfuckers, one by one."

Aymun sighed. "Your anger consumes you, my brother."

"No shit," said Vamps. "I'm putting it to good use."

"Vengeance will bring you no peace."

"It's not about bringing me peace, Aymun. It's about bringing pain to the demons. I've had enough."

Mass reached out to touch him, but Vamps waved his friend away. "Don't!"

"Vamps, man. What happened to Marcy and Max—"

"Don't!"

Mass sighed, and didn't push it, which was good because Vamp's hands had been instinctively tightening around the bloody baseball bat. Instead, he waved an arm towards the road. "Let's get off the highway. Maybe we can find a police station and some ammo. It'll save us from having to take the demons on hand to hand."

Vamps pulled the MP5 sub-machine gun from the holster on his waist and tossed it to the ground. He raised the bloody baseball bat beside his head and tapped it against the peak of his cap. "I prefer this."

Mass shook his head and exhaled.

Vamps grunted and started walking. Mass went to say something, but Aymun spoke first. "Let him go, my brother. His heart must find its own way to beat."

Vamps sneered. What was their problem? Did they sympathise with the demons? Well, fuck that. Whether his friend liked it or not, he was going to rip apart every demon he stumbled upon. And if he ever saw that angel again…

Traffic snarled ahead, making it a good time to get off the road. Bunched up cars and lorries made too good a hiding place for demons, and while Vamps wanted to kill as many as he could, he wasn't stupid. He hopped the barrier at the side of the road and pushed through a thorn bush. An old wooden fence, bordering a field, stood in their path. It was easily assailed.

Mass and Aymun followed him in silence. The rain had been falling for the last hour. The wet grass of the field was slippy and soaked their trouser cuffs.

"Looks like there's restaurants and stuff over there," said Mass, pointing to the far edge of the field where a pair of golden arches stood up high on a plinth. A giant pizza slice rose atop another.

"The people of this country eat many things," said Aymun. "Burgers, pizzas, and more. You idolise food."

Mass shrugged. "What's wrong with that?"

"When you idolise something you give it too much worth. Half the world starves because they cannot eat. They starve while others eat three times what they need. Do you see the injustice of that fact? Your large muscles come at the expense of a starving child's emaciated frame in Zambia or Eritrea."

"Not my fault," said Mass. "Besides, I don't think it matters anymore. The whole world is equally fucked."

"It matters because we are fighting to regain our world. What is the point if we re-establish old inequalities?"

"Things won't ever go back to how they were," said Vamps, sick of the chatter. "The world is dead. It ain't coming back."

"I pray not," said Aymun.

They travelled the rest of the way in more silence until they reached the fence again. Part of the wooden barrier had collapsed, probably when a starving cow clattered through it to escape— funny how a cow could escape if it wanted, yet dozily remained in captivity. They passed through the broken section and stepped into a ditch by the side of the road. They found a trading park, typical on the outskirts of most towns. Half-a-dozen themed restaurants mingled with a few large retail outlets. Bring a credit card and you could grab a light lunch followed by a king-sized bed on four-years' finance.

"Oh snap!" said Mass. "There's a bowling alley."

Vamps saw the colourful facade of three pins and a sparkling bowling ball. "Sweet, maybe they'll have a bar inside."

"You should not drink," said Aymun. "We need our wits."

Mass agreed with Vamps about the booze. "I'm tired of having my wits about me, Ay. Sometimes a guy needs a fuckin' break. Come on, we can check the place out and build a barricade. It'll be safe as houses."

"I like it," said Vamps. "Where's the harm?"

Aymun relented. "As you wish, but I will not be partaking."

"Oh yeah," said Mass. "The Muslim thing."

Aymun chuckled. "No, my brother. I am no longer a Muslim. I have seen what lies beyond this life and see that all religions are undeserving of their followers. God does not care if a man enjoys the fruits of the earth. He cares about a man's heart. My heart is pure, and I will have my head remain also."

"So, in plain words," said Mass. "That's a *no* to getting shit-faced."

"Yes, that is correct."

"Let's roll then," said Vamps, heading across the car park. "I'll check the place out. Bit of luck, there'll be demons to kill."

"I wouldn't be so eager to throw yourselves to the wolves, fella."

Vamps, Mass, and Aymun spun around as one. They had no ammunition in their guns, but Mass and Aymun pointed their weapons anyway. Vamps held his bat over his head like a samurai sword.

Before them stood two men, one gaunt and wiry with messy brown hair, the other stocky with a shaved head. The gaunt man was the one speaking, and he did so with a jaunty Irish accent that almost seemed faked. Both the men stood casually outside Pizza Hut, like they were employees on a break or something.

"The fuck are you?" Vamps demanded, waggling his baseball bat in their faces.

The Irishman grinned. "Hey, fella, I was here first, so how bout you ease off on the caveman act."

Vamps lowered the bat, but only slightly. "What are you hanging around here for? Are there other people around?"

"Alas, no, tis just me and my taciturn friend here." The shaven-headed man stared at Vamps without blinking. He had an air of menace, a genuine hard man who didn't need to waste time speaking bollocks.

Vamps narrowed his eyes. "And who might you and your friend be?"

"We're not looking for trouble," said Mass. "I'm Mass. This is Aymun, and this is Vamps."

Vamps glared at his friend. "Why you chattin' with these motherfuckers?"

"Um, maybe because they're human, and have done nothing to threaten us."

"Indeed," said the Irishman. "No threat are we. The name's Lucas, and this handsome fella to my left is Damien. Say hello, Damien."

Damien didn't move a muscle—just continued to glare.

"Good to meet you, I guess," said Vamps. "So, what's the noise around here? Any demons?"

"Ah, plenty of those. Closer than you would think. But let's not discuss mundanities. I've been waiting here for you, Jamal, lad."

Vamps gripped his bat. "The hell you know my name?"

"I know many things. More than the likes of a thug like you."

Mass frowned. "Hey man! Chill."

"Why don't you be quiet, fella, before you pull a muscle. I'm talking to your boyfriend here." He sneered at Vamps. "B'jaysus, how on earth has a cretin like you kept alive?"

"By fucking shit up." Vamps swung the bat, but before it made contact, it melted away into nothing. Like a cobra, Damien grabbed Vamps' throat and threw him into his friends. All three men ended up on the floor, and when Vamps looked up, Damien was again leaning back against the wall.

Lucas leant over Vamps, his hand extended. "Sorry about that wee spot of rudeness there, fellas. Just needed to get your attention. Plus, I knew you wouldn't calm down unless I let you take a swing and get it out o' yer system. If you're still a tad disgruntled, you're free to take another swing. Just let me know when you're done."

Vamps shook his head and swallowed. "Nah, man. We cool."

Lucas danced a jig at that. "Delightful. Now, shall we head inside this fine eating establishment and have ourselves a beer? I hate to make new friends out here in the cold."

Vamps brushed himself with his palms and got off the floor. Mass and Aymun did the same, but none spoke. They were all dumfounded—even Aymun, who had taken a vacation in Hell.

They followed Lucas into the Pizza Hut, passing through the heavy glass door. They were immediately met by a tropical heat that had no place being there. The room was dark, so the source of such warmth was unapparent.

"Forgive me," said Lucas. "I hail from warmer climes."

Mass frowned. "Aren't you from Ireland?"

"Not originally. Take a seat, fellas. I'll get us a drink." He clicked his fingers and the lights came on, and so did a television above the bar. Man Utd was playing Liverpool. Impossible.

"What the fuck are you?" said Vamps, backing towards the door, wishing he still had his baseball bat, for comfort if nothing else.

"I'm just being a good host. The match is from last year as I'm afraid all the players are dead, except for John Terry. Cheeky bugger was playing away at a secret hideaway in the highlands. He's having to spend the apocalypse with a chatty airhead half his age—and a third his intelligence."

Vamps' jaw kept working, but he had no idea what to say. "I... w-what?"

Lucas chuckled. "Never mind." He disappeared into the back and came back with an armful of bottled beer. As he set them on the table, he glanced at Damien and winked. "Takes you back, lad, don't it? Everyone sit down."

Damien gave the merest hint of a smirk, but didn't sit as requested. Instead, he moved over to the window and stared out like a sentry. Everyone else did as they were told. Lucas took a swig of one of the beers and plonked it down on the table. Vamps couldn't be sure, but he thought he saw the liquid refill itself back to the top of the neck. A useful trick if it was true.

Vamps battled the urge to leg it, but he forced himself to stay seated. "What are you? You're one of them, ain't you?"

Lucas took another swig before letting out a painful-sounding burp. "Aye, strictly speaking. But at heart I'm one o' you."

"What do you want from us?"

"Not us..." Lucas leant forward, face to face with Vamps. He gave off an odd smell... like cookies. "I just want you, Jamal."

The urge to run kept on increasing. It was getting harder and harder to stay.

"Why do you want me?"

"To give you something, lad. You seem set on a path of destruction, even before you shot that poor sprog in the chest." Vamps reached his limit. The mention of what he had done to Max was enough to make him leap up and try to leave. Lucas put a hand on his arm and forced him to remain. "Hush there, lad. Hush. There used to be a good calling for souls like yours. A good friend of mine, Daniel, used to have such a role. Angels of death we used to call 'em, but truthfully, they were beings of justice. God's way of keeping order in his absence."

Aymun frowned. "God is not absent."

"You seen him lately, fella?"

Aymun sat back in his chair and gave no reply.

"Anyway, Daniel is a good lad. When this silly little war broke out, he tried to get involved and help you small folk. He made a great sacrifice that sent him back to the cage he'd only just escaped." He took another sup of beer and then toasted the air with the bottle. "Christ, I wish I had an ounce of that lad's bollocks. I owe him more than I could ever pay."

"You're not making any sense," said Vamps. "Are you talking about angels? Like the ones walking around killing people?"

Lucas picked up his perpetually full beer again and sloshed it around like a drunken pirate. "Aye! I am talking about just that. Angels! Not just any flavour though. I'm talking about fallen angels. Hell was left in their care. Lucifer—or at least the current holder of the title was supposed to keep order—but a dirty fella by the name o' the Red Lord made a right pig's ear of things while I was gone. These gates are not just gates. They are the seals keeping Hell and the Earth separate, powered by God's willpower. But God's willpower is powered by you."

Vamps frowned. "Me?"

"No, not you personally, you daft apeth. By humanity. When he created the Adams and Eves, God placed part of himself inside them, to keep his power safe from Heavenly forces who might wish to take his throne. I tell you, Hell might be a tad shabby, but the politics and power plays in Heaven can drive a fella mad. Over time, that power passed to every little boy and girl ever born—diluting all the time. Who knew you would end up being such horny little beasts?"

"You're losing me again," said Vamps.

"I suspect I am, lad. Let's just say, there is a war going on wider in scope than you realise. The war is not against mankind, but God's power contained within you. If all of you die, God will be left powerless. And who knows what happens whenever a monarch is rendered powerless?"

Aymun leaned forwards. "Claimants to the throne make war."

"Aye, go to the head of the class, you cuddly little terrorist."

Aymun actually blushed.

"It might not bother humanity too much—on account of that you will all be dead—but if God falls, then the war of succession will get so bloody that the universe itself will end up like a Belfast brothel. There's a lot of sodomy involved, take my word for it."

"So, we're really done for then?" asked Mass. "This is too big a fight to win?"

Lucas rocked back on his chair and sloshed his beer some more. "Would you ever behave, big fella? Leave the talking to the adults." He winked at Vamps. "You lot aren't beaten yet, are you? There's a resistance. There's always a resistance, so long as someone plays the part of the Nazis. There's this one world—a place where the dead walk around like a bunch of hungry drunks—where a veterinarian is kicking ass for mankind. In fact, she even gave Damien here a run for his money once. He's still brooding about it. Another place where men and women fight a war against animals—you gotta laugh at that one. Point is, humanity never gives up. It always resists fate. In fact, this whole disaster started when one lonely soul convinced God himself to allow a do-over. It was at that moment the Great Adversaries made use of a loophole and got their hooks in the Earth. Anyway, I'm going off the topic. My point is that humanity resists. And on this earth, you three are part of that resistance. More than you know. That's why I want to give you something." He placed something heavy on the table with a thud. It was a long silver sword, covered in strange etchings.

The sword caught fire and incinerated the table.

"The fuck?" Vamps and the others leapt back from the table.

Lucas grabbed at the flaming sword several times, cursing each time it burnt his fingers, but eventually he was able to extinguish the flames and pick it up. "Bloody thing. Daniel never did show me how to work it."

"That sword belonged to the angel, Daniel?" Aymun asked.

"Aye. It was his smiting stick, or whatnot. Fella never parted with it. Was a little weird to be honest. Anyway, it's great for vanquishing evil and all that. I'm surprised it even let me touch it. I suppose I really must have changed. Anyway, Vamps, lad. You want to take vengeance on the ugly feckers, at least go equipped for the job. Embrace the rage inside and become an angel of death. Humanity needs you." Lucas looked at Aymun and Mass. "But so do your friends. This sword is powerful, and if you're not careful, it will wield you, instead of you it."

Vamps swallowed. "Really?"

"Nah, I'm just having you on. But it is really sharp so be careful. Vengeance can make a fella lose himself, and I would hate for that to happen to you. Here, take it. Tis yours."

The lights in the restaurant flickered. Tentatively, Vamps stepped forward, worried that taking the sword would somehow hurl him down a rabbit's hole he would never get out of. Perhaps this whole thing was a trick, and the strange Irishman was here to kill them all.

"Be careful, man," warned Mass.

Vamps glanced at his friend and nodded.

He grasped the sword and took it from Lucas.

Vamps lost his breath.

The sword felt light in his hand, yet powerful, like it could cut through diamond. It fizzed and crackled like a loose wire, and when he examined the fine etchings, they seemed to pulse and reorientate themselves.

"Use it well, grasshopper," said Lucas in an offensive Japanese accent. "We never had a black angel of death before. About time, really."

Vamps was about to reply, but the Irishman was gone. He didn't so much disappear as just stopped existing in the first place. Like he'd never even been there.

Damien was still present in the room, and he peeled away from the window to face them. He let out a sigh and then said, "He does that."

Then, in a blink, Damien was gone too. The room was once again dark and cold. The only proof either man had ever existed was the flickering silver sword in Vamps' hand.

Vamps lowered the weapon to his side and looked at his companions.

"Anyone else think that was really weird?"

10

JOHN WINDSOR

Things felt better now he was wearing a fresh suit. After pulling himself from the rubble of London, John Windsor had lost access to his usual wardrobe, but after finding a gentleman's retailer in Woking, he'd re-outfitted himself in the manner to which he was acquainted. He was once again the Prime Minister of Great Britain. The reins of this country were still his.

That was why his current destination was Portsmouth. The seat of Government had established itself there in the form of a Military Autocracy. That would not do. The United Kingdom was, and forever will be, a democracy headed by an elected Prime Minister. Whichever General had placed themselves in charge was going to receive a demotion. John Windsor, and only he, was head of state.

That a settlement even existed at Portsmouth was impressive. The sudden, unilateral takeover of the world by supernatural forces had been unstoppable. The world's capital cities had fallen in days. London became a ruin within weeks, and most of the nation's armed forces were abroad. What had taken root in Portsmouth was a bunch of naval recruits and soldiers on leave. Reports he'd been receiving of their numbers must surely be inflated. No way could there be substantial resistance at Portsmouth.

Windsor leant forward and took his glass of sherry from the small bar built into the centre of the long Mercedes ferrying him towards his destination. So wonderful to be free of the harping and bickering of his cabinet, his phone hadn't rung in weeks. The nation was in a chrysalis, ready to be reborn with him as saviour. That he had negotiated a small settlement agreement with the demons was the sole reason humanity would survive. If not for him, extinction was inevitable.

"You're clear what is expected of you?" asked the ancient man in the seat beside him. Oscar Boruta eyed his glass of sherry disapprovingly, which only made John sip at it defiantly. Screw the old codger and his judgement. So what if he had been drinking a little during the past weeks? It was a stressful time.

"I know precisely what is expected of me, thank you very much, Oscar. Tell your masters I won't disappoint them. Also remind them of our deal. Humanity will receive a safe zone in which to live, with me in charge.

Boruta snickered, the sound of crunching leaves. "You will have your fiefdom, Prime Minister, do not fret. A deal struck in Hell is for eternity."

"The deal wasn't struck *in* Hell. It was struck in my office at Downing Street."

"What is your point?"

"Ha! Yes, very good. I agree, Westminster is much improved nowadays."

Boruta continued to eyeball him. "You must deal with this resistance in Portsmouth. The longer it remains, the harder it will be to dislodge. You want your deal, then you must take care of it."

John rolled his eyes. He detested being ordered to do anything. "Portsmouth will do as I say."

"We will see."

John's chauffeur turned around to tell him they were reaching the security perimeter around the city of Portsmouth. A checkpoint lay ahead—the first cars in John's convoy had already reached it. The black Jaguars had been intentionally battered and dented before arriving, making their journey seem more frightful than it had been. Truthfully, John and his entourage had travelled the country unmolested. The brand on his wrist gave him free passage amongst the demons.

"You better leave, Mr Boruta…" John sniffed. The old man had gone. *Good riddance.*

His Mercedes stopped at the checkpoint where two grim-faced sentries appeared at the driver's side window. Sitting behind the driver, John opened his window first. "Speak to me, please, soldier."

One of the two soldiers frowned at John, but moved to the rear window as requested. "Prime Minister Windsor?"

"One and the same. I am here to take charge. Let me in."

The soldier raised an eyebrow. "General Wickstaff is in command here, but I'll let her know you're coming."

John gripped the seat with both hands, but bit his lip and forced a smile. There was no point chewing out this worthless grunt, so he rolled up his window without further comment. A few seconds later, the convoy continued, entering the city of Portsmouth proper. It wasn't a pretty place, but it was old and possessing of a noble history. Great Britain had been a naval empire, and here was one of its greatest ports, home to some of the nation's greatest warships. Even now, John could see multiple vessels sitting in the distant harbour, though he had not expected nearly so many. The skyline blocked much of his view, but the corner of dockland was visible upon entering the city and was bustling with military and civilian crafts of all descriptions. He thought he even saw the nose of a carrier.

Not good, that so much manpower had found its way here. Early days of war had suggested the nation's forces had quickly scattered and become isolated. How had such a force accrued? Who was galvanising resistance?

General Wickstaff, of course. The traitor claiming to be in charge. Who was this man, and how much of a problem would he be?

It took twenty minutes to reach Portsmouth's naval base. Many of the roads were blockaded with the cement debris torn from nearby buildings. A toppled church spire had blocked off a side street. *An apt image to behold,* thought John. It appeared the city had been blocked off purposely so that a few chokepoints remained, each with a heavily armed guard. Trying to breach the city would be a nightmare for an enemy. Even more reason John had to enact a full surrender of the human forces here. He just had to assume his authority first.

John's Mercedes pulled onto a concrete parade square and came to a stop. His bodyguards parked their vehicles on either side. Their arrival had obviously been radioed ahead because a contingent of soldiers were already there waiting. John adjusted his tie and stepped out into the cold drizzle. He waved a hand to the gathered men and wore his most winning smile. "Hello, thank you for receiving me. The operation you have put into place here is astonishing. You are all extremely capable men and women. Please take me to the man in charge around here so that I can applaud him personally."

A scruffy woman in a pair of oily coveralls stepped forwards and offered an equally greasy hand. "Prime Minister, it's an honour to have you on base."

John ignored the woman's hand, nowhere near willing to shake it. "The man in charge, please? I wish to speak with General Wickstaff."

"Why would you wish to speak with anyone else?" said the woman. "I am General Wickstaff, current commander of operations here. I understand you would probably have preferred to meet with my male, Etonian predecessor, but I'm afraid he's currently unavailable."

John clenched his jaw. He did not like this woman at all. The way she looked at him... Her smirk was barely hidden. "Why is he unavailable?"

"Oh, you know, dead and all that. A real bother, to tell you the truth, as I don't much like having to run things around here. But, alas, I do run things around here, so if you have anything to discuss, I'm your man—in a manner of speaking."

John grunted. "Fine. You are to step down as commander here immediately. I am taking authority of Portsmouth as is my right as Prime Minister." Unhappy grumbles from the soldiers amassed behind the general. The woman obviously had them under her thumb. He would re-educate them in due course. "You will, of course, remain informed on a majority of matters, General, particularly military affairs, and your deeds here won't be forgotten."

The general nodded, the smirk gone from her face. She seemed almost relieved to relinquish command. "I suppose it is your right to take over. I mean, the population of this country voted you in, right?"

"Yes, they did. I am their legally elected leader."

"Indeed. But, the problem, as I see it, is that when you were voted into office, the country had... what? About seventy million people? There's only thirty thousand here at Portsmouth, and about six thousand of those aren't even from the UK. We have a lot of French. Even some Korean."

"What is your point, woman?"

"That's General while you're on my base, Prime Minister. My point is you represented a vastly different people than the one we have here, and I feel your authority is no longer legitimate. Not to mention, your cabinet is dead and the country we knew is gone. There is no more United Kingdom, there's just Portsmouth—and you were not voted into power here."

"Now look here," John growled, pointing a finger in this woman's face. "You will not usurp my power."

"What power? This is a military outpost with military rule. What these people need is a steadfast leader, not a sleazy career politician. Maybe I'm acting unconstitutionally, but I don't give a shit. I don't like you, and I won't help you, however many bull-dogs in suits you turn up with. I am in charge here, Prime Minister, and if you don't like it, you're welcome to hold an inquest. Let me know how that goes."

"*I* am your leader."

Wickstaff—the insolent bitch—just smirked. She *fucking* smirked!

"Look," she said calmly. "If you want to help around here, I'd be pleased to have you. I will happily include you in my war room meetings and even defer some of the more civilian matters to your experience. What I won't do is hand over the kingdom—especially regarding military matters. Your government is gone, so accept it and move on. Help your fellow man here, or fuck right off."

John felt a drumbeat in his temples. The gun hidden at his back cried out to him, and he imagined pulling it out and shooting the woman right in her smug mouth. But when he saw the defiant glares of the armed men all around her, he reconsidered. He would not beat this woman with force. No, he must do what he did best and gather power from within the populace. Embed himself and sway the majority to his side, then he could stage a coup. It wouldn't take long. He could eat this vile woman for breakfast.

John allowed a sigh and offered his hand. "Sorry, General. I feel it is my duty to take control here and see that our nation prevails, but if the people support you as leader, then who am I to demand otherwise?"

The general stuck her greasy palm against John's forcing him to hide his disgust. She smiled at him warmly, having bought his line of bullshit. "New politics for a new world, ay, Prime Minister. I think they call that cooperation. Well done."

John kept the smile plastered on his face and shook the woman's disgusting hand harder. "Now we have reached an agreement, is it reasonable to ask to you to bring me up to date on matters here?"

She looked at the battered side panels of John's Mercedes. "Looks like you might have a few stories to tell yourself."

"Indeed. It's hairy out there, I'm sure I need not tell you. I'm not sure fighting is the right option."

"It's the only option. Especially now."

"What do you mean?"

"Come with me, Prime Minister."

John frowned, motioned to his bodyguards to follow, and then carried on after the general. Her soldiers outnumbered his bodyguards six to one, which was something he was comfortable with, or at least not in any position to change. They headed across the large quadrant of concrete towards a cordon set up on the far side. Now that Wickstaff's soldiers broke up into a looser formation, it was easier to see ahead.

"Is that a gate?" John's jaw dropped open.

"No," said Wickstaff. "But it will be."

"Well, w-w-we need to evacuate at once. You can't have people here."

The general frowned at him. "And where should we go?"

"Anywhere!" This was perfect, just the avenue he needed to dismantle Portsmouth. "Once that stone opens, there'll be a massacre. We'll be finished."

Wickstaff sighed. "I've considered all that, Prime Minister, believe me. At least we have a kill zone in place. Anything that comes through will get ripped apart. But if we leave, we go right back to running and dying."

John noticed then what must have been fifty snipers positioned around the various rooftops of the camp. There was also a trench in the process of being dug around the glowing black stone. It was true that any demon wanting to make it through was going to have a hard time, but Hell's legions couldn't be contained forever. This would still be mankind's last, losing stand if they didn't leave now.

His role became even clearer. Thousands of lives here depended on him taking charge.

"Okay," John told his bodyguards. "Pass on the word. We are implementing a mass evacuation right now. It is not safe here."

"You'll do no such thing," said Wickstaff, glaring at the bodyguards, who shamed themselves by wavering. "If I see any man passing on orders that are not my own, I will have them shot dead. You are all welcome here, but that can change in an instant."

"You don't have the right to gamble with people's lives, General!"

"Spoken with no hint of irony, Prime Minister. Bravo! Our plans here are under constant discussion, and you're welcome to voice your opinion, but you will do so via acceptable methods. You will not sow dissent here, Prime Minister. This is your final warning."

"Fine. Then I demand to be informed of all events going forward. You might think you are in charge here, but when the time comes, you will be out of your depth."

She threw her arms out. "Then help me, you stubborn fool! Stop holding onto silly notions of power and entitlement and get the Hell on board. Don't plot my downfall. Plot the enemy's downfall."

John looked at his own men and saw them nodding. The woman spoke sense to them. The lowly always saw sense in demagogues. An evacuation must happen, or that gate would open and there'd be no survivors left to form a human settlement. He had to take control of this mess. And soon.

"Inform me of everything, General, and you shall receive my advice. I won't force you to take it, but you would be wise to consider it."

Wickstaff nodded curtly. "I'll have offices set aside for you and your people. Welcome to Portsmouth, Prime Minister."

Welcome to Hell, thought John as he turned on his heel and went back to his Mercedes, *because that's what this place will become if I don't wrestle it from that mad bitch's grasp.*

11

GUY GRANGER

"I still have to go," said Guy, standing at Rick's bedside. The blowback from the stone had left the man woozy, and he had been weak for the last few hours. He didn't appear physically injured, but it had taken till now to come back fully to reality. Maddy stroked his brow and gave him sips of water, but other than Guy, everyone else was waiting outside.

Rick blinked, one eyelid slower than the other. "You'll still have my help, Guy. I'm coming."

"What?" said Maddy, pulling her hand away from his forehead and staring at him. "You can't leave now. You're hurt, and we don't know when that gate will open."

"I'm fine, Maddy. It took the wind out of me, but I'm okay now. As for the gate, it's too powerful for me to close. If it opens, there's nothing I can do."

"Why can't you close the gate here?" asked Guy. He still wasn't sure that Rick could close any gate, but he decided to take it as truth for now.

Rick sat up to answer the question, much to Maddy's disapproval. "It's different somehow. More powerful."

"Then perhaps you should stay here," suggested Guy.

"No. The plan hasn't changed. If we don't weaken Lord Amon,

then everyone here is doomed. The only good I can do is out there."

Guy had gotten so used to trusting his own people that the thought of relying on a stranger was tough to reconcile. It was Rick's condition, though, that truly unnerved him. He looked more ghoul than human. How much longer did he have?

"You know, I can't help feeling like we've met before," said Guy, now that he'd taken a long look at Rick's face. "You look familiar."

Rick groaned as if that was the worst thing he could have heard. An odd reaction. "I just have one of those faces. Now, are you ready to go? Longer we wait, the bigger chance Maddy has of convincing me to stay."

"Yes, I'm ready. Just let me get my men together."

Guy headed out of the barracks and back towards the docks. He had left his scouting party on the Hatchet to load up on supplies while Tosco readied the larger part of the remaining crew to depart for home. A final segment of men and women would stay at Portsmouth. The large family that had sailed the Atlantic were breaking up.

But when Guy made it back to his ship—or Tosco's ship now —he was dismayed to find his contingent had reduced by two thirds.

Tosco stood on the gangplank waiting for him. "The crew are anxious, Captain. They heard about the new gate."

"It's not a gate yet." Guy moved past the Lieutenant and boarded the Hatchet.

"Well, regardless, the number of men intending to return home has increased, but I'm afraid that means less people for your hunt for Alice."

Guy stopped and looked Tosco in the eye. "Did you help convince them that joining you was in their best interests, Lieutenant?"

Tosco's eyes narrowed, and he bared his teeth. "I knew you would think that. No, Captain, I did nothing to dissuade anyone from going with you."

"He's telling the truth," said Skip, heading across the deck. He had a Remington Riot shotgun slung over his shoulder that looked more than his withered frame could handle. "Everyone on board wants to get as far away from that black stone as possible."

"You too, Skip?"

"Heaven's no. I'll be right there beside you when you find your Alice. Other men too."

Guy turned to Tosco and sighed. "I'm sorry. I should have known better than to question you."

"No one is thinking clearly right now, Captain."

"How many men do we have left, Skip?"

"Six sailors and two civilians."

Guy moaned. "Including you and me, that makes ten. Rick is still coming, and if Wickstaff comes through and lends more manpower, maybe we still have enough."

Tosco folded his arms.

Guy folded his own arms in reply. "What is it, Lieutenant?"

"You're going to get them all killed. You might have twenty bodies if you are lucky. I've been speaking to the soldiers here on base, they say there's fifty thousand demons scattered around Portsmouth, with more coming every minute. You'll never make it where you're going."

Guy wished he could argue his case, but Tosco was right. The chances of finding Alice—and finding her alive—were beyond slim. But what father would not try anyway? "Way I see it, Lieutenant, we're all due to die in some fashion. The only thing we have power over now is how and why. That I have such a small amount of help is the very reason I will succeed. Smaller the group, less chance of the enemy spotting us."

Tosco let his arms drop to his sides and stood there motionless for a moment. Then he did something unexpected and snapped off a crisp salute. "I wish for your safe return, Captain. Alice's too. It has been an honour serving under you, and I hope to command the Hatchet in the way she deserves."

Guy returned the salute, then broke protocol and yanked Tosco into a hug. "You've always been built to lead, Commander Tosco. Do well."

Tosco was stiff at first, but then he put his arms around Guy and patted his back with real affection. When the men finally broke away, they maintained eye contact for a few moments, conveying their unspoken respect. Tosco and Guy had never been friends, but the younger man was courageous, and willing to die for his crew. The Hatchet deserved a leader like him.

Skip gave Tosco a quick hug too. "I hope we all meet again someday."

Skip nodded. "When the world is ours again, lad."

"It's time for me to leave, Commander," said Guy. "Permission to gather my team and disembark?"

Tosco saluted. "Permission granted, Captain. God speed."

12

VAMPS

Vamps and his crew had remained at Pizza Hut following their strange encounter with the Irishman. It had left them unsettled and unnerved so much that they had needed to collect themselves. So they stuck around for a while, digging out uncooked pizza bread that had turned blue with mould and wishing there was something fresh. Eventually, there would be nothing in the world left to eat. They had survived weeks on canned food and foil-sealed snacks, but everything else was spoiled. With no new food being produced, there was a finite supply.

While Mass and Aymun filled plastic bottles with full fat Coke from the vat behind the self-serve machine, Vamps sat at a table staring at his sword—his 'flaming' sword that was the prior property of an angel of death. Somehow, he didn't feel honoured to have been bestowed with it. All the angels could go back to Hell, good or bad, he didn't care. None of them should be here. All they brought was death. Ravi, Gingerbread, Marcy, *Max...* So many lost.

And it was only a matter of time until everyone was gone.

He looked over at Mass, his last remaining friend. The guy was an ox, yet he would not have stepped on a bug before the end of the world. Now he was forced to fight for his life every day. What did the demons want? Was it really as simple as escaping Hell? Or was there something more? Why did they have to wipe out mankind? Lucas had suggested there was some larger war going on —a war with God. Humanity was just the innocent victim caught in the middle.

When has mankind ever been innocent?

Screw it. He'd kill as many demons as he could, whatever the reason.

"I'm the Angel of Death."

Mass looked over from the drinks station. "Huh?"

"Nothing."

There was noise outside. Not so loud that it startled anyone, but loud enough that Vamps rose from his seat to take a look out of the window. The sword was automatically in his hand as if it were part of him.

"What is it?" asked Mass, moving up beside him. Aymun was soon at his other side, the three of them now in a line.

Vamps saw movement near the bowling alley, across the car park. His hand tightened around his sword. "It's him."

The wounded angel stalked the shop fronts, smashing windows and looking inside. A dozen demons scurried about beneath it—worker ants finding prey for their queen. Was the angel searching for Vamps? Had killing Marcy and Max not been enough?

It was me who killed them.

But it was because of this creature.

Vamps rushed for the exit.

"Vamps, man. Stop! We have no ammo left and we're outnumbered. Vamps!"

Vamps didn't listen. He burst out of the restaurant and stalked across the car park. His approach went unnoticed for several paces, but then the angel turned its head, singed hair flicking over its shoulders. It pointed a massive hand, and like a swarm of bees the demons charged. Vamps gritted his teeth, lowered his head, and prepared to meet them.

"Vamps, man! Get the fuck back!"

"This is folly," shouted Aymun.

But Vamps wasn't listening. He raised the sword in front of him, and it began to throb, almost jumping loose from his hands.

He gripped tighter. Preparing to swing.

The first demon was one of the hunched over primates, and like the agile beast it resembled, it leapt at Vamps.

Vamps swung his sword.

The silver blade cut through the air, and halfway through its arc it turned to flame. The primate's torso sliced like warm butter and came apart in two pieces. The steaming flesh landed at Vamps feet and sizzled. He studied his sword with admiration. "Fuck yeah."

The next demons arrived en masse, and Vamps cut through them just as easily. He wielded the sword clumsily at first—having never used such a weapon—but slowly he settled into a rhythm, swiping left and right in looping arcs. Demon torsos came apart like slurry and each one he killed made his grin wider.

"Vamps!"

Vamps was sick of hearing Mass's voice, so he tuned his friend out. All that mattered was killing demons. All that mattered was being the Angel of Death. He'd been born to violence. He'd been born for this.

Vamps swung his sword in another spinning arc, having fun and enjoying the feel of hot silver slicing through flesh. Did he actually see fear in his enemy's eyes? The demons approached more cautiously now, trying to surround him before attacking. But Vamps would not be surrounded. He spun and leapt, attacking all sides.

"Vamps!"

Spinning to catch a burnt man attempting to slash at his back, Vamps glanced back across the car park.

How had he missed it? How had he lost sight of the angel?

Because I was lost in the killing.

Enchanted by the blood in my nostrils.

The wounded angel stalked Mass and Aymun across the pavement, barging aside parked cars in its quest to crush them. Aymun caught a glancing blow and tumbled to the ground, hitting his head against a Volvo's protruding tow bar. He lay on the ground, unmoving.

Vamps rushed to help his friends, but more demons appeared in his way. A burnt man grinned with broken teeth, shrivelled lips pulled back like a Pitbull's.

Vamps snarled. "Go ahead... try me!"

The burnt man lunged and Vamps decapitated it with one quick cut. He kicked the legs from under the next attacking demon and made a gap for himself to rush across the car park. Mass was pinned against a delivery van for the bed company, with the towering angel glaring down at him. The killing blow seemed to arrive in slow motion.

Mass cowered, his courage drained.

The angel reared back, clawed hands cutting the air.

Aymun lay on the ground, unconscious, just a few feet away.

Vamps screamed.

"NO!"

The blow was so powerful that the delivery van slid sideways on its tyres a full six feet.

When it came to a stop, Mass was gone.

"I FUCKING HATE YOU!" Vamps ran across the car park, raising the flaming sword above his head. The wounded angel turned to meet him.

Vamps turned sideways, leapt, and then threw his sword with everything he had. Twenty years of anger and hate went into his throw—a lifetime of poverty and violence on the streets. The sword tumbled through the air, whirling end over end for an eternity. It left a trail of blackened air and the smell of burning in its wake.

The wounded angel bellowed.

The sword plunged into its chest.

The angel stood frozen for a moment, eyes wide open. When it fell to its knees, it did so slowly, like treacle pouring from a cup. It clutched at the weapon hilt poking up from its chest, but its fingertips blackened and burned as they made contact. Finally, it opened its mouth, but no sound came out.

"See you in Hell, bitch!"

The angel tumbled forward onto the tarmac, expiring face down. Vamps turned and saw the remaining demons coming up behind him, but he was past caring. His last friend was gone. He prepared to fight with his bare hands, but realised the flaming sword was once again in his hands. He had thrown it, but it had found its way back to him.

The demons stopped just as they had been about to set upon Vamps. They peered past him at their fallen master and faltered. As one, like a starter's pistol had fired, they turned and fled. For the first time since the apocalypse began, Vamps saw demons running in terror.

The tables had turned.

But at what cost?

Vamps hurried towards where Mass had been standing. A massive dent distorted the side panel of the truck, but Mass was nowhere to be seen. Had he been obliterated? Shouldn't there be blood?

"Shit, that was close." Mass crawled out from beneath the crumpled truck. His forehead was bleeding, but he was okay. Vamps stumbled back and lost his legs completely. He dropped his sword to the ground and collapsed, panting. Crying.

Mass clambered to his feet and pulled a face. "I froze, man. I almost let the thing swat me like a fly. Got my senses back just in time and ducked beneath the truck. Fucking thing dragged me across the ground on my face when that son-of-a-bitch hit it." He looked down at the dead angel. "You did it, man. You killed a fuckin' angel."

Vamps couldn't speak, he was sobbing so much. Sobbing like a bitch, but he didn't care. "I-I-I thought you w-w-were…"

Mass moved beside him and knelt. Then he wrapped his arms around him, and the two of them hugged it out—a long embrace that neither broke away from.

"It's okay, man." Mass patted Vamps' back. "It's all good."

"You almost died because of me. I ran off and forgot about you and Aymun. All I cared about was the fight."

Mass nodded. "You need to chill, man. You haven't been right since—"

"Since I let Marcy and Max die."

"Nah, you didn't. That piece of shit on the ground killed them, and you know it. We're all just doing our best to survive, and every death is on them, not us. You're one of the good guys, Jamal. Don't lose yourself to anger. Stay with me, man."

Vamps bumped his forehead against his friend's, both of them still on the ground and hugging. "I hear you, bruv."

"Does anybody else hear ringing?"

Mass and Vamps looked up to see Aymun staggering towards them. The guy seemingly refused to die.

"I don't hear anything," said Mass.

Aymun nodded and slumped against the bed truck and trickled to the ground. "Oh good."

Vamps and Mass hurried to help their injured brother. It was just the three of them now, but they had each other's back. They would survive. Even if it killed them.

13

RICHARD HONEYWELL

Finally being out in the world again after weeks holed up at the Slough Echo was not as freeing an experience as Richard would have thought. Death stained the landscape like graffiti. The demons had strung up humans from lampposts or impaled them on railings. Some of the bodies still twitched, but were beyond helping. Fire and buildings falling in on themselves blackened other parts of the landscape. Civilisation was dead. All that remained were echoes of humanity.

Even the soldiers were mournful as the bus hurtled through the twisted shadows of the world. They flinched each time they sped by a group of wandering demons, or whenever the bus was forced to drive across a carpet of human viscera. If not for David's confident, somewhat reckless driving, they might not have made it out of Slough. If a group of demons tried to get in their way, David ploughed right through them.

But those continuous impacts had taken their toll. The bus's engine *thunked* and grumbled, and now and then the whole vehicle shuddered. Not to mention the needle of the fuel indicator plummeted.

The tank had a leak.

Knowing the bus ride was only a reprieve from fighting, Richard took a seat with his son. Dillon, like everyone else on board, was sullen. He stared at the floor, avoiding the horrific views from the windows on either side. This was no world for a child. It was almost cruel keeping Dillon alive, but what choice did Richard have? He was a father before anything else.

"You okay, Dil?"

"Yeah."

"Good. We'll find someplace safe again soon. Safer than before."

"Will Alice's daddy be there?"

Richard glanced over at Alice. She was sitting near the rear of the bus with Carol. The old gal had her arm around the girl—giving as much comfort as she could. It didn't stop Alice from weeping into her hands. The poor child had been so close to reuniting with her father, but their phone call cut mercilessly short.

Richard put his own arm around Dillon. "David told me he's heading south. If we make Portsmouth, we might find Alice's daddy. That would be nice, wouldn't it?"

Dillon nodded. "I don't think it's fair I have my daddy, but Alice doesn't have hers. Most daddies are dead. I seen them out the window."

Richard hugged his son. "I'm not going anywhere, Dil, I promise."

"The skeleton man wants to get you."

"We left him behind. He'll never find us again."

"You promise?"

Richard swallowed a lump in his throat. He didn't want to make the promise, but what were the chances of Skullface finding them again? They could be a hundred miles away by the end of tonight. David said he would continue driving long after dark.

But the petrol was depleting fast.

"I promise, Dil. He won't find us again. We will be safe." The words felt like ash in his mouth. Was he lying to his son?

The bus shuddered again, this time without end. The passengers started to mutter. The soldiers checked their rifles.

"Okay," said David from the driver's seat. "I was hoping we

could get a little way farther, but she's giving up the ghost. We have to stop."

The passengers moaned. Some cried.

"It's okay," said Corporal Martin. "We are prepared for this. Everyone will be fine."

It was an empty assurance, but it seemed to calm many. Richard moved up to the front of the bus to join David. "What's the situation?"

David glanced up at him. "That fuel leak neither of us wanted to mention has become too hard to ignore. We have some fumes left, but there's air in the tank, and the engine is on its last legs. Apparently, running over demons doesn't do a vehicle much good."

"Will we be safe stopping here?"

"No choice in the matter. I haven't seen any demons in the last few miles. Maybe we'll catch a break."

Richard thought of Alice's interrupted phone call with her father and decided the world didn't give breaks anymore. "Did we make it anywhere near Portsmouth?"

"We're still a good fifty miles away. We can still get there, but not today."

Richard sighed. The bus's shuddering increased, and they lost speed. David maneuvered them off the road, amongst a copse of trees. The area in their rear view mirror was urban, but ahead was farmland and scrub.

"Thanks for getting us this far," said Richard.

David nodded, but gripped the wheel as if reluctant to let it go.

"Okay, everyone," said Corporal Martin. "Let's stay quiet. We'll keep off the road and take the fields. It will give us plenty of vision and allow us to pick off our enemy in the open. We have guns, they do not. So don't panic. I'll get us through this."

Richard glanced at Dillon. *You better.*

Everyone filed off the bus in silence. If they had learned to do one thing over the last few weeks, it was to keep a low profile. People helped each other over to the side of the road and stayed huddled together. Alice came and took Dillon's hand and walked with him and Richard. Carol joined them too.

"Once more into the breach, ay?" said Carol with a determined, tight-lipped smile.

Richard raised his eyebrows in reply, letting out a weary breath through his nostrils.

Corporal Martin had his soldiers surround the group of civilians, and together, they entered the fields and started walking.

It was an hour later when the dull silence turned to chitchat. It was easy to see ahead, and the coast was clear. The ground was wet, and a light drizzle fell on them, but the group moved easily and without hardship. Alice and Dillon even had space to play, chasing after one another and wielding sticks like swords. Seeing his son smile lifted Richard's soul. He never thought he'd see it again. Children playing—such a simple thing, such a precious thing. Even before the apocalypse, humanity had lost itself. Men and women forgot what was important. Cars, houses, jewellery—it was all worthless. This was what mattered—being alive, outside in the open air with smiling children playing. If mankind prevailed, what would it go back to? Would it remember the ills of the past?

Would it repeat them?

After a while, Corporal Martin spoke from the front. "There's a farmhouse ahead. We should check it for supplies."

"Is that wise?" asked David.

"It's what we will have to do while we're on the road. Who knows how long we'll have to feed ourselves?"

"I agree," said Richard, although apprehensively. "We might find other survivors too."

"More the merrier," said Carol.

"Not necessarily," said David. "We thought Andras was a survivor. Turned out he was one of them."

Corporal Martin shifted his rifle to the other shoulder. "He's right. We won't turn people away, but any newcomers need to be closely watched."

"Maybe we can test them," said Richard. "Make them hold something made of iron."

"Do we have anything?" David asked.

"No."

"Then be on the lookout."

"Maybe there'll be something at the house," said Corporal Martin.

They reached a fence at the edge of the field and climbed over one by one in a long line. As soon as he was over, Dillon raced off towards an abandoned green tractor. Richard called after him. "Dillon! We need to make sure this place is safe."

Dillon nodded sullenly and came back.

Corporal Martin and his men swept the property, circling the various outbuildings. Their search eventually caused a stir.

"What the Hell is that?" asked Carol, eyes wide.

Richard chuckled. "Sounds like chickens."

Richard took Dillon and Alice around the back of the farmhouse where a couple of soldiers stood with their hands on their hips. A family of chickens clucked about their feet. A huge bag of bird feed lay propped against the back wall of the house—it had been pecked open, and the seed fell out gradually through the small hole. The fat chickens had been eating like kings.

Corporal Martin stood watching the fowl like he didn't know what to do. When he saw Richard and the kids, he nodded. "This is a lucky find, right?"

Richard pulled a face. "You want to… you know?"

"We have to. Can't turn down the meat."

Alice petted one of the birds, which seemed very happy about it. They were tame, milling around merrily and undisturbed. "Don't kill them."

Dillon glanced up at his dad and pouted. "Yeah, don't kill them."

Corporal Martin was looking at Richard too. "Want to take the kids somewhere else?"

"Sure. Come on, you two."

"No," said Dillon, pulling away. "The chickens haven't done anything. Why do they have to die?"

"So we can eat," said Corporal Martin.

Richard put a hand up. Corporal Martin had his job and

Richard had his. His hand went to Dillon's shoulder as he spoke to him. "You've eaten chicken before, Dil, right? You know we use them for food."

"That was before."

"Before what?"

"Before the monsters started killing us. It's horrible. If we kill the chickens, we're the same as the monsters. Why are we allowed to just kill animals?"

Richard sighed. The demons killing people *was* no different to people killing animals—except animals didn't think and feel like humans.

"Dillon, if we run out of food we'll die. You want that?"

He shrugged.

"It isn't like that yet," said Alice. "We aren't hungry yet." She knelt and patted another bird on the head. "Let's just leave them."

Richard put his hands on his hips and sighed. Corporal Martin shook his head, but Richard gave it a shot. "Maybe Alice is right. Things aren't that bad yet."

Corporal Martin rolled his eyes as if Richard was the biggest kid of all. "So, we should wait until things are desperate before we start looking after ourselves? There are thirty of us, Richard. Food will run out fast. And I mean *fast*. Sorry, but we have no choice. This is how we need to travel."

Richard grunted, but nodded his agreement. The soldier was right, his pragmatism unburdened by having a son to care for. Time to bite the bullet. Richard looked at Dillon and tried to resist the pleading look on his face. "I'm sorry, Dil."

Dillon stamped his foot and ran off. Alice hurried after him. The Down Syndrome made it hard for Dillon to handle his emotions, and it had taken a lifetime of Richard and Jen helping to manage them, but now Dillon's safe and loving environment was gone. Only the hard truths of bleak existence remained, and it made Richard want to scream at the Heavens.

Corporal Martin nodded off to the side. "We haven't checked that building yet. You best go after them. Your son's making too much noise."

"You might be in charge of most things, Corporal, but when it comes to my son, keep your mouth shut, okay?" Richard turned and went after Dillon, with Corporal Martin calling after him in a placating tone. But Richard's entire body tensed, and he wasn't in the mood for rational discussion.

Dillon had run off towards an old barn. The tin roof was corroded and listing to the left, and the whole thing could slide off at any moment. "Dillon, can you come here, please?"

Silence.

Richard picked up his pace.

Alice screamed.

There was no door on the near side of the barn, so Richard sprinted around to where he found a wide-open section. A tractor trailer poked halfway out, and he almost slammed right into it as he entered the shaded interior. Movement at the back caught his eye, near a stacked pile of rotten hay bales.

Dillon and Alice were both screaming now.

"What is it?" Corporal Martin rushed in behind Richard. "What's wrong?"

"I don't know. Dillon? Dillon, come to me."

Dillon appeared from behind the hay bales and came rushing over. Richard gathered his boy to his side, but Alice continued screaming. He had no choice but to abandon Dillon and rush deeper into the barn.

Alice was frozen in place at the back, staring at the ground and screaming in terror. Richard saw the mess on the floor and had to fight the urge to scream too. Side by side, lay the ruined corpses of two children—a girl and a boy. The boy clutched a dirty teddy bear in his tiny hand. The girl wore a tartan skirt and thick white tights. Their heads had come apart like dropped cantaloupes, victims of the shotgun that lay nearby. Mum and dad hung from the rafters by their necks, contorted expressions on their grey faces —bloodshot eyes bulging. It was a scene out of a horror movie, and Dillon and Alice had stumbled right into it.

"Alice," said Richard firmly while stepping forward gently. "Alice, come over to me, sweetheart."

"Why did they do this?" she asked. "They shot their children!"

Richard glanced at the two tiny corpses but kept his focus on

Alice. "People do terrible things when they're afraid, Alice. They weren't bad people, they just couldn't cope."

Alice shook her head at Richard. Tears magnified her eyes. "That didn't give them the right to kill their children. Parents are supposed to protect their kids. They're supposed to keep them safe." Her voice was turning into a shout. "Maybe if parents did their jobs, my brother would still be alive, and I wouldn't be lost!"

Richard hurried forwards and gathered the trembling girl into his arms. She fought him like a beast, but he was still the adult here, and he kept a hold of her until her struggles and cries ceased. "We will find your father, sweetheart," he said. "Then you can tell him everything you're feeling. Until then, I will keep you safe, okay?"

"Me too," said Dillon, rushing up to join the impromptu cuddle.

Alice sobbed. "I don't want anyone else to die."

"Nobody else is going to die," said Corporal Martin, pulling them away from the grisly scene in the barn. "And that includes the chickens. We'll find something else to eat, okay?"

The kids grinned, and Richard looked at the soldier and nodded his thanks.

Corporal Martin nodded back, but didn't look happy.

14

HERNANDEZ

Commander Hernandez gazed upon England's south coast, wishing he could reach out and crush it in his fist. The craven traitor, Captain Granger, filled his lungs with air somewhere here, seeking refuge. The world was at war, but Granger cared only about himself. If not for the impertinent Coast Guard's interference, Hernandez would still hold command of his ship and crew. Instead, events the traitor set in motion had left Hernandez marooned on a fishing boat with a gaggle of stinking Englishmen. Granger needed to be stopped before his selfishness dragged more good men to their downfalls.

"Right, mate, we got you here, so now we're off, yeah?"

Hernandez nodded at the stinking trawler's skipper—sick and tired of observing rotting fish morsels in the filthy wretch's beard. "I gave my word, and I shall keep it. Drop me ashore."

The skipper began to turn away, but changed his mind and frowned. "You really reckon you'll find the geezer you're looking for?"

Hernandez clenched his fists. "The man owes me a debt, and if it takes my entire life to do so, I will collect."

"Okay dokay. We'll be ashore in ten."

"Good man." Hernandez turned back to look at the shore. To think he'd imagined the British sophisticated. They were more

Oliver Twist than Queen Elizabeth. Unwashed oafs. It made him wonder how Britain, at large, fared. Had the apocalypse consumed this country, or had it put up a fight? His fishermen companions spoke of a Resistance, but it hadn't convinced them to take their chances on land.

The scenery filling his view, he'd been informed, was called Dorset, and it seemed quiet—deserted. Granger sought his daughter somewhere in this land, but the girl might be anywhere. The only lead Hernandez possessed was Portsmouth. That was where the fishermen claimed the UK Resistance existed. There were people gathered there. So maybe that was where Granger was headed.

Yet, Hernandez didn't want to overplay his hand. If Granger was at Portsmouth, he would be well defended. Better Hernandez approach from afar and check the lay of the land. The trawler's skipper suggested a small marina here in Dorset, at a place called Poole. The journey from there to Portsmouth could be made on foot within a day. Things could be tough going, so Hernandez gave himself three days. Three days to find and kill the man who had ruined him.

The boat bumped against the docks, and Hernandez leapt out onto foreign soil. He neither said goodbye nor thank you to the native fishermen at his back. His focus was solely on what lay ahead.

Revenge.

15

LORD AMON

Lord Amon towered over his amassing army. To annihilate humanity, it had been necessary to attack on a thousand fronts at once—the primary need for so many gates to be opened —but now that the task was all but completed, the focus re-shifted. No longer did the Children of Darkness need to blanket the Earth in a quest to exterminate—most of its seven billion insects were trodden. So the Children converged instead, ready to strike at the few remaining human gatherings.

He, Lord Amon, would destroy one of humanity's most trou-blesome holdouts.

Portsmouth.

The word had fallen from the mouths of a thousand tortured humans as their innards unravelled before them. A human army in Portsmouth, with ships and planes and soldiers.

An army.

And so it would be...

A glorious battle to seal mankind's extinction.

Lord Amon savoured the prospect.

So eager to begin, he had closed a hundred gates and diverted their energy into activating a new seal—one right in the midst of the human Resistance. Even now, he could sense the new gate opening like the bud of a great, odorous flower. Soon, the malignant jaws would open, and Hell's last remaining forces would pour through to finish the rout—bellowing cavalry mopping up those too stupid to lie down. The Red Lord himself would be watching the events to follow, and Lord Amon would please him immensely. The battle's brutality would be legendary—even amongst the ancient souls of the Abyss.

Nothing could stop the Red Lord's plans. Not even Lucifer—the real Lucifer—wherever he was hiding. A thousand worlds like this one, all toppling one by one, like disease-ravaged pines.

Soon, God will be as impotent as the humans he cherishes. To think I, Lord Amon, once had to kneel at the Creator's feet before delivering the gift of a child to a whore.

Gabriel.

The name was faeces in his mouth.

I am Lord Amon: Regent of Hell. The Red Lord's most faithful.

The creatures at his feet scurried, sensing his fury. Further away, twisted beasts from the lower level stumbled about playfully like monkeys. The Children were thirsty for blood. Hungry for slaughter.

Soon would run a great red river—the herald of a new dawn.

A glorious kingdom.

A world without humanity.

16

GUY GRANGER

The roads were blocked—and too exposed—so Guy set off from Portsmouth on foot. Demons swarmed the landscape, according to Wickstaff's scouts, so keeping to the countryside and travelling at night was the smart choice. As it turned out, Guy recruited only nine men and women from the Hatchet, but another six bodies from General Wickstaff's personnel had bolstered his party. The final count also included Skip, Rick, and his brother, Keith. Twenty-one bodies in total, each armed with a fully loaded SA-80 combat rifle, or some other weapon of choice. The British soldiers also kept two grenades apiece. The party's odds were abysmal, but at least they weren't toothless.

Wickstaff had given Guy another of her oily handshakes before leaving, wishing him "the very best of luck, old chap!" It had been the briefest of goodbyes—nothing like the prolonged agony of leaving the Hatchet. That so few of the crew chose to follow him hurt, yet he couldn't ignore the good sense behind their decision. The true fight would take place at Portsmouth. What Guy was doing—leaving to find Alice—was selfish. But he was a father, and that came before all else. No choice in the matter.

So call me selfish if you must.

One British soldier, a young lad named Heath, had gone to

scout ahead. He hurried back now, exiting the tree line between a gathering of swaying elm trees. The rainfall covered the rushed sounds of his footsteps, but it did not disguise the grave look on his face.

"What is it?" asked Guy, emerging from beneath the draped arms of a willow.

The lad shook his head. "Not good, Boss. There must be two-hundred shitskins past these woods. We can skirt around 'em, but it'll be touch and go. They might spot us."

Rick overheard and came over. "We're likely to encounter demons whichever direction we go. They're heading back the way we came—towards Portsmouth."

"Preparing for battle," said Guy. "Maybe you should all go back."

"Portsmouth is screwed," said Keith, pushing up from a tree he leant on. His chin sagged and wobbled as he spoke as if he'd recently been much fatter. "Good thing we're heading away from there, if you ask me."

The soldier, Heath, sneered. "My friends are at Portsmouth, and I'm stuck here protecting you."

"Don't need protecting," said Keith before adding, with relish, "Sonny Jim."

Guy grunted and put up a hand. "No squabbles, please. It's soaking wet and about as cold as I can stand. You all agreed to this mission, but you can go back if you want."

Heath looked away, chewing his lip.

Keith shrugged.

Rick cleared his throat. "Best thing we can do for Portsmouth is close Lord Amon's gate. Heath, take us up to the tree line where you marked the demons. We should see for ourselves."

Heath nodded and headed back towards the elms. It was a good ten minutes before he got them to the edge of the woods, and what they saw was worse than what the soldier had told them. Guy glanced out from behind the wide body of an ancient oak tree and estimated at least two-hundred gathered demons separated by species—for want of a better word. The burnt men stood on one flank, the primates on another. In the middle were the more human-looking demons, the ones who taunted and sneered as they eviscerated you. What Heath omitted from his report was the huge, towering beast driving the enemy army forwards. In the dying light, the angel looked like a mirage.

"That wasn't there earlier," said Heath weakly.

"Lord Amon," said Rick in a hushed voice. "There's a hierarchy amongst the demons, and that big bugger is indisputably the most senior prick in these parts. Take a good hard look at him, fellas, because he is the enemy general dedicated to our extinction. Don't fear the reaper, fear that."

Guy studied the angel—a beast formed as a beautiful man—as it strode amongst its minions like an arrogant warlord. Did it have an agenda? Did it think and feel like a man? Or was Lord Amon as much a savage monster as the demons at his feet?

The question got answered when Guy saw the human viscera hanging around the angel's neck. Lopped off feet, hands, heads, and genitals, strung together by ropey intestines. The latest in chic-Hellish fashion. Instinctively, his hand found its way to his mouth.

How do you kill something like that?

Guy could not abandon his quest to reach Alice, but now he gazed upon the face of his true enemy, he had a new mission as well. If it was the last thing he did, he would get Rick to that gate. Then Wickstaff could shove a missile right up this angel's ass.

It rained, the *pitter-patter* amplified by droplets hitting the tree canopy. Other than that, the woods filled with silence as the group of humans watched the scene beyond.

Lord Amon threw out an arm and bellowed. The enemy army picked up speed, marching at the double.

"What's happening?" Keith stumbled back amongst the trees. "What are they doing?"

"Attacking," said Rick.

"Not us, though," said Guy. "Portsmouth."

"We need to get back and warn them," said Heath.

Rick wiped rain from his face and then blinked. "We'd never make it in time. Portsmouth is ready. It's all down to Wickstaff now."

Heath chewed his lip bloody and clutched at his rifle. "I thought we had more time."

"That's the thing about time," said Rick, "It waits for no man. All we can do now is focus on our mission: find the gate and close it."

The trees rustled.

A twig broke.

Keith spun, hands up in fists. "Fuck it. They're coming through the woods."

Heath raised his rifle, but Guy put his hand on the barrel and pushed it down. "We haven't been spotted yet."

"Then what the hell do we do?"

Guy watched the shapes in the distance, moving between trees. The demons were going to stumble right into them.

No time to think.

Pointless fighting.

"We run!"

The group sprinted back in the direction it came from, weaving through the trees. Guy's mission to reach Alice was failing before it had even started, and Lord Amon's gate was getting further away.

And Portsmouth's time had run out.

17

VAMPS

Afder the fight in the car park, Vamps and his bros had needed to nurse their wounds. Night had fallen and brought more rain, which had made taking cover an even more urgent consideration. The bowling alley had called to them as if its large neon facade was still lit and blinking. The large unit possessed only a single glass window up front, and only a single fire door. A good place to hide out for the night.

Vamps had led the way inside, his sword no longer flaming, yet it still throbbed with life, almost breathing. Holding it made Vamps feel lighter than air, yet powerful and not quite himself. Was the Irishman's earlier jest a warning? Could he really lose himself to vengeance if he wasn't careful?

"Oh, fuck yes!" said Mass. "Who's for a game of pool?"

Vamps grinned as Mass grabbed a pair of cues and tossed one to Aymun.

Aymun didn't react and instead watched the cue sail past and land on the ground. "I do not know how to play, my friend."

Mass shook his head. "You're useless, Ay. Don't worry, I'll teach you how to hustle."

The purple-baize pool table had Vamps' name on it, but the first place he headed was the long, dark wood bar. Hard liquor lined its back shelves, but he fancied something more refreshing.

While it would doubtlessly be warm, he craved beer—and beer he found in abundance. Several well-stocked fridges nestled beneath the bar. Vamps placed his sword on the bar and gathered up a bushel of the good stuff, bottles clinking as he piled them in his arms.

"Bottom's up, bitches," he said upon returning to the pool table.

Aymun waved a hand. "Not for me, thank you."

Mass took two beers and chewed off the lids with his back teeth. After taking his first hearty swig, he belched. "Shit, it's been a while, huh? Need to get a buzz on like you wouldn't believe."

Vamps understood all too well. It was good to take a load off finally and stop fighting for their lives. The beers were unlimited and the company good. He felt like a taut spring uncoiling.

Aymun grabbed a fizzy orange from the bar and also brought back an ice bucket filled with snacks. The crisps and chocolate made Vamps think about the kid, Max, but Mass noticed and didn't allow him to dwell. He threw him a cue. "You're up, man. I'll let you break."

Vamps caught the cue and grinned. He chalked up the tip and leant over the table. "Now, Aymun," he advised. "You wanna get nice and low so you're behind the cue ball. Then you just…" He fired the cue, launching the white little cannonball. Two reds and one yellow sank into the corner pockets. "Hit that son of a bitch like it fucked your mother!"

Aymun chuckled. "Such an elegant teacher of the arts."

"Swagger is as much a part of this game as skill, yo. You wanna make this shit look easy to your opponent."

Mass took his turn and sent the cue ball leaping off the table. In anger, he kicked the table and sent every ball on the table two inches to the left. "Bollocks!"

Vamps waved a thumb at Mass and smirked "See, Aymun? I put him off his game."

Mass retrieved the cue ball from beneath an X-Files pinball machine and placed it back on the baize. "Been a while, playa. Need to get my eye in."

"You ready to have a go, Aymun?" Vamps offered his cue.

Aymun waved a hand. "I shall watch a little longer."

"Suit yourself. So, what did you used to do for fun back home? Terrorist shit, right?"

Aymun pulled up a chair and sat down. "There was little in the way of fun back home. My people knew only suffering."

"Then they might have had half a chance when the gates turned up," said Mass, leaning over the table and readying himself for another shot.

"No man could prepare for such evil. We brothers and sisters have been too long distracted, fighting amongst ourselves. We did not realise the true threat that was coming."

Vamps saw the pain on Aymun's face and wished then that he and Mass weren't so dismissive of what he'd been through. It had obviously been a lot; both before and after the gates had arrived. Vamps and Mass may have been gangsters, but Aymun had his own streets to survive. "Maybe this will change things for the better, Ay. Maybe once the dust settles, we'll be better to each other."

Aymun nodded, but didn't seem to believe it. "I fear it is man's nature to self-destruct. When I entered the gate, I walked through hallways filled with the damned. There is no Hell for any animal but man. We are the only species capable of being wicked. Evil is not a part of our nature—it is a cornerstone of our nature. I have killed. You both have killed. Men kill. We condemn ourselves."

Mass took another shot and potted a yellow. He straightened up before taking his next shot. "It's our ability to be evil that makes it count when we're good though, right? Being human is a battle, man, but it's what makes us strong. It's what will help us win this war."

Aymun plucked at his beard and nearly smiled. "Perhaps you are right, my brother. I will take my shot now."

"Yeah, my playa!" said Vamps, whooping and handing over his cue.

They stood back while Aymun made a clumsy attempt at potting a ball. At least he didn't foul.

"Not a bad first attempt," said Mass, swigging the rest of a beer.

"It is a fun game. May I have another turn?"

Vamps nodded. "Knock yourself out."

This time, Aymun potted a red in the centre pocket. He straightened up and beamed. "Good, yes?"

Mass and Vamps both chuckled warmly and patted the Syrian on the back. "Well done," said Vamps. "You know, you have a friendly face when you're not frowning like a bouncer."

"That is just my thinking face. I will try to think less."

"Eh, yeah... cool."

They started a new game—practice session was over. Mass played Aymun, with the winner to face Vamps.

"So, tell us about Syria," said Mass as he lined up his break.

Aymun sat on a stool, sighed, and then gradually began. "A place of hardships, but as you say, people gain strength through their struggles. When I was a boy, Damascus was frightening because nothing ever changed. Rules were never to be broken, or the police would punish you cruelly. After the rebels rose up, it became a place of fear for other reasons. Death could fall from the sky at any moment. A quiet corridor could fall in on you from an indiscriminate bomb. Yet, in the last days of my country, there was hope. I saw the kindness God intended for us."

He linked his fingers together across his lap and glanced upwards as if picturing the story he was about to tell. "One day, I walked down a street. Once was a market street, but Assad's forces reduce it to rubble. There I see a little old lady. I know her face, for she is wife of local baker. Every morning, she sell her husband's bread, and today she does so in an empty, bombed-out street. No one else is around. I go to this lady, and I say, 'Lady, this street is safe no longer. Why do you not go home?' This lady look at me and tell me, 'Sir, my home was right behind where you stand. Now is gone. My husband sleep there in his bed, tired from baking bread. He gone too when bombs fall. All I have left is bread he make.'"

Vamps shook his head. "That's fucked up."

"That is not the point of story. I smile at this lady, and I say, I would like to buy some bread. But when I try to give her money, she shakes her head. 'No, no sir,' she say, 'this bread is for free.

People's homes have been destroyed, and they have nothing. How can I ask for their money?' I frown at her and tell her she does not even know which side of war I am on. I could be one of Assad's men who blew up her home. She just look at me, pressing the bread into my arms. 'My husband did not judge,' she said, 'so I will not either. All men fight to protect what is theirs. I give what I have for free so cycle can be broken. All that I have, I shall give, and so I will never be forced to fight for what is mine. I shall never have reason to kill.'"

Aymun unlaced his fingers and let his palms rest on his knees. The simple gesture somehow made it clear he was done.

Vamps wanted to fill the silence with words, for that was his way, but for once, he found himself silent. He thought about his own life, hanging around the streets with nothing to his name, but strutting around like he had it all. His reputation had been a facade, he realised—an imaginary possession because he had, nothing real. The old woman had been right, men fought over what they had and what they wanted. That was why the world got so screwed up. Humanity had developed through a constant struggle for possessions. Land, money, oil, power...

"It was all bullshit, wasn't it? I mean, life. The world. It was a joke."

Aymun nodded tenderly. "God gave us the freedom to work things out for ourselves, but we came up with the wrong answers. Life is a gift to be shared. Mankind is supposed to be a glorious, loving family, but instead, we allowed ourselves to become a species of individuals."

"What happened to the old lady?" asked Mass, clutching his cue against his chest and twiddling it between his palms.

"She died a day later," said Aymun. "The rebels that time. Her life was ruined by one side and ended by the other. When I find her body in the rubble, she had no more bread. She had given it all away. I placed a blanket over her and promised never to forget. I tell my brothers of her courage, and she lives on."

Vamps smiled. "Yeah, I like that." He lifted his beer. "Here's to the baker's wife. I hope she has her family back in Heaven."

The three men clinked bottles and went back to playing pool.

Vamps noticed that his sword was flickering on the bar, but he decided to ignore it. Tonight was for letting go of the fight. Tomorrow could be about killing. He placed the sword out of sight behind the bar, and then re-joined his brothers.

His family.

18

GENERAL WICKSTAFF

The ground shook. Middle of the night, but Wickstaff was already fully dressed and only half asleep. She stood outside the command block, demanding to know what was happening. The floodlights glared, illuminating bodies rushing back and forth like headless ants. Despite the several thousand soldiers under her command, Wickstaff knew most by name, which was why she quickly reached out and grabbed the nearest corporal. "Tell me what's happening, Dee."

"They're coming," the man said, looking everywhere but at her. "Christ, it's actually happening. They're out there. The demons—"

Beneath their feet, the ground shook.

Wickstaff cupped the back of the corporal's neck and pulled him close. "Calm down, Dee. Let's not shit our knickers just yet. We have plans in place, remember? Head to the drill square and ring that bloody bell. You need me to tell you the signal?"

He gawped at her, eyes twitching.

"Dee! Do you know the bloody signal or not?"

The corporal snapped back to reality and nodded frantically. "Seven peals followed by a five second pause, then another three peals."

"Good, lad. Now go!"

The corporal raced off to ring the muster bell. The brass relic was ceremonial more than anything, but in the absence of reliable electricity, it had become the agreed upon alarm. Its pealing would let all of Portsmouth know full battle-stations were in effect, and the enemy was at the gates. Luckily, those gates had been forged from iron, as had several of the barricades blocking the main roads. One benefit of digging-in at an old naval port was the abundance of iron. The city's many museums played home to iron anchors, antique ship fixtures, and even the huge iron frames from a pair of 19th century warships. Men had gathered the scrap at a collection of choke-points at the city's widest roads and thorough-fares, where the enemy could be funnelled into narrowed kill zones—spaces between rows of taller buildings where soldiers could fire down from both sides of the street. Several areas were also earmarked for bombardment from the warships in the docks. Once the bulk of the enemy forces inevitably passed into the city, she would call in the artillery to rain down death.

She was prepared for this.

She had this under control.

There was no other way.

A jeep skidded outside the command block and one of Wick-staff's lieutenants leant over and threw open the passenger door. Her chauffeur had arrived. Wickstaff nodded and got in. Her driver sped her over to the large sentry tower on the edge of the naval base. Fortifications extended another half-mile out into the city, but from this tower, she would be able to see what was coming their way. The guard tower's roof had been pulled down and replaced with a rickety platform accessed by a stepladder. It gave the tower another fifteen-feet of height compared to the orig-inal structure and allowed a sentry to see right to the outskirts of Portsmouth.

Wickstaff nodded to a group of soldiers assembled at the bottom of the tower and then started her way up the ladder. The ground continued to shake with distant rumblings. How many thousands of clawed feet were bearing down on them? Did Portsmouth even stand a chance?

Lord Amon would be among the enemy for sure, and would

be unstoppable unless Guy and Rick came through closing the gate. All she could do was try to keep her people alive until then. Was it an impossible task? She would find out.

Climbing the ladder, she reached the original crows nest and grabbed hold of the stepladder that would take her up to the roof deck. The steel rungs vibrated in her hands, and worryingly, the whole ladder wobbled when she assailed the first step.

"It's tied with rope," someone called down from the shadows. "It gives, but it won't fall. Hold on tight, and you'll be fine."

Wickstaff tried to see who was up there, but had to look away when rain started filling her eyes. She hadn't even noticed the downpour. The voice sounded familiar. "M-Maddy? Is that you? What on earth are you doing up here?"

"Wanted to pull my weight, so I've been bringing refreshments to the sentries. Arrived just in time to catch the show."

Wickstaff trotted up the ladder and heaved herself onto the cramped deck. With Maddy stood a grizzled old sergeant with binoculars in his hands. A monstrous sniper rifle lay propped up against the wooden boards by his legs. "Welcome to the eagle's nest, ma'am," the man said in a voice thick with manliness. The unmistakable tone of Carl Martinhal, an active SAS soldier who had been on leave when the gates opened. He was about as tough a man as she had at her disposal, but his skill with a rifle made him a real asset.

"Thanks for having me, Sergeant Martinhal. I hear we have guests?"

"Don't we fuckin' just," He handed over the binoculars, as casually as if they were at the opera. "Get your peepers on those."

Wickstaff looked through the binoculars and scanned the horizon. It didn't take her long to react. "Bonk my giddy aunt. Looks like they came to do more than just visit."

The city at large was poorly lit, the floodlights and petrol generators being centred on the naval base, but it wasn't difficult to understand the situation. The shifting shadows of an endless horde filled the horizon like raving highlanders. A legion of the damned.

"Get me a radio," ordered Wickstaff. "Time we teach these

dirty buggers a lesson. That, when it comes to making war, mankind has no equal."

Martinhal smirked. "Yes, ma'am."

A radio was shoved into her hand, and she gave a dozen orders to a dozen different sub-leaders in less than a minute. Then she waited. The rain pitter-pattered against the deck.

The screaming began one second before the first chattering gunfire. Muzzle flashes lit up the city like fireworks. Every gloomy alleyway now flashed like a rave was taking place. The city's darkness lifted, replaced by a radiant orange glow and white smoke. Grenades boomed. Windows shattered. Soldiers bellowed to one another, fighting together—dying together. Men wailed as terrible fates befell them, and demons screeched with delight. The demons had drawn first blood.

The battle might be lost already.

Wickstaff snatched the sniper rifle from the boards and propped it up on the railing. The weapon sported a night vision scope, which meant she got a better look at the nightmare coming their way.

It was an unwelcome sight.

Through the scope, a luminous green mass swarmed through Portsmouth's ancient streets. Frightened soldiers crouched behind cover, mostly unaware they were being surrounded. But no man or woman ran. No one threw down their weapon and surrendered.

They were ready to fight.

Wickstaff lined up the rifle's cross hairs and yanked the trigger. She took the head off a burnt man just as it was about to fall upon a stumbling soldier yet to find cover. The man dropped to the ground in surprise when his unseen attacker's skull turned to mist right in front of him. He took advantage of the rescue and got himself behind a bulky Range Rover, where a machine gunner had already entrenched himself inside the sunroof. Wickstaff took another shot and kneecapped a leaping primate and spun it like a leaf in a storm. As the creature squirmed on the ground, the machine gunner finished it off, making its corpse dance. Wickstaff wasn't quick enough to line up her next shot, and a burnt man waylaid the machine gunner and the unlucky soldier beside him.

The machine gunner took care of it with a handgun, but the distraction delayed both men long enough that a squad of demons were able to blindside them. Wickstaff heard their screams a half-mile away.

The enemy moved closer.

Wickstaff turned to Sergeant Martinhal and snatched the radio again. "All units in Zone 2, fall back to inner perimeter. Artillery Groups 2 and 4, reduce Zone 2 to dust. I want to see Australia through the craters you leave."

"Roger that."

She kept hold of the radio, but handed the sniper rifle to the sergeant who would put it to better use than her.

"Are you okay?" Maddy asked, suddenly reminding the general of her presence. A civilian.

Wickstaff nodded. "The whole humanity in peril thing is old hat now, my love."

"What can I do to help, General?"

"Keep a clear head for me. Giving orders is a lonely business. I need someone I can curse at if the need arises. Sorry, Maddy, but you've got that job."

"It's an honour. Mind if I swear back at you?"

"Fire away."

"Send those fuckers straight back to Hell, General."

Wickstaff chuckled. Maddy was exactly what she needed right now—an anchor to keep her feet on the ground while she made decisions that could end the human race.

Or save it.

Somehow that was the prospect that scared her more.

"By the time I'm through with these bastards, Maddy, Hell will look pretty goddamn inviting. Speaking of which, I think I hear the gods whistling."

Maddy frowned, but then tilted her head as she too caught the sound. Overhead, the starry sky lit up as a dozen fireflies sliced gracefully through the air. Fireflies that whistled as they fell.

"Cover your ears," barked Sergeant Martinhal.

The gods roared.

A massive wall of fire leapt up from the heart of the city.

Buildings tore apart like matchstick models and abandoned cars cartwheeled twenty feet through the air. The massive heat and ensuing concussion vaporised the demons so quickly that they didn't even have time to scream. They were simply gone, replaced by a flaming crater.

The guard tower wobbled, and the stepladder swung to-and-fro on the rope it was secured with. Wickstaff and the others hung on for dear life and almost fell to their deaths by the time the second barrage was through. Wickstaff had to blink several times just to work out which way she was facing. Once she reoriented herself, she turned the air blue with cursing.

A dozen infernos lit the night brighter than day now, and the full enemy force revealed itself.

Thousands.

Tens of thousands of the wretched monsters.

Wickstaff knew she had sentenced soldiers to death with the artillery barrages, as not all would have escaped the blast radius, but she understood now it had been the right decision. The massive bombardment devastated the enemy vanguard and tore apart several-hundred demons at least, but it had done something even more important: bombed-out buildings crumpled and fell across the roads. Massive piles of masonry blocked the enemy approach and bought Portsmouth more time.

Wickstaff studied the battlefield and felt a mixture of hope and despair. The first round had gone to mankind, but their real foe was only now approaching. Lord Amon stomped towards his front lines, demons parting before him like butter on each side of a hot knife. Once he reached the ruined outskirts of Portsmouth, he stopped and stared. Wickstaff was certain he was staring right at her.

Then the angel took another giant step forward and grabbed hold of an upended camper van. With terrifying strength, Lord Amon plucked the van up off the ground and held it over his head, before launching it like a javelin. The boxy vehicle struck the roof of a nearby office building and shattered a vast chunk of it. Wickstaff covered her mouth as three soldiers plummeted to their deaths from their hiding places. The angel's message was clear:

"You can't hide. You can't run."

Before Wickstaff looked away in total horror, she watched Lord Amon pluck a fourth soldier from a hiding place inside a shop doorway. In one giant hand, he clutched the woman by her ankles and bellowed with laughter as he tore her torso in two. He tossed the pieces into the air like bread for the birds.

You can't hide.

You can't run.

19

RICHARD HONEYWELL

Corporal Martin had been trying his radio for the last two hours, but Portsmouth didn't respond. Richard wanted to say something encouraging to the soldier, but there was nothing that would be believable. He grew more and more desperate by the minute.

Their one hope was fading.

Dawn broke, but the rain remained a downpour. Puddles formed sucking quagmires in the mud, sapping the group's strength and making walking a chore. The group's mood had been sullen since the grisly scene in the barn, and necessity had forced them to spend the night there inside the house. Everyone had been eager to depart the exact moment the first bird chirped. Now the farm lay several hours in the group's rear mirror, but still their spirits remained low.

Richard put an arm across Dillon's shoulders, trying to keep him dry. With his other hand, he shielded his eyes. "We should find more shelter or go back to the farm. This rain will be the death of us."

"Portsmouth is only a half-day away," argued Corporal Martin. "We can't afford to stop now."

"But they haven't responded since last night. We don't know Portsmouth is safe anymore."

"It's the only destination we have, Richard. We won't be safe anyplace else. We've endured worse than a little rain."

Richard sighed. True, a bit of rain seemed silly to complain about considering what they had survived, but his instincts were to keep Dillon warm, dry, and fed. Difficult to override fatherly instincts, and he looked at his son now, he found it hard to consider enduring anymore of this weather.

"Dillon, are you okay?"

His son glanced across at him and nodded. His thin blonde hair was plastered to his scalp with rainwater. "I want to go somewhere with more people. I want to keep on going."

"See!" said Corporal Martin. "It's only you being soft, Richard."

Richard grunted. "Like with the chickens, you mean?"

"Let's just get to Portsmouth, okay?"

The march continued in silence, the only person talking was Carol. The old editor regaled Alice of her time in Africa as an aid worker. Alice responded that her father helped people too, and that they would get along when they met. Richard admired the American girl's defiance, still believing she would get her happy ending. Meeting her father was a matter of *when*, not *if*.

The countryside ceased and they entered a built-up area leading to the South Coast. The first things they scouted were a Ford dealership and a set of train tracks. Blocking their view further was a massive plot of half-built houses. Ironic, as there would now be far more houses than there were people living. It would be a long, long time before people ran out of living space again—and that was only if humanity survived.

"Think we can grab ourselves some motors?" asked David. "I've always fancied one of those big Ford pickups. They seemed built for banging up and getting dirty."

"Ranger," said Richard.

"Huh?"

"The pickup that Ford makes is called a Ranger. I impounded one a few months ago on a drugs bust. Proceeds of crime seizure."

"Well, maybe we can rustle up a few Rangers then and drive the last stretch to Portsmouth."

"We'll check things out," said Corporal Martin. "Might not be a bad idea."

Talk of procuring a fleet of cars lifted the group's spirits, and people started nattering again, sharing stories of vehicles they had once owned themselves, as well as cars they would have liked to own. The apocalypse wasn't all bad. You could take whatever you found, and a car dealership became a playground.

The group reached the dealership's cement forecourt and spread out, searching. Men and women both stopped to glide appreciative hands over shining bonnets and boots.

Richard wasn't much of a car guy, but he allowed Dillon to run off with Alice to climb and play. It seemed safe enough. David ran off too and gave a triumphant cheer when he found a brand-new Ranger in white. The paintwork was filthy from dust, but the placard's exorbitant price betrayed its unused condition. David leapt up into the rear bed and bounced like a clown. Dillon and Alice saw him and quickly climbed up to join. The three of them laughed like idiots.

Richard smiled.

"David always did like his toys," said Carol conspiratorially. "He used to be a right pain in my arse, always moaning about his pay, like he was bloody Louis Theroux or something."

Richard nodded, eyes still on the two children and childish adult. "I forgot you two go way back."

"Way, way back. I still remember hiring the arrogant sod. Wet-behind the ears graduate who thought he knew it all, he was, but I always knew he would make a good journalist. Contrary to what one might believe, the best reporters are the ones with the biggest moral compasses. David lost his way for a while, let his ego rule him, but I'm proud of how much he's risen to this challenge. After Mina died…"

"I never met her, but I've heard about her."

"A nice girl. Real shame what happened to her. David took it hard. The anger inside him… When he took it out on the demon, we had tied up… I won't deny it frightened me. I think being around your son and Alice pulled him back from the brink."

"Andras…" Richard remembered what a mess David had made of the angel, disguised as a human. A real mess.

Carol nodded, her voice a whisper. "We all lost something after Andras. It made us realise how evil those bastards are. Just look at what they did with your wife."

Richard grunted.

"Sorry. I'm just saying, we owe it to all the people we've lost to make those bastards pay, but it's important to keep a hold of what makes us human. Or else what's the point?"

Richard continued watching Dillon and Alice bouncing alongside David and saw the truth of it. The children kept everybody's hope alive. They were a reminder of what they were all surviving for.

Carol half-turned, her attention moving someplace else. "Now that is a thing of beauty."

Richard followed the woman's gaze until he saw what she was referring to. He let out a whistle. "It certainly is."

Sitting inside the glass-fronted showroom was a low-slung sports car in fire engine red. The modern blue Mustang parked beside it looked bulky and unsophisticated by comparison. Carol rushed inside; not even checking the front door was unlocked as she charged through it. Richard gave chase, worried for her safety, but also eager to see the beautiful piece of human engineering for himself. He wasn't a car guy, but he wasn't blind either. Some things were just indescribably flawless.

Carol clapped her hands like an excited schoolgirl. "Ford GT 2016. This baby must have made it here just days before the world ended. Who knew it would be one of mankind's final accomplishments? A beast hiding beneath a masterpiece."

"She sure is beautiful, Carol. I never pegged you as a petrol head."

She ran her hands over the curved bonnet. "Are you kidding? When I was a younger gal, I owned a Lotus Esprit. Payments cost more than my mortgage, but damn if it wasn't worth it. My old Lotus was nothing compared to this though. The original GT was a beauty itself, but somehow they improved on it."

"It's beautiful," Richard said again, not knowing what else he could add. If he had known anything about engines, he would have spat out some specifications, perhaps.

"It's mine," said Carol with a grin. "Find me the keys."

Richard chuckled. "Erm, okay."

Luckily, the keys were hanging from an open lock box in the back office. When shit had gone down, the staff had obviously fled without giving a thought about locking up. It worked out well for Carol.

Richard handed over the key ring with the car's registration number on it. "I think this is the key, but it's weird."

Carol snatched it like Gollum grabbing his Precious. "It's an e-key," she explained. "You only need to have it on you to start the car."

"Neat."

She pulled open the driver's door and pointed at the dashboard to a large red button that said START, then jabbed it with her finger. The engine roared to life, and she seemed to breathe it in for a moment, closing her eyes and smiling serenely. "Isn't that the most beautiful sound you ever heard?"

"Hey, hey!" Corporal Martin came striding in. "Turn that thing off. The noise will attract every demon for a hundred miles."

Sheepishly, Carol thumbed the START button again, and the dragon went back to sleep. "I suppose it is a little impractical."

"You think? Come on, we've found a couple of panel vans around back. Three should hold everyone, so we'll divide into teams. Me, David, and you, Richard."

Richard raised an eyebrow. "You want me to lead a team?"

"I just want you to drive a van full of people, but yes you should also lead. You're a police officer."

"*Was* a police officer."

"Whatever. Just get away from that teenage wet dream and come help with something useful."

Richard and Carol exchanged chastised glances, and both fought emerging grins. Corporal Martin stormed off, leaving them alone a moment to get their giggling over with.

"Suppose we should do as we're told," said Richard.

Carol patted him on the back. "I think that lad fancies me, you know?"

"Ha! I think you might be right. Come on."

They went outside and headed after Corporal Martin who was disappearing around the far side of the showroom. Most of the group were already out of sight, likely assembled near the afore-mentioned vans. David, however, was still in the back of the truck with the kids. They had stopped their jumping and were now just sitting and talking.

"You'll have to start paying him for babysitting," said Carol.

"Yeah, I think I wi—" Richard flew forward as something struck him between the shoulder blades. He tried to stay on his feet, but his balance had deserted him and he ended up on his hands and knees.

Carol cried out.

David shouted.

The kids screamed

Dazed, Richard rolled onto his back. Carol struggled a few feet away from him, demons closing in from all sides. They seemed to be emerge from the landscape itself, filtering from the distant tree line or from behind abandoned vehicles. Of the ones who had already got close, Carol cursed and kicked at them, but a clawed hand shot out and snapped her wrist. A tirade of foul language spewed from her mouth in reply. Richard clambered to his feet, rushed to her aid, yanking a knife from his belt and burying it in the chest of the demon that had broken her arm. The blade stuck, so he threw a punch at the next demon. A third leapt out of the crowd and pummelled him before he could defend, knocking him to the ground.

More demons snatched Carol, yanking her arms at unnatural angles.

"Get off her, you bastards!"

David appeared and launched himself into the fray, tossing aside one demon then head butting another. With his ruined, snarling face, he looked like one of them. Carol had only one good arm, but she swung it like a club. Richard tried to get up and help them, but a demon leapt on him and pinned him down. Far off, he heard Dillon scream.

"Daddy, Daddy."

More demons swarmed the dealership, scurrying between cars and leaping the low chain-fence separating the forecourt from the road. Demons everywhere. Where had they come from?

Richard squirmed, managing to avoid a sharp swipe aimed at his jugular. The foul creature on top of him was too strong to escape, and each swipe got a little closer. He fought back with his fists, but it was only delaying the inevitable. He tasted blood when a claw finally sliced a burning canyon from his eyebrow to his lip.

The creature stunk of piss and shit.

"Fuck you!" Richard spat. "You'll always be damned. Hell will follow you wherever you go. So... Fuck... You!"

The demon glared, blackened teeth thick with decay. Its eyes were human, but whatever lay beyond them was anything but. Nothing existed inside this creature but the darkest and most base instincts of a predator. The need to kill and devour.

Richard closed his eyes. It was over.

Dillon continued screaming, even more distant.

Gunfire pierced the air. The weight fell away from Richard's chest, and he was back on his feet, confused. He spun around, trying to work out what had happened. A demon now lay dead at his feet.

Carol was sprawled on the ground. David fought to get to her. When he saw Richard standing, he yelled. "Help her, man. Get her out of here."

Another gunshot took the head off a demon coming towards Richard. He glanced back to see Corporal Martin and his soldiers taking aim and firing in a line.

Richard dropped his shoulder and barged a demon aside as he made his way forward. Carol bled from a wound on her neck, and was cradling her snapped wrist, but she was alive. Still swearing like a trooper. He reached out with both hands and grabbed her around the waist, pulling her to safety. She was stick thin, and with the adrenaline in his system, he was able to scoop her up like a baby.

More bullets tore up the demons.

Richard staggered back with Carol in his arms. She muttered to him as he dragged her away. "D-David. You have to help David."

"One thing at a time, Carol."

David was surrounded, his burnt face contorted with rage. He was lashing out with a blade, slicing the demons left and right, or shoving them back so Corporal Martin and his soldiers could take a clear shot.

But it was useless.

A dozen monsters closed in on David at once, and Richard lost sight of him in the pack. He did not scream, only shouted and swore, insulting the monsters even as they surrounded him. Eventually, his curses stopped and thick red blood rolled across the concrete beneath the demon's clawed feet.

Victorious, the monsters turned around to face Richard and Carol who were still yet to escape. Richard held Carol against his chest and whispered in her ear. "Don't look, sweetheart."

"Don't call me sweetheart, shithead."

The demons surged across towards them, wailing with blood lust. Richard closed his eyes and buried his face against Carol's. Her breathing was rapid and hot in his ear. They had seconds left.

Less than that.

The demons roared.

Dillon still screamed from somewhere.

And then the demons hit an invisible wall.

Corporal Martin and his soldiers let loose with all they had. The demons danced and reeled, like fish on the line. Heads exploded. Limbs tore away from torsos. "Take that, you monkey shits."

The demons fell rapidly into a pile. Somewhere beneath them lay David. When Richard saw an argyle sock without a shoe poking out from the bodies, he knew the old chap was gone for good.

Carol shrugged out of Richard's gasp and spat at the dead demons. "Rot in Hell, you fucks." Then she turned sombre as she saw the same shoeless sock that Richard had. She put on a taut smile. "David, you saved my silly old behind. I always knew I'd be glad I hired you one day. You took your sweet time."

Then she turned her head and sobbed into her shirt cuff. Everyone else remained quiet, reflecting on the moment and trying to come back down to earth. The smell of gun smoke made all of them cover their mouths.

The battle had come out of nowhere.

They had won. But they had lost.

When would it end?

The dead demons cartwheeled up as if a grenade had exploded beneath them, corpses flying in a dozen directions. David rose up in what had been the centre of the pile. He looked only at Carol.

"Don't miss me," he said in a rasping voice. "Join me!"

Carol stumbled back in fright, but was not quick enough to avoid her old colleague's grip as he reached out and grabbed her around the throat. One-handed, and with sickening ease, he crushed her neck to pulp before she even had time to scream. The old editor's lifeless body slumped to the floor. The back of her skull cracked open on the pavement.

Richard's eyes bulged. He clenched his fists. "Nooooo!"

"It's not him anymore," Corporal Martin barked. "Take him out!"

David cackled, arms out to the side like he was being crucified. To complete the picture, he let his chin drop against his chest and closed his eyes.

Corporal Martin and his soldiers unleashed Hell.

In the shape of the cross, David's corpse danced and jiggled. Blood spurted from a dozen places, but he would not break from that sacred pose. His already-ruined face chipped away piece-by-piece, first his jawbone, disintegrating into mush, then both eyes. Another two-dozen bullets in his torso eventually turned him to mincemeat and dropped him, but he still maintained that position, even as his insides drooled out on the pavement.

Jaw locked, Richard stomped over to his friend's corpse and kicked one of his bleeding arms against his side, breaking that mockery of Jesus on the cross. After a few seconds, he was able to unclench his fists. "How? Who raised him from the dead? I thought..."

More screams.

Dillon and Alice—thought safe behind the line of soldiers—they were not safe.

Skullface yanked the children away from safety and scooped them up. At seven-feet tall, the creature didn't even struggle as he tucked them under each arm.

Richard shoved the soldiers out of his way and sprinted across the forecourt. Skullface raced away, the children screaming. Richard gave chase, gaining even, but a pair of primate demons leapt into his path. They'd been hiding behind a billboard. He fought to get past, but took a sharp swipe across the thigh, which dropped him to his knee. Corporal Martin appeared and took them both out with the last of the rounds in his magazine, but it was already too late. He offered a hand to Richard, but he refused it, remaining on his knees, watching his son disappear. "Skullface! He has Dillon and Alice. We..."

More demons raced towards the car dealership. Skullface disappeared behind their lines. Impossible to pursue.

More demons came. They came from everywhere.

"Take cover," Corporal Martin shouted to his men. "Pick your shots, and we might live through this."

Gunfire, screams, and car alarms filled the air.

20

GUY GRANGER

Guy broke from the woods, ran across a cluttered road, and found a gap in a wooden palisade wrapped around a three-story building. Not knowing what lay inside, he threw himself through the opening and waited for the others. A stream of bodies squeezed in after him. Rick came through last. He was sluggish and bent over. Guy pulled him over to one side, so he could shove a spare wooden panel across the gap and complete the barricade.

He turned to Rick and assessed him. Not good. "You okay?"

Rick was panting, doubled over, but he waved a hand. "Yeah, sorry. I'm not as fast as I used to be. Must be getting old."

Yeah, thought Guy, *or dying of some weird demonic virus.* His biggest concern was not Rick's health though. "Did any of them see you?"

Rick shook his head, hands on his back as he creaked upright.

"You're sure?"

"If the demons had seen me, I would know. Don't ask me how."

Guy allowed himself to relax. "Okay, good. We'll lie low here, stay quiet, and set off as soon as the coast is clear."

"The coast isn't going to be clear," said Keith. "It sounded like an entire battalion is coming this way. The shits are everywhere."

"We're safe," said Rick calmly. "Guy is right. We just need to lie low. What is this place anyway?"

They were outside a small, provincial cinema. Its roof timbers lay exposed, and scaffolding scaled the front of the building. The wooden palisade was in place to keep the public away from the building work, and for now, it would keep them hidden. "If we can get inside, we can stay warm and sheltered from the rain."

Rick nodded. "We'll keep a watch from the top of the scaffolding. There's a bunch of tarps up there, so staying out of sight shouldn't be too hard."

Keith folded his arms as he looked the building up and down. "Wouldn't be so bad if there was power. We could watch a movie. Doubt there'll be much to do but twiddle our thumbs. Did anybody bring cards?"

"Staying alive is enough to occupy us for now," said Rick. "Try not being negative for a change, Keith."

"We'll have plenty to do," added Guy. "If we spend any amount of time here, we will need to make the place defensible. I intend on leaving the first chance I get, but I won't reach my daughter if I'm dead, so let's be safe. There's a pile of spare scaffolding poles over there, and more wooden panels. We can build an inner wall and set up a kill zone in the space between. Any demon creeps over the first palisade will find themselves trapped against the inner walls. There's not enough wood to make an entirely new perimeter, but we can place a new wall between the palisade and the cinema's front entrance."

Rick sat down on a pile of breeze blocks, still trying to catch his breath. "All sounds good to me, Captain."

"I am not Captain anymore, so call me Guy." He walked away, but Skip broke from the crowd and joined him.

"We will find Alice, Guy. I can feel it."

"I know, Skip, but what then? My son is gone. Alice's mother is probably gone too. I'm all she has left. How do I go back to being a father after all this? What the Hell do I say to her?"

Skip scratched at his beard. "Words don't in any way matter. What matters is you've travelled halfway around the globe to get to her. She won't be expecting anything from you, Guy. Just being with her after all this is enough. A girl needs her daddy."

"Really? I wasn't there for her in the past. I spent most of her childhood away on a boat. Kyle is gone, and I'll never get to make that time up with him. Alice is still alive, but what does she have to live for? All the things I planned on doing..." He sighed. "There's no more Disneyland, no more school plays or sports days. I missed it all, Skip, and there won't ever be a chance to catch up."

Skip paused for a moment, like he didn't know what to say, but then the words spilled from him. "The world is what we make it, Captain. Maybe you weren't there in the past, but the past is over. Memories are just nature's way of taunting us. Even if the future is difficult, we all find moments to be human. History is full of war and bloodshed, but even in our darkest times we have created art, music, culture. You can't suppress the human race, and life being difficult is not the same as life being worthless. Find your daughter and keep her alive, and she will flourish, even in darkness. Maybe more so."

"Damn it, for a grizzled old seadog, you speak a lot of sense. You're right. I can't change the past, or even the present, but I will make the future my own. How would you feel about being an honorary uncle, Skip?"

He patted Guy on the shoulder. "I'd say poor Alice has things bad enough."

The two men re-joined the others, smiles on their faces. Rick and Keith were working with the soldiers and sailors to hastily erect scaffolding poles against the palisade to reinforce it. They already had an L-shape in place and were propping up a panel of wood against it. Guy knew his sailors weren't the best field engineers, but Wickstaff's infantry seemed rather handy at the task. Rick, himself, was digging a hole for the next length of scaffolding to sink down into. Sweat beaded from his forehead and each movement seemed to make him shudder, but he was still on his feet. The man did not quit.

Guy reached out and took the shovel from Rick's hands. "You look like you need to rest."

"I'm fine. I should help."

"You're too important to get injured. Just take a rest. What happened to you anyway? What made you... like this?"

Rick gave up the facade and handed over the shovel. He leaned back against a cement mixer with obvious relief. "I got infected by an angel is the best way I can put it. I died, but a fallen angel called Daniel brought me back. I came back wrong."

"Brought you back? Why? The angels want us dead."

"Not all of them." Rick motioned to the floor, signalling that he would sit down, and he did. Guy nodded and crouched to stay on his level. "I don't know for sure, but I think there's some kind of war going on behind the scenes. Whoever runs things in Hell has led some sort of uprising that has brought all the demons here. Not all the beings in Hell are onboard though."

Guy sighed. "Seems like enough are."

Rick folded his arms against his tummy as if in pain. "I suppose the notion of escaping Hell is too good to refuse. Anyway, there's a minority sympathetic to us worthless humans, it seems. Daniel was one of them. He brought me back from the dead, but to do so he had to transfer some of himself to me. He died helping me, but his time was limited, anyway. The human body he possessed was too weak to contain him. It was breaking down. That's what's happening to my body now. Whatever power I have inside me is too much. I'm dying."

"How long do you have?"

"I don't know. As much as Daniel's power is killing me, it's also keeping me alive. It's getting stronger as I'm getting weaker."

"Stronger how?"

"The last few days, I've been able to sense the demons like a radar. I almost know what they're thinking. That's how I know we're safe right now. You already know I can close gates from a distance, but I can also wipe out a group of demons if they get close enough, although it wipes me out, big time."

"Does using your powers make you worse?"

Rick swallowed and stared off into space. "I... don't know. I think I'm dying either way. All I can do is try to do as much good as I can before that happens."

Guy's calves ached from squatting, so he copied Rick and sat right in the dirt. "That's a large burden, Rick. I'm sorry."

"Don't be. I was dead, and now I have some extra time. Most people don't get that. Just get me to that gate, Captain."

Guy thought about Alice, but he knew this mission of Rick's was equally important. "I'll get you there, Rick. I promise."

Keith stormed over to them then, kicking up dust in his wake. "Hey, you two! Sorry to break up your chitchat, but you think you could lend the rest of us a hand?"

"Coming right over," said Guy. He raised an eyebrow at Rick. "Is your brother always so..."

Rick nodded. "Yeah, always!"

21

RICHARD HONEYWELL

The last demon bled out at dawn. Now, morning sunlight illuminated a grisly tapestry across the forecourt. The rain had finally taken a break. Bleeding, grey corpses—both human and demon—littered the pavement. Corporal Martin's soldiers had held their own, but the demons had been too many. Each time a man had stopped to reload, a foul creature had pounced and tore off their screaming faces. By the time Corporal Martin expelled his final round into a demon's neck, twelve dead men joined the four-dozen demon corpses. Tired and injured, the survivors had collapsed where they'd stood, and remained there overnight.

Richard, too, was exhausted; for he had fought the demons with everything he had as well. With just a blade, he had gutted two demons, before snatching the rifle from a soldier dead to a throat slash. Then he had taken out three more.

The fighting had taken less than an hour, but it had taken a week's worth of strength from everyone involved. Now, beneath the warm sun, Richard looked off into the distance, wondering where the Hell his son was. Skullface had taken Dillon, but why? Was the suffering already wrought on Richard's family not enough?

What did Skullface want with children? Why not just kill them?

The possible answers were too painful.

Whatever the reason, taking Dillon was the biggest mistake of Skullface's existence. Richard would find him and rip the grotesque abomination apart. But first, he had to put his affairs in order. He went to where Carol had fallen and stayed throughout the cold night, the rain hammering at her lifeless body. Her expression now was peaceful, and her sodden hair made it look like she just got out of the shower. Richard lifted her easily, so much of her blood having leaked out and formed a crust on the floor. "You had a good inning, love, but we'll take it from here."

When Corporal Martin saw Richard carrying Carol across the forecourt, he frowned. "Where are you taking her?"

"Some place she'd like to be."

Corporal Martin seemed to understand and showed Richard so by giving a respectful nod before turning and walking away. Richard continued into the showroom, ignoring the beastly Mustang. The GT's driver door still hung ajar, which made placing Carol inside easy. Richard positioned her upright and held her in place with the bright-red seatbelt. Death had stiffened the old girl's limbs, but he could still position both her hands on the soft leather steering wheel before closing the door. "Drive safe, Carol."

Back outside, the remaining men and woman gathered. There were less than twenty of them now. "We're out of ammo," said Corporal Martin. "We're fucked. Totally fucked!"

Richard shoved the soldier, shocking him. "We're alive, you fool. Maybe we'll be dead tomorrow, but right now we're alive. Let's use that time to make as many of those bastards pay as we can. We lost a dozen good men and women last night, but not before we took fifty of the enemy. Next time, we'll take a hundred."

"What's the point, Richard? They outnumber us by thousands. We have no chance. Fighting them is suicide."

"You said we're fucked. It's not suicide if we're already dead. I'm going to find that bastard who took my son and destroy him. I will do it for Carol and David, and everybody else. That thing killed my wife, and it still isn't satisfied."

Corporal Martin swallowed, and he even looked worried. "Calm down, Richard. We have no ammunition, or any idea where that thing took Dillon and Alice. Let's just bide our time a little and regroup."

Richard shook his head. "You really think I can do that? My son is out there. I get that you want to stay and lick your wounds, but I'm going." He raised his voice as he moved out into the open. "Do you all hear me? I am sick and tired of hiding, waiting to be attacked. How long did we cower at the newspaper office? What good did it do? If we act like frightened cattle, then it's just a matter of time until we're slaughtered. But I won't go out afraid and hiding. I will go seek the bastards out and make them pay. I am a father whose son was taken by a monster. What can I do, but try to find him? The question is, what will you people do with your last days? Are you going to lie down and die while the monsters who took your families— your children—inherit everything we built together? Or are you going to take as many of those bastards down with you as you can?"

One soldier present cheered, and his reaction pushed the group to do the same. Heads nodded and muttered curses flew. Somehow, despite all the misery and loss, people were no longer afraid of the demons.

They were angry. Enough was enough.

Corporal Martin chuckled. Richard frowned. "What's funny?"

"I was wondering when you'd step up and lead people."

"You're in charge, Corporal. I just want revenge."

"A corporal is not a commander. We take orders from Sergeants. I believe that was your rank in the police force?"

"I don't want command. There's nothing *to* command."

Corporal Martin shook his head and kept that annoying grin on his face. "Then you shouldn't give rousing speeches. That's the thing about strays—you offer your hand once and they follow you forever. These people belong to *you* now. Good luck, Richard. I'll be right beside you."

Richard studied the group of survivors, horrified to see their attention had somehow shifted from the corporal to him. Fine, if they wanted him to tell them what to do, no problem. They would all be dead before the day was through.

Not before I find Dillon though.

"Grab your stuff, people. Say your goodbyes to those we leave here in our memories because we head out in ten minutes."

22

HERNANDEZ

Hernandez found navigating England easy. While the narrow and winding roads were most un-American, the street signs were clear and easy to follow. As Portsmouth seemed to be the biggest city in the area, all signs pointed there.

All roads lead to Rome.

All roads lead to vengeance.

The closer he got to his destination, so far unaccosted, the surer he became he would wrap his hands around Guy Granger's throat. The countryside teemed with rabbits, and even the occasional deer, but there were no people. If anyone was left, they were at Portsmouth, a place the fisherman who brought him here fancied the last Bastion of their ancient land. Hernandez's ancestors hailed from Catalonia, Spain, and he wondered how well his ancestral home was faring. Better than here, he hoped.

Where are you, Guy? Have you wormed your way into safety, or are you out here somewhere in the wild?

I'm coming for you.

Hernandez knew he had lost his mind to an extent, but it wasn't mental illness. It was a lack of anything else to occupy his mind. Focusing on punishing Guy was all that was left for him. His old life, his career, his family, were all gone. The only goal still attainable—killing the man who caused his downfall.

How had life come to this? Hernandez had dedicated his life to saving people, and now he was a nomad promising murder. He was supposed to be a hero.

Really? A voice in his head asked him. *Do people join the Navy to save people? Doesn't the Navy kill? Make war?*

Hernandez bit at his lip and asked himself a question out loud. "Am I some kind of psychopath?"

"I believe the prevailing term is sociopath?" came a husky voice through crackling leaves. "But the desire to see one's foes reduced to viscera is as old and as human as civilisation itself. Do not admonish yourself for it."

Hernandez's heart burst through his chest. He had not heard a human voice in more than a day, and for one to suddenly pierce the silence out here among the trees and fields was jarring. He looked at the old, hairless man and raised his unsure fist. "Who the Hell are you?"

"My name is Oscar Boruta, and you are a foolish man. This is the End of Days, yet you stroll through the countryside without a care for your own safety."

Hernandez looked around at the open countryside. "All seems pretty safe to me, old man. Your concern is unwanted."

The old man grinned. Burnt abominations in the shape of men emerged from the landscape, seeping from the bushes and stepping out from behind trees. The old man's grin turned to a scowl. "You haven't taken a single step without it being seen, fool. It is only your outright foolishness that has allowed you to live this long. I admit to a certain curiosity. You wear anger around your neck like a leaden torc. Your soul reeks like smoking, black oil. A dark heart like yours is a shame to waste."

"What are you talking about?" Hernandez eyeballed the demons coming closer on all sides. "You're human. What are you doing with these creatures?"

The old man blinked, eyelids moving sideways like a lizard's. He flicked a forked tongue. "We were all human once, fool, but no more. I am something greater now, a ruler of a new earth. Your life is mine, fool, as is all life fated to tremble beneath the gaze of the Red Lord."

"Who is-"

The old man ignored him. "That black chain around your neck—who put it there?"

Hernandez frowned, then realised the man was referring to his anger. "A man who wronged me. A traitor."

"There's a place for traitors, but it's been recently relocated."

Hernandez was tired of being spoken to like a child. "Leave me be, Mr Boruta."

"Do not make demands of a Lord, you worthless insect. I could crush your skull with a blink of my eye. Your insolence amuses me, though, as does the blackness of your heart. I will allow you to take your revenge, fool, for the spilling of human blood honours my master. Go! Go and spread your suffering."

Hernandez nodded, strangely thankful that someone supported his mission. He took a step forward to leave, but then stopped. He realised he was surrounded by hundreds of demons. They would rip him apart, surely. "How do I—"

"Come here, fool."

"W-what?"

"DO NOT MAKE ME REPEAT MYSELF."

Hernandez stumbled towards the frail old man, almost wetting himself, as even the sun seemed to flee. As soon as he got near, Boruta lashed out and nearly broke Hernandez's wrist, clutching it in a crushing grip. Hernandez wanted to scream, but he knew it would only shame him in the eyes of this wicked creature disguised as a man.

Boruta gritted his sharp, rotting teeth and raised his free hand. The nails on each finger lengthened like retractable blades. He sunk them down into Hernandez's exposed wrist.

This time, he had no choice but to scream.

After several seconds of excruciating pain, the old man shoved Hernandez away who bent over double, clutching his burning flesh. "Keep your arm attached, and you will be safe, for now."

Hernandez rubbed his burning forearm and felt ridges. When he examined, he noticed strange markings scored into his flesh. Scar tissue had already formed over the wounds.

What had the old man done?

Boruta waved a hand dismissively. "Go!"

Hernandez began walking, his legs hollow and unstable. The demons in his way glowered, but they moved out of his path. Within seconds, a dozen of them had scattered, leaving a clear passage through their centre. Hernandez then realised what the old man had done.

The markings on his arm...

He was untouchable. Free to move amongst the demons.

For now, the old man had said. *You will be safe, for now.*

Better make the time count, Hernandez thought, making his way towards Portsmouth with both hands clenched in fists.

23

SKULLFACE

Skullface grew tired of battling with the children, so he shoved them aside and into the arms of his minions. Let them restrain the snivelling worms, he had preparations to make. Children of his own to nurture. Their arrival would be glorious. Their plague of pain a joyous event.

Beedle. Molok.

The original connoisseurs of agony.

Skullface trod on the disembodied skull of a dead human and enjoyed its hollow crunch. The corpse was not his doing, but it still pleased him. This field, with its gaudy fairground rides, had laid witness to some wonderful atrocity in days past. The brethren had swarmed here and left a meadow of human corpses behind them. Every seat on the Ferris Wheel had a body hanging from it. The coconut shy's bristly fruit had been replaced with open-mouthed heads; eyes gouged out and placed between the teeth. It felt like Lord Amon's work. Had his army been here? Scouring the land clean?

Skullface sought to honour the Red Lord with the greatest gift he could give: the gift of his son and daughter, Beedle and Molok. The first humans ever to bask in the suffering of others. Humanity's first serial killers.

Beedle and Molok, twins alike in looks and spirit, had

tortured and gutted a mongrel before they turned six years old. He, their father, had found them playing amongst the animal's innards in the hills beside their home. The murder had not disturbed him, no. He was a proud father.

He was Cain.

His children had murder in their veins.

They killed their first woman at nine years of age. Beedle had wept in the forest, yelling that she was lost and afraid. A nearby shepherd's wife heard her cries and came to help, but Molok waited nearby with a club and cleaved her skull in two. The children played in the woman's insides until dusk and even took the intestines home to attract more hungry mongrels to kill. Sometimes they ate the mongrels. In years later, they would eat their human victims too.

While Cain had lived a thousand years, his children were young, less blessed by the pure life force of God passed down through Adam and Eve. Every line of descendants diluted that essence and therefore, Cain would watch his children age and die. Before that happened, though, they would show the world true darkness. Humanity could only know light if it cowered from the shadows. That was Cain's gift to the world.

Balance.

Evil needed to exist for good to flourish, and his children would provide it. It was as God intended.

Yet it was all ruined by a motherless widow. Her tears burned Cain's memory even now, millennia later.

That whore.

Beedle and Molok were in their twentieth year when they brought home the twin girls. They had never killed fellow twins before, or even seen such an oddity repeat itself. Such a thing was rare, and the villagers exalted any children that came in pairs. Beedle and Molok had tortured them for days, cutting off parts and strangling them half to death before bringing them back again. All the while, Cain tended his cornfield, readying the year's harvest.

The children's mother had returned home from a walk that evening to find her husband dead—his skinless body propped beneath a nearby willow tree. Screaming without relent, she had feared finding her precious twin girls the same way, but merely found them missing. The men from the village saw the devastation wrought upon the woman and set out with torches and clubs. Rumours had fluttered for many a year that innocent souls fell to the creatures at the shack upon the hill—the one surrounded by the cornfields.

Cain had hidden his identity for many years, known only as a quiet man who traded corn. That he even had children was unknown to most, which was why, when the widow and the mob fell upon Beedle and Molok in the midst of peeling off the dead girls' faces, they had been horrified. But their horror had quickly turned to fury.

Cain had tried to intervene, but he was restrained by too many men and forced to watch while his glorious progeny were strung up by their ankles as the snarling widow hacked away at their torsos. Cain winced as his children's ribs broke, fought his captors tooth and nail for the three hours it took for the widow to murder them. Then, when the whore was done, the men had pulled Beedle and Molok down and set their corpses on fire.

Mankind had learnt murder that night, and let the darkness in willingly.

The mob left Cain with two broken legs and both hands cut off, a dead man unable to even staunch his own bleeding. But he had left the wretched earth with a grin, for, using the last of his strength, he had visited the murderous widow at dawn, found her sleeping on a patch of hay in her barn. He set upon her with handless arms and floppy legs, yet had successfully impregnated her by the time her screams brought help. Before anyone could drag him away, Cain bled out right there on top of her.

The widow had kept the child.

Enoch.

Sent to Hell to burn with Lucifer and the rebelling angels, Cain found himself unable to locate his children. From Lucifer himself, he learned that God had banished them to the darkest pits of the Abyss, a place he could not enter.

Why God? Why did you punish my children for their nature? They brought darkness to your earth so that mankind could truly enjoy the warmth of your glow. You punish innocents.

You punish my children?

Then the Red Lord had burst forth from Hell's centre and invaded God's many paradises—each one in turn. Now, Cain would use his captured prey to finally free his children from the undeserved prison. He glared at the two snivelling children now and wished there had been more to pick from. The boy was defective, but would have to do. Children were scarce in any form. The girl was pure, yet resembled his daughter in no way. Again, compromises had to be made. Soon their bodies would play host to Beedle and Molok and humanity's original serial killers would return.

This time their lives would be glorious and without end.

24

RICHARD HONEYWELL

R ain poured again, the sky so grey, day felt like night. The van's automatic headlights came on and cut a shaft through the silvery sheets of falling rain. Wipers lunged back and forth furiously to keep back the tide. Richard's followers were able to cram themselves into a single vehicle—so few of them left.

Richard rode up front. Corporal Martin had the wheel. "Which way?" he asked Richard as they approached a T-junction.

Richard closed his eyes and listened to his blood pulse in his ears. If God existed, this was the time to lend a hand. *Please, just show me the way? Which way do I go? Give me a sign. Please.*

Movement caught his eye. Corporal Martin leant forward over the steering wheel. "Is that…?"

"Yes," said Richard, a bemused expression on his face. "That there is a chicken crossing the road."

Dillon and Alice had fought to save the lives of a group of chickens because they were innocent children who still valued life. If Richard was hoping for a sign from God, this was about the best he could imagine. The chicken bobbed its head without a care in the world, despite the heavy rain, and then disappeared into a nearby hedge off to the left.

"That way," said Richard, pointing to the left. "We go that way."

Corporal Martin gripped the wheel and took the turn. As they passed by the hedge, the chicken was nowhere to be seen. Richard was unsure if it had ever been there to begin with. They headed down the road for the better part of a mile before they were forced to stop. An overturned lorry, its cargo spilled across the road, blocked their way ahead. A small slip road led down a woody embankment on the left.

"Skullface could have blocked the road ahead," said Corporal Martin. "Could be an ambush."

Richard thought about it but disagreed. "He didn't go that way."

"How do you know?"

The lorry's fallen cargo contained vegetables, fruits, and grains. A miasma of mould festered on the road—blackened bananas covered in fuzz, dried out apple husks withering away like cancer-infected hearts. Yet none of it had been trodden on or disturbed. No apple or banana lay squashed or kicked aside.

"Skullface has demons with him," Richard explained. "A lot of them. If they came this way, they would have trampled through all this mess. Nothing is crushed or splattered though. A horde of demons did not come this way. If they went anywhere, it was down this slip road."

Corporal Martin looked at the small road leading down the woody embankment and apparently thought about it. Stapled to a tree, a fading blue poster flapped against the rain's onslaught. CASTLE FAIRGROUND. BANK HOLIDAY WEEKEND.

"I suppose we should visit the fair, Richard."

"I doubt there'll be candy floss."

They pulled away from the main road, leaving the overturned lorry in their wake.

THEY TOOK THINGS SLOWLY, the battering rain making the journey no easier. The slip road was old and cracked and led down into a quaint village with white-painted cottages with thatched roofs. The tallest building was a stone church, but even that was small by typical standards. Desiccated corpses littered the small grassy common in the village centre.

Corporal Martin groaned. "There must have been a bunch of people holding out here. How long did they survive before... this?"

Richard bit his lip and imagined Dillon like this, dead and rotting. "This has to stop."

"No shit."

"I wish I could kill every one of them. They deserve to pay."

Corporal Martin sighed but said nothing. What could he say? That humanity had lost, and the demons would never pay? It didn't need saying.

It didn't need fucking saying.

"I think the fairground is over there," said Richard, trying not to let his mind fly away. "Takes us in."

They took a turn and headed towards a Ferris Wheel peeking out behind the church. They found it standing in a wide-open field, alongside Waltzers and Bumper Cars, a Fun House and Ghost Train. The Ferris Wheel took up the centre of the fairground, and from each of its spokes hung a corpse. Inside its bottom capsule, Alice and Dillon sat in traumatised silence.

"We found them," said Corporal Martin, mouth agape. "They're here."

Richard put his hand on the door release, but fingers appeared around his other wrist.

"Just wait a minute," said Corporal Martin. "Look!"

There were demons everywhere, hidden amongst the grisly ornaments and dilapidated rides. Dozens. Not hiding, just dormant.

"We have no ammo," Corporal Martin added. "They'll rip us apart if we go down there."

Richard tensed his arm where Corporal Martin was grabbing it, wondering if he should pull free and make a run for it, but then he calmed down and took a breath. "My son is right there, alive. How much longer until that changes?"

"If Skullface wanted to kill him, he would have already done it, surely. Something else is going on."

He was right. Something else *was* going on.

Skullface appeared then from behind the Ferris Wheel, flicking blood from the gaping throat of a severed head. It hadn't belonged to a human, but a demon. With the blood, Skullface seemed to be making a circle around the ride. Inside the capsule, Dillon and Alice remained sitting in terrified stasis. Richard couldn't sit idly by while his son endured such horror.

"It looks like he's performing some kind of ritual," said Corporal Martin.

"I don't care what he's doing. This is the end for that abomination. Whatever it takes, I will kill him."

There was a bang on the back wall behind them in the van. The rest of the group, riding inside the cargo space, no doubt wanted to know why they had stopped.

Richard winced. "Shut them up before—"

The banging turned frantic. The van rocked on its suspension so violently that Corporal Martin and Richard fell against each other, knocking heads.

Terror filled Corporal Martin's eyes, and he pointed through the windscreen. "Shit! They've spotted us!"

Sure enough, Skullface stopped before the Ferris Wheel and stared right up the hill towards the van.

"Shit!" Richard pulled the door handle and tumbled out as the van continued rocking. He stumbled around to the side and then to the back door, which was still closed. The men and women inside were screaming. What was going on in there?

Hands trembling, Richard grabbed the rear latch and yanked open the back.

Chaos met him.

"Help!" someone screamed, but it was already too late. Two primates tore through the van's cargo bay like the wild animals they were, slashing throats and raking eyeballs. Together, and in such close confines, the demons could slice apart the trapped humans with ease. The metal bed of the van grew slick with blood, and it began to pour from the rear lip onto the grass at Richard's feet.

One soldier slumped to his chest on the van's floor and

crawled towards Richard with his arms out imploringly. "W-we opened the door. W-we thought it was you."

Richard choked on his own vomit. Skullface had known the entire time they would be coming. Had probably known of their presence the moment they arrived in the village.

"Come on," shouted Corporal Martin in his ear. "It's too late. We have to get out of here."

Richard clenched his fists and bit his lip hard enough to taste blood. "No. I'm tired of running. Dillon is here." He pulled the combat knife from the sheath at his belt and left the bloodshed in the van. The screaming victims were bleeding out and the demons would silence them within the next few seconds. In the end, they had died as he'd feared they would, like frightened lambs. And he had played a part in that. They had followed him to their deaths in less than a day.

So, it was left up to him to make the bastards pay.

Corporal Martin dodged out of Richard's way as he sped down the grassy embankment towards the fairground. The demons below gathered to meet him, but they underestimated his furious haste. He passed by the first bunch of demons before they had a chance to grab him, and the next group that got in his way found themselves barged to the ground like kittens hit by a locomotive. Skullface lay right in his path, and he raised his knife, ready to bury it in the bastard's eye socket.

Dillon saw him coming and screamed. There was hope in his voice.

But there was no way to save him.

Richard would at least get them both a little payback. He threw his body through the air, knife out in front of him. The bellow spilling out of him sounded like it came from a bear.

Skullface raised an arm to protect himself, but it was too late. Richard had the force of a broken man behind him, and he would not be denied his vengeance.

Something struck Richard in mid-air, knocking the wind from him and sending him into a spin. A demon appeared in front of him and tackled him to the ground while another set upon his wrist and wrenched away his knife. Within a single second, he was being held down by the arms and legs, a demon crushing every limb.

Skullface glared at him and cackled. "You're just in time. Say goodbye to everything your son ever was."

Richard fought and wept, wept and fought.

From up on the grassy hill, the screams from the van had stopped.

Everyone was dead.

25

GUY GRANGER

The earth shook and the pouring rain formed vibrating puddles on the ground. Guy wondered if the explosions coming from Portsmouth were the drumbeats of humanity's last moments. Was this the end of the End?

Alice? Where are you, girl?

Rick snatched the radio from one of the soldiers and tried to get through to someone on the other end. Wickstaff answered. "Bit busy right now, chaps."

Rick seemed surprised to get an answer, and it took him a second to answer. "W-What's happening?"

"The buggers are storming the walls, what does it sound like?"

"Do we need to turn back, come join the fight?" asked Guy.

Silence... Then: "We're holding our own, for now. They might have the numbers, but they're as thick as shit sandwiches. Our big guns are flattening them. We're not out of the woods, but—" a massive explosion rumbled in the background, "— but our tactics are working. What you chaps need to do is close that sodding gate and let us kill Lord Amon. He's keeping his distance, but—" another explosion "—but once he joins the fray, we won't be able to do anything to stop him. Close that gate, Rick. Be the rock star you were in a previous life."

Guy's eyes went wide. "That's why I recognise you!"

Rick waved his hand at him irritably. "We're a little stuck at the moment, General. The demon horde coming your way formed up around us and we had to go to ground in an old cinema building."

"The Trescott?"

"Um," Guy looked up at the scaffolding; he thought he spotted a faded sign. "The name is covered up by construction at the moment, but I think I see a picture of a popcorn carton."

"Yep. I know where you are," said Wickstaff. "Hold on to your arses, chaps."

The radio clicked and hissed. Rick lowered it and frowned at Guy. "She cut off the call."

"Maybe the enemy broke though. The fighting sounds bad." It was an understatement. Gunfire, explosions, and screams mingled like a clash between dragons. Or gods. The urge to go back and join the fight was persuasive, but Wickstaff had been clear. She wanted that gate closed.

And Guy wanted his daughter.

"Incoming!" One of the soldiers in their group shouted.

Guy glanced up and saw a streak in the grey sky.

The ground leapt beneath their feet, and a soul-rattling roar obliterated their hearing. Fire leapt up in the distance, visible over the palisade walls. Every man and woman hiding out at the cinema tumbled to the ground.

Rick covered his ears as he lay face down in the mud. "What the Hell?"

"She's buying our escape," said Guy, understanding what Wickstaff had meant when she said to hold on to their arses. "She's pointed some of Portsmouth's artillery our way."

"She'll bloody flatten us," said Keith, lying nearby. His hair had slipped, exposing an impressive bald spot.

"No," said Guy, shouting over the din as another shell hit nearby. "She knows the area. The shells won't hit us. We need to leave while the enemy is distracted."

Rick climbed onto his knees, sweat beading on his temples. He didn't look good. "Keith's right, we'll die if we go out there."

"What other chance will we get?" Guy stood up and brushed

himself off. Disturbed air buffeted his untucked shirt. "Everyone get to your feet, we're getting out of here, right now. Keep your heads down and pray."

Nobody looked happy, but nor did anybody argue.

Guy knew he would have to be the first out of the parapet, so he approached the wooden palisade and started stripping away the barricade the men had built. His hands turned to ice beneath the onslaught of icy rain that had come back with a vengeance in the last hour, and his fingers were clumsy and numb. Rick came to help, and together they shoved the obstacles aside moving the wooden panel they had placed over the gap.

Fire and brimstone awaited. The world was flame and screaming beasts ran rampant.

A demon leapt at Guy standing in the gap. Rick threw up his hand, and the creature blinked out of existence.

Guy stared at Rick in awe. "Neat trick."

"Tricks are for kids. What I have is *moves*."

"Nice moves, Rick Bastion."

Rick groaned, but he smiled too.

Keith collided into the back of them. "Move your arses!"

The group put their heads down and piled out into the road. Nearby, concrete curled up in a flaming crater and a single-story garden centre collapsed in on itself. If another shell hit within fifty metres of them, they were done for. More demons lay in their path, but the creatures were shaken and confused. Some burned to death on their knees. Wickstaff's reign of fire was enough to terrify the minions of Hell. The woman was a force.

Soldiers opened fire and Guy had his sailors—now marines—do the same. Combined, they cut a path and moved onwards.

Another shell exploded. The air grew hot and whipped at them. Burning demons squealed like Guinea Pigs.

Keith laughed, popping off shots from a revolver. "Enjoy your agonising death, you fuckers."

"Come on," Guy urged. "We have to be gone by the time the demons recover."

Everyone moved. Ahead lay the countryside, farmland separating Portsmouth from the next towns over. If they could just get to the tree line...

More demons formed up ahead, reinforcements coming from outside the blast zone. Unlike their shell-shocked brethren, these creatures still had their wits about them.

"Form up," Guy said to his marines. The soldiers readied themselves, too, happy to take orders.

The demons approached slowly. Their black eyes smouldered. Rancid hides slick with rain.

Guy raised his hand, then dropped it. "Fire!"

The demons screeched. Gunfire replied. They danced frantically as bullets tore up their bodies, but they moved forward relentlessly, bodies piling up in a carpet. As soon as one demon fell, two more would clamber over its corpse. It was a surge, an enveloping wave that could not be held back.

"They keep coming," said Keith, firing endlessly from his large revolver, which he reloaded after every six shots. For a civilian, he was rather adept. "We can't hold them off."

Keith was right, and Guy hated to admit it. More demon reinforcements were arriving and seemed to have no end in sight. Soon, the soldiers would run out of bullets. Guy glanced over his shoulder, searching for a retreat, but the demons scattered throughout the blast zone had started to recover.

Guy breathed heavy. They were surrounded.

I'm sorry, Alice. I wish I could leap into the sky and fly to you, but instead, it looks like I will die right here.

The explosions had stopped, not just nearby, but at Portsmouth too. The fighting had entered a lull, as prolonged battles often did. But the men at Guy's side continued firing whatever rounds they had left.

They would go out fighting.

"I'm out of bullets," said Keith, turning his revolver sideways so he could use it as a bludgeon. "Nice plan, Rick. We almost made it ten miles out of Portsmouth."

Rick glowered at his brother. Instead of firing a weapon, he waved his hands like a magician, and demons cartwheeled as if struck by invisible wrecking balls. "Stop being so negative, Keith. For once in your life."

Keith huffed. "What's there to be happy about? We're about to get torn apart by monsters."

"Good point."

The soldiers ran out of ammo, one by one. Each now held their rifles like clubs, ready to fight till the end. It wouldn't be long now. They looked at one another, bracing themselves.

A shadow fell over them.

The rain turned sideways as a mighty wind displaced it.

Guy glanced up and saw a roaring beast.

A dragon had left Portsmouth.

And the dragon spewed fire.

The duel rotary guns mounted beneath the Apache attack chopper's wings unleashed a swarm of hornets at the ground, spitting up dirt and cement, and beating two dancing trails towards the enemy.

"Thank you, Wickstaff," said Rick. "I could kiss her."

"She'd knock your block off," said Keith.

A crimson cloud formed as demon flesh disintegrated. Twisted limbs shattered and heads exploded.

Within seconds, an entire legion of demons had been reduced to a writhing stream of leaking flesh.

The Apache tilted, swooped upwards, and disappeared back towards Portsmouth.

"Let's go," said Guy. "We can thank that pilot later, after we win."

The soldiers and marines cheered. Then they got the Hell out of there—double time.

26

GENERAL WICKSTAFF

W ickstaff could barely speak her mouth was so dry. It felt like she'd been shouting orders for days, but the fighting had been going on less than two hours. In that time, she had barely lost a man. Most of the human casualties had occurred in the opening moments of the conflict, after the demons first attacked, but now, her forces were entrenched, expending an endless supply of ammo. The naval artillery had proved the real boon. Whenever an enemy came at you en mass like the demons were, you could easily flatten them with overlapping spreads of bombardment. And they had plenty left in reserves. At this rate, the naval guns could keep firing all day, and the demons would lose long before that.

Already, she estimated a thousand enemy dead at the cost of only two-dozen men. She'd even found time to rescue Rick and Guy, encircled up at that old cinema house. Her scouts had mapped out the entire city for her weeks ago, which was why she'd had no problem finding the right coordinates to suppress. She'd spared a chopper too to check out the results. The pilot reported seeing Guy and the others making a break for it.

If they close that gate and we take down Lord Amon, we might just win this. Should it be this easy?

"We're holding our entire perimeter," one of her Lieutenants reported. "We lost Ingress 6 early on, but we set off the charges and blocked it. Since then, the enemy have been wading into our kill zones like lemmings."

Wickstaff nodded curtly. "They've won every battle until now because of sheer numbers. Their army is grunt heavy, and all they know is how to overwhelm and terrorise. But we will not be overwhelmed, and we will not be terrorised. We cannot afford to be. Inform all squad leaders not to grow complacent. The enemy are not out of ideas yet, I assure you. We must be ready for whatever they try next."

"General! General Wickstaff!"

Wickstaff sighed, wishing for just a single second to breathe and relax. The battle was non-stop.

Maddy was the one calling her. The younger girl with blonde hair hurried alongside her. *Diane, was it?*

"What is it ladies? Can't you see I've got a war on?"

Maddy tittered, but none of the fear left her eyes. "It's the stone in the parade square."

"What about it?"

"It's opening a gate."

Wickstaff cleared her throat and spat. The chance to take a breath would not come today, or maybe not ever. She had known the stone would open at the worst possible moment—why wouldn't it? Its entire purpose was to fuck Portsmouth up right when it looked like there was a chance. She'd taken preparations, of course—placed mines around the gate and set up machine gun nests on every roof. She'd intended to erect a mesh cage around the stone, to trap whatever came out, but the battle started too soon. Now Portsmouth was invested upfront, with a threat at its back. The worst thing that could happen in a battle. The effect on morale would be devastating.

She had to take charge and deal with the situation.

She had to show her men they could win any battle, and surpass all odds, just so long as they remained calm and focused.

Maddy stepped up in front of her, regaining her attention. "General, there's another problem."

"What else?"

"I think you better come."

Wickstaff found herself running after a civilian, eager to find out what the problem was. This Maddy was a calm mind, and obviously meant a great deal to Rick. She was beginning to see why.

Maddy took them to the parade square—and the imminently opening gate.

"Fuck me sideways," said Wickstaff.

This gate was three times the size of the ones Wickstaff had seen in reports and media snippets, and twice as big as the one she had seen first hand from the deck of an Apache helicopter. That gate had been the one Rick and Guy were hopefully on their way to destroy. Weeks back, Wickstaff had led an assault on the gate herself, from the air—launching live goats through it to see if it would implode the same way other gates had when humans entered. But when they had swung a goat into the gate from a winch, a torrent of bloody giblets spat right back out. The gate had remained open, and they had learned a lesson that day about closing gates.

Only a human life would do.

Or Rick Bastion's power.

Christ, does that washed up rock star really have the power of an angel inside of him? The world has flipped its lid. She reminded herself that she was at war with Hell, then Rick didn't seem such an oddity anymore.

The massive gate in front of Wickstaff was four-stories high, and it shimmered and rippled like a rain-spattered pond. It resembled a hungry mouth, ready to lurch forward and devour the world itself. Any attempt she made to see inside left her confused and sickened, with strange thoughts that urged her to kill herself. It led somewhere unfathomable, a place where only ever-lasting torment and horror existed. A place she hoped never to know.

She'd hoped to contain this. But it was too big. Looking at it now, she knew that hanging around and fighting on two fronts was impossible. But it was the only chance they had. This was their last stand.

Too late now to do anything else but fight.

Prime Minister Windsor appeared, racing across the square and yelling commands. "Fall back. Evacuate right now. By air or by sea, we are leaving Portsmouth. The fight is lost, so let's live for tomorrow."

For a moment, Wickstaff stood there, bewildered, but once she got a hold of herself, she went and grabbed the wretch by the back of his collar. "What the hell do you think you are doing, Windsor?"

The man shrugged her away and snarled, his teeth like tiny pegs between his thin lips. "What do you think I am doing, woman? This gate is about to open any minute. I am trying to save us all while there's still time."

"If we leave now, we'll always be running, and the enemy will pick us off one by one until there's no one left. They've been wiping us out that way since the beginning. This is the first time we've held our own; the only time we've had a line of fortifications between them and us. I realise that having a gate behind our lines is unfortunate, but I have prepared for it."

"Prepared for it? *Prepared for it?* What the hell is there to prepare for? The enemy will stream right through our middle." The Prime Minister dismissed her with a petulant wave of his hand and resumed barking orders at anxious soldiers. Send them the wrong messages now and they would break. She needed to get ahold of the situation.

Wickstaff grabbed Windsor by the throat and shoved him away from her. He rubbed at his windpipe and stared daggers at her, but before he managed to berate her, she cut him off.

"Running will not work. We have to turn the tide now while we still have something resembling a Resistance. If I hear you try to evacuate any more of my men, I will shoot you dead right here."

Windsor sneered, not taking her threat seriously.

So, she yanked the sidearm from her holster and pulled the trigger.

The bullet struck the concrete next to Windsor's foot and sent him leaping into the air like a flea. He yelled defiantly, yet his tone lacked his earlier arrogant authority. The man was a coward at heart—as Wickstaff suspected a great deal of career politicians were. Men and women far happier sending kids to war than going themselves. She, however, was most certainly no coward. Her threats were not idle.

"Do not test me, Windsor. Our nation is in ruins, and all that exists is Portsmouth," she waved an arm, motioning to the rushing soldiers and zooming Jeeps, "and Portsmouth is my fucking kingdom until I say otherwise. Get out of my sight!"

Hot air blasted from the gate and threw Wickstaff sideways. She stayed on her feet but needed several steps to regain her balance. When she looked back at the gate, it was shimmering madly. Something was about to come through. The Prime Minister was laughing.

"What are you laughing at, you halfwit?"

"You're finished, General. Your kingdom is about to burn."

"What are you talking about?" Wickstaff kept one eye on the gate. Soldiers rushed to form a perimeter around it, rifles at the ready.

The Prime Minister was still smiling. He was insane. No point wasting time with a mad man, so she hurried away from the gate and re-joined her squads. There was fear in her men's eyes but determination too. They would all love nothing more than to run, she knew, but each of them understood there was no longer anywhere to go. This was it—their last bastion. Hers too. Wickstaff raised her sidearm and pointed it at the gate.

A charred corpse spewed onto the parade square. Then that corpse rose to its feet and snarled at them.

Wickstaff pulled her trigger and placed a bullet right inside its mouth. The back of its neck exploded, and it slumped to the ground like a good corpse should.

Then all Hell broke loose.

Wickstaff's men made her proud. Not a single one turned and fled, even as a surge of demons spilled forth into their reality. They picked their shots with deadly aim. Demons spun and collided with one another. Dark red blood filled the air, mingling with the rain. The loud report of sniper rifles and machine guns soon joined the cacophony of rifle fire, and a full-scale battle commenced.

Wickstaff's men held their own, cutting down demons as soon as they landed on the concrete.

The problem, as always, was ammunition.

Each magazine held thirty-rounds. Each soldier had between two and five spare mags. Picking their shots at around one per second, it would take half a minute before the firing lines were forced to stop and reload.

The demons kept coming.

Unable to reload quickly enough, several soldiers pulled out bayonets and screwed them onto their barrels. They formed up like Roman legionaries, shoulder to shoulder, stabbing with their blades rhythmically. But the demons were fearless, and ploughed into the wall of soldiers like an avalanche, driving them back and impeding their balance. As soon as one soldier stumbled, a domino effect started and men were dragged down on either side. The demons shredded them like slow-cooked beef.

Maddy appeared at Wickstaff's side and grabbed her arm. Diane grabbed the other. "We have to get everyone out of here."

"Fall back!" Wickstaff screamed, holstering her empty handgun and using both hands to amplify her voice. "Get your fucking arses to the docks. Fall back. Full retreat."

The men turned and fled, some throwing their rifles to the ground in an act that was anathema to most soldiers—the same as throwing down their pride. Wickstaff did not blame them.

"Come on," said Maddy. "We can't lose you, General."

"I have to make sure everyone gets out."

The men turning their backs presented easy prey to the demons, which leapt upon them with glee.

"My men!"

"General!" Maddy shoved Wickstaff hard in the chest, hurting both of her tits. Enough to snap some sense into her. She allowed Maddy and Diane to pull at her again, and the three of them ran for it.

Prime Minister Windsor blocked their way. He was still smiling, not concerned at all about the demons surrounding him.

Wickstaff shouted at him. "Run, you damn fool!"

"No need." Windsor pulled up his shirtsleeve, revealing a strange insignia scored into the flesh of his wrist. It meant nothing to Wickstaff, but then she saw the man stroll calmly towards the demon horde. The creatures dodged around him, acting as though he wasn't even there.

Windsor was one of them.

How?

Wickstaff spat at the weasely bastard, even though he was out of reach. "You son of a bitch!"

Windsor said nothing. He raised one hand and wiggled his fingers in a mocking wave.

Maddy shoved Wickstaff again, always there, it appeared, to keep her mind focused. Along with Diane, the two women chased the retreating soldiers towards the docks—the last place still under human control. Perhaps the last place they would get to see alive.

The bellowing war cry of ten thousand demons ruptured the air.

The ancient city of Portsmouth filled with blood.

27

GUY GRANGER

Guy was out of breath by the time he and the others made it to the tree line. The panic had caused them to scatter, which was why they now called out to each other, seeking one another out. The noise didn't matter—no demons would hear them, because the world was at war. Hell clashed with the forces of man and the ground shook for miles. Heaven must be weeping, for the rain fell in buckets. Smoke stained the sky black and blotted out the sun.

Guy wiped moisture from his eyes and licked his lips.

This is it. Our final moments.

I have to find Alice.

I have to be with her before it's too late.

But what about the gate? Would closing it really give Wickstaff a chance?

Guy shook his head. Of course it wouldn't. Things were too far gone. Even if Guy made it to the gate and Rick closed it, there was barely any chance the general could make use of the advantage.

It was too late for Alice as well. The best Guy could hope for was a few moments with her before the darkness curled up around them. But it was something. A chance to make up for all the times he hadn't been there. With all the disarray, and everyone being separated, he finally had a chance to break away and try to find her. He could just run for it right now and pray God would lead him to her.

"Don't go," said a voice behind him. Guy turned around and saw Keith standing in the woods. Sweat and dirt stained his face. "Don't abandon my brother."

"Why not?"

"Because you're better off not knowing if your daughter is alive or dead. My Max and Marcy are out there somewhere, and I can tell myself they are alive. If I find them though... If I find them and they're not alive. Well, that's worse than the not knowing. Knowing for sure they're dead is worse."

"Alice is not dead."

"Exactly! But if you keep looking for her, she might be. Let her live by never knowing. Stay and help my brother. There are families at Portsmouth who need you more. Help them."

Of all the people to be hearing this from, Keith was the last one Guy expected. "It's pointless," he said. "Things are too far gone."

"Then let's do one last thing that matters before we bite it. Let's give Wickstaff a chance to kill that bastard, Lord Amon."

"Why do you care?"

Keith wiped at his filthy cheeks, rivulets of rain dropping onto his collar. "My whole life, I've played things safe—taken the smart option. Spent my life chasing money, the big houses, the nice cars. Look at me now, as poor and as wet as anyone else. I wasted my life on the wrong priorities. Max and Marcy should have been everything to me, but I'll never see them again. Why do we only realise who we are at the end of a long journey in the wrong direction?" He sighed. "Help my brother, Guy. Make your last act a good one."

Guy wiped rain from his face as he spoke. "Rick doesn't need me."

"Rick can barely wipe his own arse. He's dying. I don't want him to go without doing what he was meant to do. He spent his whole life following his dreams, and all I ever did was criticise him. It's time for me to help him achieve his goals instead of resenting him for being the better man. My brother is a fucking rock star, and I can't believe it took me so long to be a fan."

"You don't think we will live through this, do you?"

"Ha! Open your ears. That's Armageddon."

"I don't think we have a chance either. That's why I want to find my daughter."

"You want to meet her after turning your back on those relying on you? Wouldn't she want you to stay and fight, even if it meant not getting to her?"

Guy thought of his daughter, imagined her spirit. She was a feisty little thing, unwilling to be dominated by her older brother. She had always been fearless, even as a toddler, yet she was kind too. While some kids had gone through phases of hitting and snatching from other children, Alice would always share. She followed Kyle around constantly, ready to lend a hand with whatever was going on.

Alice was brave.

So Guy had to be brave too.

"Let's go find your brother, Keith. We have a gate to close."

28

RICHARD HONEYWELL

Inhuman arms dragged Richard to his feet, dragged him before his nemesis. Skullface lacked flesh on his face—and lips, yet he was undeniably grinning. Had this all been one last game to torment a beaten father? By trying to survive, Richard succeeded only in increasing his suffering.

Richard's head dangled, but he fought to raise it and look the bastard in the eye. "Just finish this. Get it over with."

Skullface's lower jaw unhinged, and a voice spilled out from the dark space. "You demand nothing. You live only so long as it pleases me. Before I end you, I wish to witness my own majesty reflected in your pleading eye." He rushed forward and grabbed Richard's head with both hands and drove the pointed shard of his thumb bone into Richard's left eyeball. Blood and ocular fluids flooded Richard's cheek, and he screamed.

Screamed.

Screamed.

"Quiet! I left you sight enough to see your child die."

Richard lurched, arms still behind his back, and vomited in the grass. His head spun, and his eardrums pounded. Strangely, his mangled eye felt numb. He held his breath, bit down on the pain, and somehow managed to look up towards the Ferris Wheel.

Dillon and Alice stared back at him, but their expressions had gone blank.

Their eyes were lumps of coal.

"What have you done to my son?" Richard found a reserve of strength and tried to fight free of his attackers, but a blow to the back of his head reignited the pain in his eye socket and stunned him.

"Be still," said Skullface. "Sit and watch your child get taken from you. An exquisite torture I know all too well."

A pair of demons unlocked the capsule and released Dillon and Alice. Both continued staring blankly. Something was wrong. The demons led the children gently to Skullface's side, acting almost reverently. Affectionately, Skullface placed a bony arm around each of them.

Like a father.

"Beedle and Molok," said Skullface, peering at each child in turn. "Your souls will soon be tethered permanently, and I shall unleash you upon this world like a plague. Your first victim will be the pathetic father of the vessels you take. Make me proud. Show me your art."

Dillon and Alice grinned like hyenas. Something dark and primal dwelt inside them, something that chilled Richard to his core. For the first time ever, Richard wanted to be far, far away from his son. "D-Dillon?"

In a raspy voice, his son answered. "Dillon is lost. He wanders Hell's hallways screaming your name and watching his mother please others on her knees."

Richard vomited again. "Just... Just finish it."

The thing inside Dillon cackled. "Not for hours."

"Shit, there's a dude over there!"

Richard was too weak to lift his head, but he strained his eye upwards. A commotion grew and some of Skullface's minions were peeling away. Dillon and Alice stopped in their tracks, too, suddenly unsure. Skullface actually rose onto his tiptoes to see what was happening.

The snap of a heavy blow echoed off the steel struts of the

Ferris Wheel. A smoky stench filled Richard's nostrils. *What is happening?*

"Wow! You took out three in one swing," said an unknown voice.

"Yeah, man. Let me try to beat that shit."

"This is not a competition, my brothers. Do not let battle consume you."

Skullface threw out his fist and struck the ticket booth outside the Ferris Wheel. Its front window shattered, and the roof fell in. "Deal with them now!"

"Richard! Richard, get out of there!"

Richard blinked his one eye and looked around. *Is that... is that Corporal Martin?*

The demons were distracted. The grip on Richard's arms faltered. Fighting the weakness in his legs, he pushed up and got standing. The sudden movement took his captors by surprise, and he was able to turn the tables on them. He grabbed one demon by the back of the neck and whipped him into his partner. The two collided together like pro-wrestlers in a ring. It was only enough to stun them, but it gave him what he needed.

Richard ran, heading towards the sound of voices.

Human voices.

"Mass, watch out, man. You got one trying to grab a feel of your ass!"

The sound of wood against bone.

"Ooo, shit, dawg. Did you see his head go?"

"Richard, over here!"

Richard turned and saw Corporal Martin fighting over by the candyfloss booth. He wielded a wicked-looking machete that Richard hadn't seen before. He used it to lop the head off a primate, and then beckoned to Richard urgently.

Richard raced through the fairground, dodging demons and debris. When he reached the solider, he collapsed into the man's arms. "Dillon! I need to help Dillon."

"There's too many. We can't fight them."

"Speak for yourself," said a voice Richard didn't recognise. When he looked over, he saw an Arabic gentleman and two younger men—one black, one barrel-chested and white. The black man held a sword that was... on fire!

"W-who are you?"

"The cavalry!" said the obvious weight lifter, swinging a base-ball bat wrapped in barbed wire.

"We are friends," said the Arab. "Brothers."

"I met them on the road," explained Corporal Martin. "I told them what happened, and they insisted on coming to help. They... hunt demons."

Richard looked at the three men. "That's stupid."

The black kid held up his flaming sword and swung it at a demon leaping towards him. It ended up as a charred lump on the ground. "Name's Vamps. These are my bros, Mass and Aymun. Brothers in a non-biological sense," he added. "We're fighting back against these things, and G. I. Joe here tells me you were part of a group doing the same. Sorry there's only you left."

"And the children!" Richard pointed back towards the Ferris Wheel. "We have to help them."

Vamps nodded. "Alright. Nobody gets left behind. We'll go get 'em."

Before he could thank them, the three men took off—fearless or stupid, he didn't know.

Corporal Martin handed Richard a second machete secured to his belt. "Our new friends came well-armed."

Richard appraised the blade but didn't take it. Instead, his trembling hand moved up to the slick hole where his right eye had been. One more thing Skullface had taken from him.

No more.

He snatched the blade and turned back towards battle. A demon was already upon him, so he thrust the machete through its guts and tossed its corpse into the grass. Dillon and Alice still stood in the field by the Ferris Wheel, and that was where he headed.

Beedle and Molok?

No, Dillon and Alice. It can't be too late.

The blade in Richard's hand felt good—more empowering than a gun—and he swung it left and right, an explorer hacking vines. Only, instead of plant life, he sliced the flesh of monsters. But for every one he killed, Vamps' flaming sword scored three. The weapon was a living thing in his hands, wielding the kid as much as the kid wielded it. The air turned black and singed demon flesh reduced to ash. His buddy, Mass, picked off stragglers with that vicious baseball bat of his.

Yet the demons were endless. They were *always* endless.

Legion.

Richard made it within a few feet of the children. They looked at him without recognition. "Dillon, Alice! Come to me!"

They did not move.

A demon leapt at Richard, and he ducked just in time. If he had come from the other side—the side where he had no eyeball—he wouldn't have seen it coming. As it was, he sprung sideways and buried the machete in the demon's neck. The dying creature spun, which yanked the machete from Richard's hand. He reached to his son.

"Dillon! Come with me, please!"

More demons attacked. He had nothing to defend himself with. Dodging one demon, he was soundly struck by another. His legs gave out, and he found himself on the ground, scurrying to get up.

"Get off him!" Corporal Martin arrived. He sliced open a demon and locked up with another.

The demons closed in, surrounding them.

Corporal Martin fell as a demon tackled his legs. He ended up in a heap beside Richard, panting and grinning.

"Why are you laughing?" asked Richard, certain the two of them were about to die.

"Because you were right, Richard. The best way to die is like this—after killing as many of these fuckers as we were able."

Richard smiled too. "Was good knowing you, Corporal."

"You too, Sergeant."

Vamps appeared in the space two demons had occupied a second earlier. Their corpses lay in smouldering piles. Mass stood a few feet away, obliterating the skull of a skulking primate about to pounce. Aymun completed the hat trick by hacking a demon's throat wide open with a hatchet.

"I'm beginning to love you boys," said Corporal Martin.

Richard clambered to his feet and made it over to Dillon. He almost felt a spark as he wrapped his arms around his boy, but Dillon gave no reaction.

"Release my children!" Skullface bellowed, smashing aside his own minions to get at Richard.

Richard grabbed Alice and pulled her next to Dillon. "Fuck you!"

Skullface roared. "I shall hang you by your own intestines."

"Fuck you!" repeated Richard, calmly, coolly.

Skullface strode towards him furiously, but Vamps stepped into his path. "Homie? Take those kids and get out of here. Me and the big man are going to work things out in private."

The towering demon looked at Vamps as if he were an ant, but something caused him to take pause.

"Where did you get that sword?"

Vamps shrugged. "Some Irish dude. Told me to find freaks like you and make you sit on it. You ready?"

Skullface sneered. "*Lucifer Primus.* He will pay for helping you maggots. I shall see to his eternal torment myself. The Red Lord will enjoy the offering when he becomes King Reality."

"Didn't you hear?" Vamps raised the sword. "Our Royal family is just for show. Only one who bends the knee around here is your cock sucking mother."

"Shit, man," said Mass, moving up beside him. "Let's leave mothers out of this, yeah?"

Vamps nodded. "My bad. You get out of here, bro. I got this. All of you should get gone."

Skullface peered past Vamps at Richard. "You shall not get far."

"We'll see." Richard grabbed the children and fled. Corporal Martin hacked at any demons that got in their way, but most were distracted by the brave lunatic facing down their leader.

Richard glanced back one time on his way out of the fairground and saw Mass and Aymun were not part of the retreat. The three brothers remained together.

Crazy idiots, thought Richard as he got his son to safety behind the grassy hill.

Thank you.

29

GENERAL WICKSTAFF

Wickstaff grabbed a young soldier shoving to get himself onto the docks and punched him square in the mouth. "Next person you shove will get you a bullet in your head."

The young soldier clambered and nodded his head over and over. "Sorry, sir, I mean miss, I mean ma'am."

"Just get out of my sight."

Maddy was on the radio beside Wickstaff. Diane, too. Both women were helping coordinate the mass retreat to the docklands. There were squads marooned all over Portsmouth, and the gate on the parade square continued vomiting Hell upon them. The scales were tipping away from humanity's favour. The rain beat harder, like it was leading up to some great finish.

Maddy ended a call and gave a report. "We have teams coming in from everywhere. I think we got the word out to everyone."

"Excellent. Thank you. You and Diane should get yourselves on board a ship now. The enemy will break through any moment."

"I think we'd both prefer to stay by your side."

Wickstaff raised an eyebrow and surprised herself by smiling. "Women united, huh?"

"Something like that," said Diane in a voice far meeker than the steely look in her eye suggested she was. "We don't fancy living on a ship with a bunch of sweaty men."

"Let the men take cover," said Maddy. "While the women organise what needs to be done."

Wickstaff grabbed both women and pulled them in for a three-way head bump. "Glad to have you, ladies. Now, let's save some lives."

The docks were the most heavily defended of all locations, backed by water and a massive flotilla of warships. The Port Administration buildings helped shore up one of the two vulnerable sides, and a tall mesh fence reinforced with concrete pillars spanned the other side that butted up against the city. In weeks past, Wickstaff had ordered additional steel fences be erected in weaker areas of the perimeter, and the docks' one main entrance was defended by a pair of Challenger 2 tanks returned to the UK for a weapons system upgrade. Their presence had been a gift from the gods. Fully armed, and ready to vaporise anything they deemed a threat. To complement security, several guard towers housed snipers and grenadiers. Wickstaff congratulated herself on keeping her heaviest assets guarding the rear. It meant they had half a chance of escaping.

But she had meant what she'd told that weasel, Windsor—that running would be the end of their Resistance, and that once they turned their backs to flee there would be no way back. But what choice did she have anymore? As much as she'd love to go down in a defiant blaze of glory, she could not condemn tens of thousands to death. There were too many civilians. Maybe a life at sea would be the new future of mankind. As she looked upon the water, she knew living space wasn't an issue. The carrier alone was enough to house a thousand in cramped confines.

But for how long?

They couldn't live on fish and rainwater forever.

So much gunfire filled the air that both the smell and sound had become part of the background—like traffic fumes had once been. The rain puddles everywhere were slick with mud and motor oil. Wickstaff made herself focus on the realities of war. "There's nothing we can do now but join the fight. The men know they need to retreat. The ships know they need to leave as soon as the enemy breaches our last lines." She turned to Maddy and Diane. "I will join my men at the front. This is your last chance to leave. Following me will get you killed."

Both women folded their arms and said nothing.

"Very well then."

The three women moved away from the waterfront and headed for the perimeter fence. The first shots from the Challenger 2's main cannons caused them to cover their ears.

"Wow!" Diane blinked as though she was seeing stars. "Do those things have a volume control?"

"I think they're stuck at eleven," said Wickstaff. She ran up a steel ramp onto a firing platform perpendicular to the mesh fence. Already, she could see the demons slaughtering their way to the docks, hacking down men and women fleeing for safety. A pair of shotguns lay stacked against the shelter's wall, and Diane and Maddy picked them up. For herself, Wickstaff pulled her Glock from its holster. "Know how to use those things, ladies?"

Maddy thumbed in a shell. "You don't survive an apocalypse without firing a shotgun or two."

The three women lined up at the rail. What they saw was not good: demons swarmed everywhere, filling the gaps between buildings and vehicles. Men and woman screamed. The Challenger 2's massive shells put craters in the enemy advance, and grenades exploded constantly as heavy gunners and their squads defended the perimeter fence.

The demons approached en mass. Wickstaff took one out with a well-aimed shot from her Glock. Maddy and Diane took out another with combined blasts from their shotguns. The recoil rocked Diane's small frame away from the rail, but she hurried back to take her next shot. Wickstaff gave the girl a nod.

The three women fired in time, picking off demons one after the other. Gunfire lit up the fence for a mile, soldiers mounted all along it.

This was their final stand. They had to hold the line long enough for the boats to fill up.

Something struck the fence. Wickstaff's hip struck the rail.

Before she knew what was happening, she fell. The ground rose up and hit her with an almighty smack and rattled her entire skeleton. She lay on her back, staring up at Maddy and Diane twelve feet above. They had fear in their eyes.

Wickstaff turned her head—glad she still could after such a fall—and saw the front end of a bright yellow Volkswagen Beetle sticking out of the fence. A decal of a swan decorated the rear bumper. One of the fence's concrete pillars had snapped, and a massive section was now sagging. Maddy and Diane fired their shotguns. Wickstaff rolled onto her side, wincing as her hip roared, and stared back towards Portsmouth. Lord Amon had another car clutched in his long fingers and hurled it through the air like he had the Volkswagen Beetle.

Another section of fence collapsed as the vehicle crashed into it. A pair of soldiers spilled from their perch and tumbled into a writhing mass of demons.

Wickstaff's time was also at an end. Monsters surrounded her —foul flesh stinking. When she craned her neck, she saw a wall of demons, enough to tear every scrap of skin from her bones while she lay paralysed on the ground.

Would she feel it?

Good luck humanity. Sorry I won't be there to see the final score.

Despite her best, she hadn't been the leader Portsmouth needed.

The demons closed in. Their shadows engulfed her.

"Send them back to Hell, boys!"

An American accent?

Gunfire erupted right above Wickstaff's head. She looked up again and saw the expressions on Diane and Maddy's faces turn from fear to urgency. They fired their shotguns again and again. A demon dropped on top of Wickstaff, teeth against her throat, and she didn't even realise it was dead until a strong hand tossed it off her.

"We need to fall back," said the American voice. "Firing retreat. Firing retreat. Someone help me get the general to safety."

Wickstaff felt herself lifted, and her saviour finally appeared in her view. The man was young and handsome, with a mildly arrogant smirk tickling the corners of his mouth. "Y-You?"

"Lieutenant Tosco at your service, Ma'am. I believe you know me as a pain in the arse?"

Wickstaff grinned. "Get me out of here, and I'll kiss your arse."

"It's a date. Glad I stuck around to lend a hand."

Wickstaff was dragged away in a fashion that had her womanly pride yelling, but she couldn't deny how much she wanted to kiss every man there. They were literally pulling her arse out of the fire.

But it was only a reprieve. The fence was falling, and Lord Amon was already picking up another car. An artillery shell struck the angel's chest, but didn't even break its stride.

Rick and Guy hadn't come through in time.

Time had run out.

30

VAMPS

Mass and Aymun were bogged down by demons, unable to dispatch them with as much haste as Vamps could. His flaming sword allowed him to cut through the enemy like butter, and he had successfully cut a path to the big bastard with a skull for a face. The scowling beast towered over all else, a full seven-feet tall.

Vamps was unimpressed.

He had a flaming sword.

"You wield something of which you are unworthy," Skullface mocked. "I shall take it from your corpse and use it to carve your friends.

"You can try pulling it out of your arse once I shove it there." Vamps dodged aside and avoided a swipe. "What you want with a couple kids, anyway? That your thing?"

"Children are meat, same as adults. You shall all rot and fester in time. Lay down your weapon, and I will make your death quick."

Vamps dodged again, but kept his sword lowered, not wanting to strike until it was right. "Very merciful for a demon," he said. "I think you're scared, bro."

"I fear nothing. Blood ran through my veins before humanity was even an idea. You are bacteria to me."

A demon appeared and slashed at Vamps. Its sharp talon tore open the flesh on his shoulder, making him cry out. Skullface took advantage of the situation, springing forward and attempting to grab Vamps by the throat. Vamps ducked, pivoted, and leapt aside, avoiding the large demon like a matador dodging a bull.

He swung his sword.

Skullface folded himself out of the way.

Not quick enough.

The flaming sword struck bone.

Skullface roared. His disembodied left arm tumbled into the grass.

Vamps chuckled. "Your 'armless, mate."

Skullface staggered, the stump of his left arm smoking. Vamps swung his sword again—the flaming weapon raging in his hand, seeking more demon flesh. Skullface grabbed the sword with his remaining hand. His exposed jaws clamped together in agony. But he did not let go.

The sword twisted in Vamps's hands and wrenched free. It twirled in the air and buried itself in the mud, pommel pointed towards the sky like Excalibur. Skullface kicked Vamps and floored him with a devastating blow that knocked the wind out of his unprotected lungs. "Your eagerness to kill will be your downfall, worm. Patience is a virtue beyond humans. Your lives are short. Every second is an eternity to you, but fleeting to me. Your sins have not been undone. Your life is unpure. Dear little Max was only your latest misery shed upon the world. Hell awaits you, worm. Glorious suffering."

Vamps tried to catch his breath, writhing in the mud and clutching himself. "H-how do you know about Max?"

"Sins decorate your soul. They will comfort you while you burn in hell."

Skullface moved over to the Ferris Wheel and ripped free a steel spoke as if the thing was made of matchsticks. Vamps tried to get to his feet, but his chest sucked inwards like a vacuum and dropped him back to the floor. He tried to call out to Mass and Aymun, but they were too far away—too surrounded.

"Send my regards to the Red Lord." Skullface raised the steel bar over his head and plunged it downward.

Vamps cried out.

The sharp steel stopped inches from Vamps' heart, hovering there, trembling.

Slowly, Vamps took his eyes away from the deadly spike above his chest and looked at Skullface. The demon lord was shaking. His oily eyes shimmered in confusion. Then, gradually, his chest began to open—ribs snapping and falling away. Something forced its way out of him. A silvery snake.

Then the silvery snake ignited in flame.

The flaming sword pierced Skullface's chest, shoved in from the back. The stunned demon dropped the steel bar and clutched the flaming sword point with his hand.

Richard appeared and yanked Vamps to his feet.

"You saved my son," he said. "I couldn't run away while you fought my battle. This was something I needed to finish myself."

Vamps heaved in a painful breath and thanked him. Skullface had dropped to his knees, the flaming sword still jutting from his chest. Then, all of a sudden, the air became super-heated and Skullface exploded.

Vamps and Richard covered their faces and turned away until the blast ended. All that remained of Skullface was a blackened scorch mark in the grass. The flaming sword once again stood up in the mud.

"What the hell just happened?" said Mass, running over to them. "All the demons just dropped dead."

Vamps looked around the fairground and saw it was true. Demon corpses lay scattered everywhere. There was nothing left alive except for the four of them. He looked at Richard. "Where did soldier-boy take the kids?"

"They're hanging back by our van on the hill."

Mass nodded. His meaty forearms sliced up badly, and a bite wound glistened on his neck. "You got wheels, man? Great, 'cus I could use a rest."

"Me too," said Aymun, sitting cross-legged on the ground with his head in his hands. "That fight *shagged* me, yes?"

Vamps chuckled. "Maybe leave the slang to the natives, Aymun. But, yeah, I agree; we should rest up a while."

"Thank you for what you've done," said Richard.

"It was *you* who just saved *my* life."

"Your life was only in danger because of your bravery. You're the real deal, aren't you?"

Vamps went and sat on the steps leading up to the Ferris Wheel. He rubbed at his forehead as he frowned. At some point, he had lost his green baseball cap. "What do you mean?"

Richard pointed to the flaming sword. "That weapon has a life of its own. When I picked it up off the ground, it almost seemed to speak to me. I felt sick the moment I held it, but it kept speaking to me. It told me what to do. It wanted you to live, Vamps. You're important."

"I've been called a lot of things, man, but never important."

"I'm just glad you were here when we needed you. Good to know our side still has heroes."

Mass joined the conversation, addressing Richard. "Your kids, they... they were possessed or something, right? We've seen it before. I'm sorry."

Vamps saw the sadness in the man's eyes—the angst of a father —and felt bad. "Yeah, man. Condolences."

It was clear, the man was fighting tears. "Do you... do you know if anyone ever comes back?"

"I think it's a one-way street," said Vamps. "If you need me to do what needs to be—"

"Richard! Richard!"

Vamps leapt up from the steel steps and went for his sword. When he yanked it out of the ground, he wondered briefly why he didn't hear the voices Richard spoke of. The sword never spoke to him.

Corporal Martin was sprinting down the hill towards them. His panic was obvious.

"What is it?" Richard shouted at the soldier. "What's happening?"

"It's Dillon and Alice. You need to come with me, right now."

Richard was running before Vamps could shout a warning to

him. The father was blind to any danger if it involved the kids. He needed to step back and let others handle it. Mass and Aymun tried to keep up with him, but they were both too beaten from battle. Vamps, too, was weak. His ribs cried out anytime he tried to take a full breath.

When he made it to the top of the hill, Vamps found Richard on his knees. He had both children hugged against his chest. "Thank you," he kept on saying. "Thank you, thank you, thank you."

The boy with Down syndrome was sobbing on his father's shoulder, different now from the dazed, black-eyed entity from earlier. His eyes were now blue and innocent. The girl was turned away from Vamps, but the sight of her arms wrapped tightly around Richard was enough to show she was just a frightened little girl again.

"They have returned to us," said Aymun, a huge smile on his face.

"Fuck yeah," said Mass. "You must have saved them when you killed *Skeletor*."

Vamps corrected his friend. "I didn't kill the demon. Richard did. He saved the kids, not me."

The flames on Vamp's sword went out. They were safe.

For now.

31

GUY GRANGER

"I've never seen one this close," said Skip, shivering against the rain. His long white beard was sodden.

Guy swallowed and wiped water from his face. It was difficult to see far in this downpour, but the massive gate lit up the dusky horizon like a beacon. "The one in New York was big, but not this big."

"They differ in size," said Rick. "But they're all connected through some kind of grid, with power being diverted where it's most needed. Now that we're close to a gate, I can tap into the whole grid."

Guy frowned. "With your mind?"

Rick shrugged, but it was a subtle gesture, seeing as how his shoulders were so narrow and weak. "Hey, I don't understand it either. I can just sense things. The grid is currently shoving power to two main points, diverting it away from other gates. One of the focal points is that gate over there, and the other is—"

"In Portsmouth," said Guy. He sighed afterwards and looked back the way they came. Was Wickstaff holding out? Or was everyone already dead?

"The gate in Portsmouth is open," said Rick. "I can feel it. It's big."

Everyone fell silent as they absorbed that information, and

what it meant. It meant Portsmouth was probably gone. It made their mission pointless. But they still had to try.

Guy had set up a scouting position on the roof of a large supermarket. They had scavenged supplies from inside and were taking a short rest before they made their assault. The gate, about a mile away, was what they had expected—large and surrounded by demons. At least ten times the number Guy had with him.

But Guy's group had guns. And they had Rick. Rick, who looked as though he might drop dead any moment.

Keith caught Guy's eye, and the two of them shared an unspoken agreement: their lives were less important than the mission, and if they had to carry Rick to that gate, they would.

It was almost time to go.

"It's getting dark," said Rick. "If we are going to do this, we should do it now. Guy, you're the military mind here. You need to own this."

Guy nodded. He was the only one capable of taking charge, whether he liked it or not. Relinquishing the Hatchet had not relinquished his responsibility it seemed.

"Okay," he said. "Final weapons check. I want us to get within fifty metres of the enemy before we engage. Once the enemy spots us, use your grenades, then form up into an advancing line. Step kneel fire, step kneel fire. Keep things slow, calm, and together. The enemy needs to be close to hurt us, so we keep our distance. There are more of them than us, but not more than we have bullets. If we keep our heads, we can cut the enemy apart like a surgeon removing a cancer. No emotions about this. It's just a job that needs doing."

The motivational speech seemed to do its job. The soldiers and marines nodded and checked their weapons. The tactic of emotional detachment was the right way to go. This would be the first time these men had sought to engage the enemy out in the open. Fear would be their greatest enemy.

They fought monsters.

Guy gave them ten minutes to prepare, but no longer. Too much time to think would be a bad thing as anxiety could kill a soldier before the first shot got fired.

The rain continued to fall.

Time to go.

"Move out men! Keep low and keep calm. The sun is behind us, which will cover our approach. But a cough or a sneeze will give us away. I want silence. Don't even scratch your balls."

The men formed a wide line, six feet between each of them.

They started marching.

Demons huddled around the distant gate like ants around a melting ice cream. How long before one of them spotted their advance? Too soon, and the men would be too far away to launch their grenades. That initial moment of surprise would be gone, along with Guy's best chance at inflicting mass casualties upon the enemy.

The formation exited the shadow of the large supermarket and crossed the car park. At the edge, they stepped onto a grassy embankment. Then another road. Then a basketball court followed by a stretch of wasteland. Their boots clomped and echoed. Guy winced and prayed it didn't announce them.

Not yet. Just a little longer.

The demons grew larger on the horizon. The massive gate propped up the darkening sky.

Just a little longer.

The march continued. Soldiers and marines held their rifles firmly, lifted the muzzles towards the enemy. Each man was eager to pull the trigger, to end the apprehensive state of pre-battle and begin the unthinking frenzy of battle. Their fear would evaporate once the first shot fired, and adrenaline would take its place. This tense moment, seconds before the fight began, was the worst. Every soldier wanted it to end—that rising urge to flee in the pit of their stomachs. A soldier always fought with himself before he fought with his enemy.

Guy lifted his own rifle, placed his finger over the trigger. *Almost there. Nearly. Just a few more seconds.*

More loud, marching footsteps. More ground made up on a still unaware enemy.

The formation exited the wasteland and entered a plush green field. The sound of the gates buzzing became detectable, growing louder with every step closer. The sound of benign demon chatter grew in their eardrums. Curses and cackling.

The line of men kept marching, their rifles pointing ever higher.

Grenades were unclipped from belts.

A demon screeched.

Then all of them did.

"Engage! Engage!" Guy pulled up his rifle and took a knee. He fired a three-round burst and then moved forward one step, kneeling and firing all over again.

Grenades sailed through the sky, coming down fifty-metres ahead, right amongst the enemy. Demons flung to the ground as insides tore apart. Bullets dropped even more to the ground.

"Let 'em have it, lads!" Keith yelled and fired a handgun. As a civilian, he was meant to stay back, but he behaved the most fervently of all, like a drunken cowboy. His wild yells were infectious and persuaded the other men to yell too as they took down their enemy. Their collective roar gave them all confidence. Solidarity.

The demons hadn't seen it coming.

Guy would win this battle. Rick would close that gate.

No more lying down for these monsters.

The gate flashed.

Something came through. Something huge.

The angel was thirty-feet tall and wrapped in a pure-white bearskin. It stumbled at first as if disorientated, but then it spotted the humans and bellowed and stamped.

"Andras," said Rick, touching his fingertips against his temples. "He is Andras—a knight of Hell. I hear his name echoing though the hallways of Hell."

Guy had stopped firing, just staring up at the colossal beast. "Is he friendly?"

"No!" Rick threw out both arms like a sorcerer and great jets of white flame shot forth from his fingertips. A dozen demons caught fire and fell to the floor roasting. Soldiers resumed their fire, reloading quickly, and pulling the trigger all the way. More demons fell.

But the giant standing amongst their corpses was the real threat now.

"Fire on the angel," Guy shouted. "Everything you have."

Keith stepped forward and took the first shot. His handgun bucked three times. The angel didn't react. Even when every soldier opened fire, Andras looked down at them with indifference. Indifference bordering only on annoyance.

"We can't hurt it," said Rick. "It's tethered to the gate like Lord Amon. We need to close it first."

Keith appeared and looked Rick in the eye. "Then we have to get you closer, brother." Then he raced off towards the angel. Rick reached out to stop him, but was too slow and too weak.

"W-What's got into him?" Rick asked.

"He's trying to atone," said Guy. "And live up to his rock-star brother."

Rick only frowned.

Guy led a charge surrounding the angel, firing at all angles and trying to at least disorientate it. It worked, because Andras kicked out in all direction, missing the small group of ex-Hatchet crewmen creeping towards the gate with Rick. A smattering of demons still survived, but Rick swatted them aside easily with magic. He made it to the gate. Guy felt his stomach tense.

"Look out!" Guy shouted a warning to a one of Wickstaff's soldier's but was too late. He was forced to watch as the man's spine snapped beneath a huge stamping foot. Andras then crushed three more men with a massive swing of his arm. It was like trying to fight a mountain with the speed of a lion.

Guy fired off a few rounds, but was forced to retreat. Andras ran toward him and almost trampled him. Instead, he missed Guy and caught Skip. The old man threw his arms in the air, but did not yell. His death was near silent—just the delicate crunch of bones turning to dust beneath Andras's giant foot. To add to the injury, the angel stood in place, reducing Skip's body to liquid. Guy clenched his jaw so tightly a tooth cracked. The old sea dog deserved better. A death at sea, not ground into the dirt.

"I'm going to kill you," Guy shouted at the angel, then sprinted away. He headed for the gate where Rick was currently reaching out with his right arm. He had his eyes closed in some kind of trance.

The gate began to flicker.

Its translucent lens turned black.

The gate was somehow fighting Rick, but it was losing—dying like a wart tied off at the stem.

Then Rick began to shake. Blood seeped from both ears onto his collar.

Guy turned back, saw Andras frozen in place, watching. Was the angel worried?

"You're doing it!" Keith shouted maniacally. "That's it brother, do it! Keep—*Shit!*"

Something flew out of the gate and struck Rick hard enough to launch him backwards.

Demons poured out of the gate.

Several soldiers fell to the sudden ambush, and only half could get their rifles up in time to defend.

Guy fired off a shot and downed a burnt man, then ran to Rick, lying unconscious on the ground. A bone stuck out of his stomach, spat out of the gate like an arrow. The gate had defended itself. Their chance of closing it was over.

Guy groaned.

Movement in the distance.

The sound of a vehicle coming to an abrupt stop.

Guy saw a small group of men alighting a large white van. They quickly headed in the gate's direction. Guy leapt up, grabbed a hold of Rick's wrist and started dragging him away. Andras was only metres away, but was distracted by the new arrivals.

The newcomers were human, and apparently coming to help, but who were they? And what could they hope to do?

One man was a soldier. He ran over to Guy and helped him pull Rick out of harm's way.

"Who are you?"

"Corporal Martin, a man without an army, but it looks like you have a small one here."

"Getting smaller by the minute. We need to get away."

While they dragged Rick away, the remaining soldiers fought to survive.

"Were you trying to close this gate?" the soldier asked. "How?"

Guy shook his head. "Our secret weapon is bleeding out in our arms."

"This man was planning to jump into the gate?"

"Something like that."

They reached the spot where the other newcomers waited. Besides two tough looking lads, there was a middle-aged police officer and a guy who looked like he'd stumbled right out of the desert.

One of the lads held a long silver sword, and he nodded to Guy. "Looks like you could use help."

"Only in getting away from here. How did you find us?"

The lad raised his sword, and to Guy's absolute shock, it caught fire. "I had a feeling we should head this way. Guess this thing does talk to me after all."

"Y-your sword speaks to you?"

"Long story," said Corporal Martin. "We need to deal with that angel."

"How? It can't be killed," said the police officer. "Doesn't someone have to give their life to close the gate? Even then..."

"I will do it," said Aymun. "I have done so before."

"No way," said the lad with the sword. "I'll do it. No one else dies on my watch. If anyone is gunna commit suicide by gate, it'll be me. I'll own this. It's on me."

The other kid shook his head hard. "Vamps, get it through your head that Max and Marcy weren't your fault. You did everything you could for them."

"What?" Guy looked up and saw Keith rushing towards them. "Did you say Max and Marcy?"

The kid with the sword nodded. "Yeah, a mother and her boy. We found them about a week ago."

Keith put his hand against his mouth. His eyes bulged.

"Can we do this later," said Guy, looking back towards the angel slaughtering its way towards them. The soldiers firing at it scattered as they each ran out of ammo. Some even ran for the hills. Guy didn't blame them.

"I need to know where they are!" Keith yelled. "Where are Max and Marcy?"

The lad with the sword swallowed, looked left and right like he wanted to be anywhere else. But then he focused on Keith and spoke in a soft tone.

"I'm sorry, man. They're gone."

"An angel killed them," said the other lad, bigger with muscles. "We were trying to keep them safe, but we failed. I'm sorry. We got the angel that did it though."

Guy stared. "You killed an angel?"

"Yeah. Took some doing, but yeah. My bro here has a magic sword."

"That is not a euphemism," said the man dressed for the desert.

"They're dead. They're dead." Keith kept saying the words over and over. After a while he turned and wandered off like he'd suddenly lost sight of the fact their lives were in danger.

Guy heard a scream and turned around just in time to see the body of a soldier flying towards him. It landed on top of him like a sack of potatoes. Corporal Martin rolled the corpse away and pulled a dazed Guy back to his feet. "Come on!"

"I got this," said the lad with the sword, rushing off towards the massive angel like a fearless barbarian.

The big lad went after him, shouting all the way. "Vamps, man. Wait up, I got your back."

"You should leave," said the desert man to Guy. "Your people are hurt."

Guy looked at the fallen soldiers, and the Hatchet's marines who had served with him since this whole thing began. "My people are dead. I gave up on my daughter to be here..."

Corporal Martin picked up a rifle from one of Guy's dead soldiers. "We have civilians in our van back there. Wait for us there. Keep them safe if things go bad."

Guy shook his head. "No. There's still something I can do here."

The middle-aged man, who had said nothing since arriving, stepped aside and let Guy past. From the look on the man's face, it was clear the fellow had been through some shit. Despite that, he nodded to Guy. Guy nodded back.

The gate shimmered and spat more demons to the earth, but they came less frequently now. How many were back there, queued up in Hell's hallways ready to leap through and destroy whatever stood in their path? Was there a finite number, or were the legions of Hell endless? Where did the demons go when you killed them? Did they go back and join the queue, an endless recycling of the damned?

Guy stared at the gate and made up his mind. He would never see Alice again, but if she still lived, maybe he could give her a chance by doing something. The demons might be endless, but if the angels were not, then maybe taking one out would make a difference. Wickstaff might still be counting on him. So he would leap through the gate and accept whatever came after. Strangely, his legs weren't shaking as he took his first steps towards it, and the closer he got to the gate, the surer he became about what he needed to do. No more fighting to survive, just one last meaningful act. He had become a Coast Guard to protect people.

Vamps and his friends danced around the angel, firing from rifles they found amongst the corpses. The angel was uninjured, but at least occupied.

"Granger! You traitorous pig."

The voice sounded familiar, and it caused Guy to turn around with a frown on his face. The man he saw rushing towards him was oddly recognisable but not immediately placeable. It was only when the man spoke again, that it all clicked into place.

"Lieutenant Hernandez? W-What are you—"

"That's Commander, to you, Granger."

"What are you doing here?"

"I came to right a wrong. I find you guilty of abandoning your country in its darkest hour and impeding a senior officer of the US Navy. The punishment for treason is death."

Guy did not understand. He had met this man in the middle of the Atlantic, on a ship, amongst a crew. What was he doing here in England, alone, and with a crazed look in his eyes? What answer would make any sense?

Hernandez lifted a revolver from his side and pulled the trigger.

Guy spun a full circle before his legs finally deserted him. He slumped onto his back in slow motion and was unable to get up again. Every time he tried to rise, he lost track of which way the sky was. Hernandez stood over him and raised the revolver again. The black eye of its muzzle resembled the eyes of the demon. "Any last words, Granger?"

Guy looked up at this strange, angry man he had met only once, and tried to understand what was happening, but all he could say was, "Sorry."

The word seemed to take Hernandez by surprise because the gun in his hand trembled for a moment. "An apology? What are you sorry for?"

"I'm sorry I didn't do more for the people I care about. I'm sorry that, even now, with everything that's happened, there's still someone who hates me enough to kill me. I'm sorry I didn't get to say goodbye to Alice."

"Who's Alice?"

"Alice is his daughter, now step away from him, sir."

Guy turned his head and saw the middle-aged man who had nodded to him earlier. "H-how do you…?"

"I suspected you might be Alice's father when I heard your accent. She's alive. In our van and very much alive."

Despite the numbness in his body, Guy gathered a smile to his lips. He stared at the horizon, at the large white van sitting there idly, and asked himself if it was really true. Was his little girl truly inside?

"Alice? Alice?"

The police officer nodded, tears in his eyes. "I promise you she's okay. My name is Richard, and I was at the Slough Echo when you called."

Guy smiled, his whole body relaxing as the fear for his daughter finally left him.

"Too bad you won't live to see her," said Hernandez, pointing the revolver at Guy's face. He pulled the trigger.

"No!" Richard leapt in front of Guy's body and reached out to Hernandez.

The gunshot echoed.

Guy felt no impact, but then his whole body was already numb. He saw Richard's body buck, like he'd been punched in the gut. Both he and Hernandez fell down in a heap as they struggled with one another, but Hernandez was the only one to scurry back to his feet again. Richard stayed down on the ground.

"Time to die," said Hernandez, his lip bleeding.

"For you maybe!" Corporal Martin fired a burst from his rifle and opened Hernandez's chest. There was no question that he was dead by the time he hit the ground beside Richard.

"Are you okay?" Corporal Martin asked Guy, but looked like he already knew the answer.

Guy's head dropped, too heavy to lift any longer. His strength faded rapidly, and he felt sleepy. "I... need... Alice..."

His eyes closed, and it was too hard to open them again.

32

VAMPS

Vamps hadn't felt afraid for a while. That emotion had calloused over when his first friends died—Ginger and Ravi —and had all but evaporated after Max and Marcy. Losing so many people had broken something in him. He was no longer afraid to die, because it felt like he deserved it. Every minute he stayed alive was borrowed time. The more demons he killed before he met his maker, the cleaner his soul would be. That's why he was so determined to take out as many as he could.

He had meant it when he'd said he would go through the gate, and give his life to close it, but he hoped it wouldn't come to that. He had killed an angel before, so maybe he could kill this one too. It was taller than any he had seen, and so far, Mass and Aymun's attempts to hurt it with gunfire had failed. Maybe his sword would be enough. It certainly worked on the demons.

Killing them was almost getting too easy.

Mass backed off from the fight, panting. "This shit is wearing me out, man."

"You're too big, man. Fewer reps and more running, yo. Look at Aymun."

Aymun was running circles around the angel, dodging all attempts to stamp him out. His dress flapped and whirled around him almost majestically.

"Take care of any demons, Mass. I'm going after the big guy."

"Be careful."

"You know me."

Mass frowned. "Better than anyone."

Vamps rushed the angel, taking advantage of the fact Aymun was still distracting it. There was no way to reach its neck, thirty-feet up, so he aimed for more accessible meat. He loosed a running swing, arcing his sword like a golf club, and struck the angel's left ankle. It rebounded so hard it flew right out of Vamps' hand. "Damn it!"

The angel roared, then spun around to face Vamps.

The sword had done nothing. Not even a scratch.

Vamps' leapt aside as a giant foot tried to stomp him to dust. He landed badly on his heel and ended up crawling to safety. Mass came to his aid and dragged him away. "It's no use. We can't hurt it."

Vamps nodded, and then saw someone stagger towards him. At first, he thought it was a demon, but then he saw it was the man who had been injured when they arrived. He had a sharp bone sticking out of his chest, but looked like he had already died weeks ago and had been rotting ever since.

"Hey, man, I thought you were a goner."

"You should maybe remove that," said Mass, pointing to the bone sticking out of his chest.

"My name is Rick, and I need you to get me in front of that gate. I think I can close it."

Vamps looked back at the angel. It was coming towards them. He didn't understand what the guy was planning to do, but nobody else was coming up with any ideas. So he grabbed Rick and dragged him towards the gate. They moved in a small group, Rick a dead weight between them. Aymun saw they were in danger, and tried to distract the angel again, but it was no use. They would have to move fast.

"Get to the gate," said Mass, letting go of Rick and stepping away.

Vamps groaned with the extra weight. "Mass! What are you doing, bro?"

Mass stood his ground in front of the angel, buying them some time. For a moment, Vamps didn't know what to do. His best friend was throwing himself in the way of a stampeding angel, but if he didn't get Rick to the gate now, the guy might not make it. "Fuck it," he said. "Come on, Rick. Pick up the pace."

Rick moaned in agony, but he did move faster. They were almost at the gate.

But someone else had made it there first.

Rick gasped and almost fell to his knees. Vamps had to fight to keep him standing. "Keith, what are you doing?"

The man in front of the gate didn't look at Rick. He looked at Vamps. "They're really gone? Both of them?"

Vamps realised he was talking about Max and Marcy. "I'm sorry. Max was a great kid, but I couldn't save him... or his mum. I-I'm so sorry."

Max's father had tears streaming down his cheeks, but he gave a little smile. "It's okay. I'm glad someone was looking out for them at the end. It should have been me, and that's not your fault. Thank you."

"Yeah, bro, no problem. We can talk about it later..."

Rick pushed away from Vamps, standing under his own strength. "Keith, get away from that gate."

He shook his head and took a step backwards even closer to the gate. It pulsed and shimmered two feet away from him. "I love you, brother. I was always jealous of you, but I'm proud now, and I hope that counts. See you in the next life."

With that, and before anyone could stop him, Keith stepped back casually into the gate.

"Get down!" Rick shouted.

Vamps threw himself away from the gate. Mass was on the ground too, about to get crushed by the angel that had him pinned. Vamps reached out towards him and yelled, but there was nothing he could do. "Mass!"

Rick dove on top of Vamps and then threw his arms up towards the angel about to kill Mass. A thick, twisting streak of light shot forth from his fingertips and struck the angel fully in the chest. The impact launched him high into the air.

Then the gate exploded and filled the air with deafening screams from another world.

33

VAMPS

Vamps spat dirt and tried to see past the dust in his eyes. The ground shook beneath his fingertips, but the energy was fading. All was silent, except the sound of rushing wind returning to fill the void left by the exploding gate. When he dared to take a glance, he saw only a sunken divot in the earth, twenty-metres wide. His feet lay only centimetres from the crater's edge. If he had been standing inside the blast radius, he felt sure he would be in pieces right now.

Rick sat in the grass nearby. He had his head in his hands and was muttering to himself. "Keith! Keith, you idiot. I could have closed it. You didn't have to do that."

Vamps crawled on his belly over to Rick and noticed the change right away: the sharp bone no longer jutted from his chest and he looked healthy. "Rick! You're better."

Rick examined himself and saw that his skin was no longer pallid or bleeding. He nodded slightly as if the change was of little interest to him. "I got caught in the blast," he said. "I absorbed some of its energy. God's life force powers the gates. They were formed from the seals He placed between realities to protect us. It must have healed me."

Vamps was too confused to respond—not just confused by the

man's words, but by the fact his brain had been shaken around in his skull like a marble.

They had done it.

Actually, Keith and Rick had done it. Had that dude really been Max's father? Vamps' failure to protect his family had led to him killing himself. More blood on Vamp's soul. "Keith killed himself because I let his family die."

"He was my brother, but no, he didn't blame you. He blamed himself. Trust me, he failed his family long before they ever met you. What he did was an attempt to make it up to them, to be the good man in the end."

"He succeeded," said Vamps.

Rick nodded. "Yes, he did."

"YOU MAGGOTS! I AM ANDRAS, MARQUIS OF HELL, THE DISCORDANT. BOW DOWN NOW, AND I WILL END YOUR WORTHLESS LIVES QUICKLY."

The angel stomped towards them, having recovered from the blast Rick had hit him with. Vamps stood up and clenched his fists. *"Eat shit motherfucker. Your gate is dust."*

Rick clambered to his feet beside him and shouted up at the great beast too. It was absurd, like two ants heckling a brown bear. "You will not win this war. There are others in Hell who oppose you. I see your fear. This close, I can see how unsure you are. You thought wiping out humanity would be easy, but you have discovered strength and defiance where you thought none existed."

The angel strode forward, crushing human corpses beneath his feet. The demons' bodies had all vanished. "I SHALL ENSNARE YOUR SOUL IN THE GREATEST OF HELLS. I SHALL PRESENT YOU TO THE RED LORD AS AN OFFERING. YOU HOLD THE POWER OF DANIEL, AND FOR THIS, THE FALLEN BROTHER WILL BE PUNISHED."

Vamps shook his head. *More talk of Daniel? Who the Hell is that guy?*

Rick threw up his hands, but this time nothing came out of his fingertips.

Andras cackled. "DANIEL'S POWERS MAY ONLY COME TO THE SURFACE AS YOUR HUMAN VESSEL BREAKS

DOWN. YOU ARE FULLY HEALED, AND SO YOUR POWERS ARE NULL. YOUR FLESH BETRAYS YOU, HUMAN."

Rick glanced at Vamps. "You might want to run now."

Andras stomped towards them, massive hands clenched.

Vamps tried to flee, but he was battered and bruised. His skeleton felt like mushy peas. "I can't run anymore, man. I'm done."

"Then it was nice knowing you. Wish I could have asked you about that flaming sword of yours."

"Let me know if you see it. Could use it right about now."

"I have it right here, bro!" Mass rushed up on the angel's left flank. He held Vamps' sword, but it wasn't aflame. Even so, he lifted the weapon over his head and hurled it forwards with all of his massive strength. It sliced the air like a javelin and pierced Andras, the Marquis of Hell, right in his perfectly chiselled chest.

Then the sword ignited.

Flames erupted from the silvery shaft and covered every patch of skin on Andras's body. Within seconds, he became a massive, thirty-foot fireball. As he flapped about, screaming like a thousand babies, his angelic body began to disintegrate like a burning paperback. Scraps of black flesh turned to ash and flew away in the wind. Piece by piece, Andras disappeared.

It was over.

The flaming sword fell to earth, once again standing upright with its pommel in the air.

Vamps really loved that sword.

"The rest is down to you, Wickstaff," said Rick, a grim smile on his face.

34

GENERAL WICKSTAFF

Wickstaff was walking, but she sported a limp. Each step drove a spike of agony into her hip, but she strode with determination alongside Maddy. She asked a question. "I wouldn't be mistaken in thinking the entire earth just shook, would I?"

Maddy shook her head. "That was one heck of an earthquake. You think Rick came through for us?"

"I say we find out. Still have your radio?" Maddy handed it over right away, and Wickstaff put through the call. "I want all birds up in the air. Target is Prime 1. Keep me posted."

"Roger that," came a haughty voice at the other end.

Now all there was to do was wait. Wickstaff watched the darkening sky, certain she had seen a bright flash moments before the last embers of daylight had disappeared. The rain was stopping, too, and she hoped it was a good omen. Inside, she felt something she thought she'd lost—hope.

Maddy had her arms folded, chewing her lip. Wickstaff reached out to her. "I'm sure Rick is fine."

Diane came over to join them. "The ships are filling up slowly, and our defences are falling. It's not good."

Wickstaff had known there would be victims of retreat. Someone had to hold the line while others fled. Was it time to order a full retreat and let people take their chances, or did she tell those remaining men to keep holding until the death? She got on the radio again. "Rear Guard, I need you to hold for five more minutes. Just give me that long."

There was no reply. Anyone left was too busy fighting to talk. Gunfire continued to echo, but it was quickly diminishing as the enemy broke through.

The radio screeched to life in her hand. "Air Squadron One, about to engage."

"Roger that."

The three women stood in a huddle, war going on all around them, and waited. First, they heard the whooshing noise—the sound of rockets leaving canisters. Then they heard the insane chatter of cyclical machine guns. Eight attack choppers were unleashing Hell.

Let's hope it makes a dent.

"Prime 1 is down. Repeat Prime 1 is roasting on an open fire."

Wickstaff felt her eyelids stretch wide, and she stared at Maddy as she spoke into the radio. "Can you repeat that one more time for me, please?"

"Happily. The big bastard is on the ground and bleeding. He's dead. Lord Amon is dead. I fired a hellfire into his smug face myself."

Wickstaff was beaming. "Roger that, and God bless you!"

Wickstaff ended the call. For a few moments, she just stood there in dumb silence. Maddy and Diane did the same. Eventually she lifted the radio and gave a new order. "Men and women of Portsmouth, on ship or on land, Prime 1 is eliminated. Pick up your weapons and fight. Find the nearest enemy, and kill it. Today is the day we earn our survival. Today is the day we prove humanity deserves custody of the earth. We will win this day, and through victory we shall renew our future. We have come together from many places, and speak several tongues, but fight now beneath a new banner. Fight for humanity."

Wickstaff gave more orders in quick succession, the last being to her naval artillery. "Flatten the city, chaps. I want nothing left beyond the docks."

And so, the night sky lit with fireworks and shooting stars, plummeting towards the city that had kept humanity safe for so long. Buildings toppled, petrol stations exploded, and on the docks of Portsmouth, men and women spilled back off the boats to reengage the enemy. Wickstaff stood amongst it all, firing a pistol with a dodgy hip, a smile on her face because, live or die, humanity was standing up for itself. And she was the woman in charge.

35

VAMPS

As the sun rose, bringing with it dawn, the dirty white van snaked through the ruins of an ancient city. Portsmouth was gone, a flaming crater blighting the land.

"This shit is bad," said Vamps, sitting up front with Mass and Corporal Martin, the driver. The others huddled in the back, a mixture of wounded and shell-shocked. Aymun was tending to them as best he could, but he was no doctor. Their victory at the gate had been costly, but it paled in comparison to what they saw now. A large, spiny tower deep in the city rose out of the ruins, but its top had been lopped off by the fighting. A thousand fires blazed, and the roads choked up with bricks and blood. Several times they had to stop to clear a path, and when they finally made it to the gates outside the docks, a pile of corpses met them.

Vamps felt sick and knew Mass felt the same because he covered his mouth. The two of them looked at each other and then embraced with tears in their eyes. Was it all over? Had anything survived?

"Hold on," said Corporal Martin at the wheel. "It's going to get bumpy."

And bumpy it got as the van's large tyres crushed human and demon viscera like they were off-roading through Hell. Vamp's sword lay across the dashboard, and it rattled and sparked now as if woken from sleep. Sickening crunches accompanied every second of their harrowing journey, and it seemed to go on forever. Then, just when it appeared the van might die on them and maroon them amongst the death, the vehicle lurched forward and found solid earth again. They picked up speed and headed for the docks. Here, the various buildings were still intact and nothing was burning.

Corporal Martin stopped the van outside the Port Authority building, which itself lay next to a large open space. He turned off the engine, and the three of them up front disembarked. The air felt hot—the heat of so many fires blazing behind them. The water beyond the docks laid still, a hundred hulking vessels unmoving. Where were all the people?

A middle-aged woman appeared, flanked by two younger ladies.

"Who are you?" said the older woman in a plummy accent that Vamps would've hated in a past life. Now, such things didn't matter.

Corporal Martin stepped forward. "Are you... Are you General Wickstaff?"

"I am."

"It's so good to put a face to the name. I'm Corporal Martin."

The woman beamed and rushed forward. She gave Corporal Martin a great big hug and then winced in pain. "Forgive me, I'm a tad sore. It's wonderful to meet you at last. You must have survived an awful lot getting here?"

"We have others with us," he said, ignoring the question that would take too long to answer.

One of the younger women, a brunette, lit up at the mention of that. "Is Rick with you?"

"Yes. Let me take you to him," said Corporal Martin, a smile on his face.

And so they moved to the back of the banged-up van. Mass grabbed the door latch and yanked it open. Rick was already on his feet, and when he saw the brunette, he leapt out and hugged her. "Told you I'd be back."

"Rick! You... you look..."

"Great, I know! It's just a reprieve, but it's good to feel good."

"I never thought I'd see you again."

"I'm glad you're okay," said the third lady, the youngest of the three, and blonde. Still a girl, really.

Rick smiled and gathered the blonde into a three-way hug with the brunette. Vamps chuckled—*a real lady's man.*

"You closed the gate," said Wickstaff to Rick. "Amazing."

Rick broke away from his group hug and shook his head. "No, it was my brother, Keith. These guys took down an angel though. May I introduce Vamps, Mass, and Aymun."

"Taking down the angel was all him," said Vamps, pointing to Mass who immediately blushed.

Wickstaff folded her arms and whistled. "I took one down, too, but it took eight attack helicopters to do it. Well done, you."

Mass tried to make eye contact, but ended up staring sheepishly at the floor. "Thank you, General. It was my pleasure."

Vamps nudged his embarrassed friend and laughed.

"We have casualties," said Corporal Martin, turning serious. "Do we have anyone left to see to them?"

"Yeah," said Vamps. "Where all the people at?"

"Back at the old naval base," came Wickstaff. "I came from there when I saw you folks entering the city. It's good you're still alive, Rick, because we have one more problem for you to deal with."

THIRTY MINUTES LATER, the survivors from the van were being triaged. A few soldiers had lived through the battle at the gate, but far too few. Vamps was glad to see the two children were still okay. Though, after being possessed, neither seemed to have any memory of it. What concerned them most was that both their fathers were wounded, shot by the same man. A man nobody could identify. He had just appeared out of nowhere and started shooting people. Richard had taken a bullet shielding Guy from a second blast. Corporal Martin had seen the whole thing and had been the one to put the stranger down.

Now both men laid out on the ground while a pair of medics saw to them. The brunette Vamps met outside the Port Authority building was a medic, too—apparently—and she lent a hand too. Alice and Dillon rested on their knees, holding their hands out to their respective fathers.

Richard was awake. A medic had attached an IV of morphine, which meant he was drowsy, but he gazed at his boy and repeated over and over that everything would be alright. The medic concluded the bullet had struck his collarbone and gone through his shoulder tissue. Barring infection, Richard should recover.

Guy, on the other hand, had taken a shot right to the stomach. The round was still buried somewhere in his intestines. Vamps overheard the medics appraising Wickstaff of his condition, and it hadn't sounded good. "Best I can do is wake him up," one medic had said. "I'm not a surgeon, and neither are Chris and Samantha. We can't dig the bullet out of him, and it's probably blocking something important, considering where it is. He's already lost too much blood, and I think he's getting septic."

Wickstaff sighed and looked over at the little girl bent over her daddy. "Wake him up. Let him see his daughter. I owe him that."

Vamps took Mass by the arm and moved him away from the scene. When Mass saw Vamps was about to break down in tears, he pulled him into a hug. It was something he never would have done back in the old days.

"It's okay, man. It's okay."

"It's not okay, man. I can't take any more death. It's the kids. When I look at those two kids, I think about how many millions are lost. How many of them died in terror, or starved to death waiting for mummy to wake up. I can't get it out of my head, Mass. It's like ants in my mind. What do I do?"

Mass rubbed his back. "You go on living. We keep fighting so that tomorrow's children live. Those two kids are the reason we stay strong. They're alive because of something we were a part of."

"I wish I hadn't failed Max."

"I wish we hadn't failed him, as well. But it's done. Let's do better tomorrow."

Guy was suddenly awake. Vamps heard him moan and cry

out, "Alice!" He blinked several times when his daughter leant over and smiled at him as if he struggled to believe what he was seeing. "A-Alice?"

"Yes, daddy. It's me."

"You found me?"

"I got tired of waiting for you to come." She kissed his forehead. "You promised me we'd see each other again, and that I would be okay. You were right. It's safe here."

Vamps wondered if she truly believed that.

Guy was smiling dozily. "You look just like your mother. Getting so... grown... up."

"Daddy. Daddy, please stay awake."

But Guy couldn't. He closed his eyes and didn't open them again. The only thing he left behind was the smile on his face.

Alice slumped over his dead body and wept. After a few moments, Dillon left his own father to cradle her in his arms. They were siblings now—brother and sister in a new world—like Mass and Vamps were now brothers in more than just street terms. Family wasn't about blood anymore—or maybe it was more about blood than ever.

The blood of battle.

The reason everyone gathered in the ruined naval base was because the biggest gate of all still towered into the sky there. Nothing was coming through, but that could change at any moment. A thousand soldiers encircled it, ready to rip apart anything that dared step foot on the parade square. Vamps dreaded, all over again, that they had only won a single battle, and that the war would rage on. That was why he held his sword at the ready—the gift given him by a strange Irish man in an abandoned Pizza Hut.

Life had gotten screwed up somewhere along the line.

"Can you close it?" Wickstaff asked Rick.

Rick shook his head. "My power is gone. It'll be awhile before I can close gates—maybe weeks."

"We don't have that time. The enemy scattered after we beat them, but we can't stop them from regrouping if we have to worry about this thing in our midst. Can you at least try?"

Rick raised both arms towards the massive gate, but ended up looking like a confused mime. He let his arms drop with a sigh. "I'm sorry. Daniel's powers took weeks to grow inside me. They withdrew when I got healed by the blast."

"There is one way to close it," said Aymun. "One we are all aware of. I shall pass into the gate as I did the one in Syria. I lived through Hell and returned. What lies beyond this gate does not scare me."

"I sensed something before I left," said Rick. "This gate is the largest of them all. It leads somewhere far worse than wherever the gate in Syria did. I wouldn't recommend anyone steps through."

"Yet, this thing must be done," said Aymun, "and I would be honoured if the burden was mine."

"I'll go with you," said Rick.

"No way," said Maddy.

Wickstaff agreed. "We need you here, Rick."

Rick spoke sternly, all his vitality returned. "For all we know, General, I could do more good on the other side of this gate, behind enemy lines. I'm dying anyway, so I can only help you for so long. If I still have my powers on the other side, maybe I can stop whatever caused all this in the first place."

"I agree," said Vamps. "But you'll need more help than just Aymun. You need a badass from the streets. Maybe a guy with a flaming sword."

Mass was already shaking his head. "I don't want to go inside that thing, man. That's crazy."

Vamps turned to his brother—the little boy he had grown up with, now a man. They had fought for survival their entire lives in some form or fashion. They never imagined escaping Brixton, but things had changed.

They had changed.

Vamps most of all.

"Not us, just me, brother. I'm going. The things I've seen and done… I have to leave it all behind me. I need to do some *real* good to make it right. No more kids dying, right?" Mass nodded sadly. "You got things here, Mass, so let me take care of business on the other side. The hero today was you. You killed the angel when it was about to stomp me. It's not me who got us this far, Mass, it was you. Stay here, and be a hero for these people. But I'm not a hero, I'm a killer. The best place for someone like me is amongst the enemy—somewhere I don't have to worry about losing people I'm trying to protect."

"Vamps, please don't…"

"This feels like what I'm supposed to do, man."

"Are you gents really serious about this?" Wickstaff asked, looking at Vamps, Aymun, and Rick.

All three men nodded.

"Then say your goodbyes. It needs doing sooner rather than later."

"I'm ready now," said Vamps, swinging his sword like he had been practising his whole life.

Rick looked at Maddy and swallowed, tears in both their eyes. "If I wait," he said. "I'll lose my nerve. I'm ready now."

"I too am ready," said Aymun. "Hell awaits me for my sins. May I atone for each and every one."

Vamps moved away from Mass, not sure if he was strong enough to stay the course if his friend tried to talk him out of it. The two of them nodded at each other and said their last goodbyes silently.

Rick took longer, holding Maddy and Diane in his arms and exchanging words for what seemed like an eternity.

Aymun stood beside the gate peacefully, hands clasped at his front, waiting to leave.

Ten minutes passed, and they were finally ready. They discussed taking weapons, but decided that restocking ammunition in Hell might be troublesome.

Vamps tried not to think as he looked at the flickering lens of the gate. *Hell! Shit, am I really about to leap, willingly, into Hell?*

Hell yes! Can't be any scarier than Brixton.

Wickstaff stood in front of them as they lined up in front of the gate. "You will have to pass through at the exact same moment because the gate will explode as soon as someone passes inside. We will take cover, if you don't mind?"

"Of course not," said Rick. "Good luck to you, General."

"And you, gentlemen. If humanity survives, your sacrifice will be the foundation upon which our future is written. You are martyrs and heroes both, and I will ensure you are never forgotten."

"Make sure they mention how handsome I am," said Vamps. He flashed his gold fangs. "And don't leave out the teeth."

Wickstaff nodded.

Then everyone in the parade square departed to take cover. With such a large gate, they headed out a long, long way. The three martyrs were left standing utterly alone in front of the gate.

"You ready for this?" asked Rick.

"I'm shit scared," said Vamps, realising he had regained the ability to fear. He looked up at the shimmering gate and imagined the horrors waiting to meet him. "I'm ready though."

"I have done this before," said Aymun. "Is okay. We hold hands now."

Rick and Vamps looked at each other and exchanged frowns. Vamps shrugged. A little human contact wouldn't go amiss.

"Why not, I suppose. Might keep us together as we pass through."

"Okay," said Rick, shuffling up in front of the gate while the others joined him. "After three, okay? One... two... three!"

The three men linked hands, took a breath, and stepped forward.

36

MASS

"Let 'em have it, lads!" Mass threw a grenade far enough to impress an Olympic shot putter, and it landed right amongst a horde of demons besieging a small zoo where some survivors had taken refuge. One of Wickstaff's helicopter scouts had spotted their SOS sign from the air two days ago. The survivors had used red paint atop the glass roof of the zoo's atrium. Now Mass was here to rescue them—just in time by the looks of things.

He lifted his radio and asked for a favour. "Tosco, I need the ground to shake. Can you help a brother out?"

Tosco chuckled on the other end of the line. "For you, anything. Hold onto something, Mass."

Mass ordered his lads down, and they took cover. Moments later, Commander Tosco rained fire from his fleet ten miles away on the coast. Two-hundred demons turned to ash in an instant. They still hadn't learned not to huddle together, and since all the angels in the UK had gone, they had only gotten stupider.

Once Tosco had tilted the odds in their favour, Mass led the final assault. His soldiers had no military experience, but they were all survivors. Taken from the civilians of Portsmouth, Mass selected most of the remaining youth. Now, kids who had been thugs, criminals, students, slackers, or anything else in their past lives, were fearsome warriors, respected and relied upon.

They had survived Hell. What else was left to fear?

Mass pulled a machete from a sheath and held it in his left hand while he fired a black-market Uzi with his right. His body armour split at the seams as it tried clinging to his massive body, but it was only there as a last resort. With his blade and machine pistol, nothing was getting near him. He was a war machine.

His lads charged alongside him, each of them with a machete and pistol of their own. They liked to get in close, shoulder to shoulder, where they could cleave the enemy apart like a line of Roman legionaries. It had been remarkably effective against the demons, which knew no tactic but to throw themselves at their prey. Some were smart enough to grab weapons, but as ammo became scarcer, it was a rare problem. Weeks now, since a full-sized horde had posed a threat. Wickstaff's forces were picking the enemy off in groups; killing stragglers just like the demons had once done to them. The victory at Portsmouth had changed everything.

Mankind was the hunter again.

The last remnants of the demon horde staggered in a frenzy, but they did not surrender. It seemed like something they were incapable of. Not that Mass would show mercy if they did throw their arms up. He jabbed his machete in front of him and disembowelled a primate.

Within minutes, the battle was over and two-hundred demons lay dead. Of his thirty-six men, Mass had lost not a single one.

Shit was getting too easy.

"Target secured," Mass said into his radio. "No casualties."

"Roger that," came Maddy on the other end. "Good work, Mass. I'll let Wickstaff know."

Mass sheathed his machete and holstered his Uzi. He placed his hands up as he approached the fence around the zoo. It wouldn't be the first time survivors had shot at him out of fear.

A woman in her late thirties stood on the other side of the wire mesh. Her eyes were wide with fear, but the corners of her mouth lifted hopefully. "Are… are you friendly?"

"Of course we are. We're all in this together. How you people doing?"

The woman huffed. "Starving. Sick. You know, not bad."

Mass tutted. "That sucks. How 'bout you come with us. We have food and medicine, and about thirty thousand people all armed and ready to kick demon arse."

The woman frowned. "Come on!"

Mass reached into his pocket, making the woman flinch, but when he pulled out a roll of paper, she relaxed again. He pushed it through the fence, and the woman took it and unrolled it. Her eyes went wide.

The package Mass had given her was the same handwritten note from Wickstaff he gave all the survivors he found. It read:

DEAR FRIEND,

RIGHT NOW, *you may be in the presence of men and women you do not know. That must be frightening. Your suffering these last months has been endless and awful, but I promise you, it is ending. Humanity is fighting back, and it is winning. We have slaughtered the angels and closed dozens of gates. Great sacrifices are required in the days ahead, but the choices you make are now your own. I beg you to join us at Portsmouth, the new cradle of civilisation. There, we are rebuilding. We need teachers and carers for our children, soldiers for our cause, and experts in all fields. If you would like to help humanity thrive once again, please trust whoever gave you this note and come join us. If not, I have enclosed directions and a map to our nearest outposts. Once again, I promise you your suffering is at an end. The enemy is on the run. We have beaten our extinction and tomorrow is arriving.*

YOUR FAITHFUL SERVANT,

244 IAIN ROB WRIGHT

GENERAL AMANDA WICKSTAFF.

THE WOMAN inside the zoo shook her head as if she couldn't believe it. She looked at Mass, and then at the army of lads standing in a line behind him. "This is real? Portsmouth is real?"

Mass nodded.

"Okay, so... who are you?"

"We," said Mass, waving a hand at his lads, "is the Urban Vampires."

The lads grinned, exposing the gold fangs that each of them had. Mass smiled too, his own gold teeth glinting in the afternoon sunlight.

37

GENERAL WICKSTAFF

Wickstaff was stressed, as she had been every second for the last three months. Still she waited for that beautiful moment of silence when she could take an undisturbed breath.

Maddy approached with a satellite phone. "Chancellor Capri on the line for you, Ma'am."

"Oh, how splendid!" The German leader was not Wickstaff's favourite person, but he was too important to ignore. She did her best to work with the various groups they'd made contact with, but she feared the old power mongering of the past would return.

Putting on her happy face, she took the phone from Maddy and spoke into it.

"Chancellor Capri, how good to hear from you. Things fare well on the Continent still?"

"We have things much in hand. I hear you are faring well also, *ja*?"

"We've got the buggers on the run. What can I help you with, Chancellor?"

"I've been getting some concerning reports."

"Such as?"

"General Wickstaff, are you in possession of nuclear warheads?"

Wickstaff looked at Maddy. To those in her council, it was no secret Portsmouth possessed eight nuclear warheads housed on their German sub. It wasn't something she shared with anyone else though, but it was hardly surprising that the German submariners had relayed the information to their homeland.

"Where would you get that idea, Chancellor?"

"We have brought our Intelligence systems back on line. The tracking unit for one of our nuclear submarines is firing off the coast of Portsmouth. I have tried many times to raise the submarine's crew via radio, but they refuse all calls. Did you dispose of them and take possession of the vessel yourself? If so, that sub is the property of the Sovereign nation of Germany, and it must be returned."

Maddy tutted. Wickstaff waved at her to keep quiet. "Chancellor, I assure you the crew on that submarine are the original German men and women it belonged to. That they haven't answered your calls is the decision of Commander Klein. I was unaware you'd tried to get in touch." She let a grin escape. Sounded like the German submariners were happy right where they were. Their loyalty would not go unrewarded.

"Nonetheless, General. That sub must be returned."

"I'm afraid not, Chancellor. You see, the idea of possession, or even sovereignty, is a concept of no import to me. That submarine is part of my naval fleet—the biggest fleet in the world, I would wager—and it will remain so. The crew are not German, they are men and women of Portsmouth, and they will remain where they wish. You will not make demands of them or me, and we shall make none of you. I think that would be best, don't you?"

"Be careful, General."

"Be careful of what, Chancellor? Are you threatening war? Are you seriously making threats against your fellow human beings after what we have all been through? Do you think that is what your people need right now? Be a leader, Chancellor, and fight for peace, not war. And keep your bloody eyes off my toys because you're not having any of them."

"General—"

She ended the call and almost threw down the phone. "Bloody imbecile. Can you believe him? Nothing's changed."

"It's just a submarine," said Maddy. "What does he even want it for?"

"It's not the sub, it's the warheads. We might have the only armed nuclear weapons in the world, and that makes us undeniably powerful—something the Chancellor does not like in the slightest."

Maddy folded her arms and seemed to shiver. "You would never use them, would you?"

"Seeing as how Commander Klein and I have already discussed dropping them into the ocean, you may rest assured that they are not in any of my future plans."

Maddy lifted her dark eyebrows. "You want to chuck them in the sea?"

"With men like Chancellor Capri, I feel it best they were lost altogether. He won't make a fuss about something we don't have. Commander Klein agrees with me, and after he hears what his Sovereign leader has been demanding, I imagine he will make his way to the middle of the Atlantic very soon."

"Do you really think the Chancellor would start trouble with us?"

Wickstaff sat down at her desk and rubbed her forehead. "No, not yet. His land forces in Central Europe are larger than ours, but they also have war against the demons on a dozen fronts. The German Federation will be occupied for years to come. But while men might gain power slowly, they can abuse it in a second. I worry about our future, Maddy. Will it be any different from our past? If so, then I ask, what are we even fighting for? Humanity is a bird with a broken wing, and there's no point healing if we end up flying sideways."

"It won't be the same," said Maddy. "We won't let it. We fight for each other here at Portsmouth, and we will build a world people deserve. Chancellor Capri can suck our dicks."

Wickstaff smirked and got up from her chair. "He most certainly can. I'm going for a coffee. You want one?"

"I wouldn't say no."

They exited the Command tent set up at the docks and headed for the coffee shop. While the city itself was in ruins, the docks had become a small settlement, full of canvas roofs and lean-tos housing families and loners alike. This was the seed from which a nation would once again grow.

People milled about everywhere, shoving past one another, but always nodding politely. They didn't curse or anger one another, not anymore. They were forever bonded. Family. One man, however, marched stiffly towards Wickstaff without stopping to apologise to the people he shoved. People hopped out of his way, confused by what would make him push so rudely.

Wickstaff stopped her walk and reached out to grab Maddy's arm.

The man wore a grimy hoody, and he pulled back the hood to reveal his face. The snarling jaws of a demon opened. A handgun emerged from the hoodie's pocket and pointed at Wickstaff. An assassin.

The creature hissed with delight as it sighted a clear shot at Wickstaff. She could do nothing but throw her arms up vainly. Maddy cried out and tried to leap in front of her. But she was too slow. Too many steps required.

An almighty gunshot echoed off the parade square.

The demon slumped to the ground. Its mushed head splatted its grimy hoodie.

Diane stood over the corpse with a smoking shotgun. "Fucking bastard! That's the third one the guards have missed this week." She looked up at Wickstaff. "I'm so sorry, Ma'am. They just keep coming. Dozens each day. They want you dead. I almost let them get you this time."

Wickstaff waved her hand. "Better late than never, Diane. We're going for a coffee. Fancy coming?"

Diane nodded. "Best stay close to you until we get a handle on all these assassins."

"Don't worry so much, Diane. It takes a lot to keep a good woman down, and with you two watching my back, the demons have no hope. Now, let's go get that coffee before the next crisis begins. I swear, a woman's work is never done."

38

LUCAS

"Hello, Danny Boy."

Daniel slumped in the corner of his cell, maggots festering in his flesh. His golden hair was filthy, and the stumps of his wings were sore. It hurt Lucas to see. It had been his actions that led Daniel here. When the Fallen Angel looked out through his bars and saw Lucas, he began to weep. "Lucifer? Are you here to torment me?"

"Behave, lad! You been locked away a long time, brother, and for that, I'll be eternally sorry. But much has changed. Name's Lucas now, if you don't mind. Gave my former mantel to some no mark from the Pits. This whole war on God thing is partly my fault. The new Lucifer turned out to be a bit of a wet fish, as it turns out. He let that bloody eejit, the Red Lord, get his hooks into the place."

Daniel nodded. "I heard you'd changed. Wasn't sure I believed it."

Lucas waved his hands, and the iron bars melted away into nothingness. Then he blinked, and the maggots disappeared from Daniel's flesh.

"Come here, brother. It has been too long."

Daniel rubbed at his now-healed flesh, then crept apprehensively towards Lucas. As soon as he was near, Lucas reached out and pulled him into a hug.

Daniel sobbed loudly.

Lucas held him tight, trying to absorb his suffering. "I am sorry, brother, for leading you to your downfall. All of your sins, I own fully, and one day, I am sure Father will let you back into paradise. But that can only happen if he remains in power."

"I tried to help," said Daniel thickly. "The humans."

"Aye, you did at that. Your actions made all the difference, lad. You did good."

"Good?"

Lucas chuckled. "Takes a while to sink in at first, doesn't it? Yes, you did good, and can continue to do so. For a long time, I owned what I was, acted the Devil I was named, but one day I came to a remarkably simple revelation. I realised that what we were yesterday is set in stone, but what we are tomorrow is up to us. We were angels once, Daniel, and we can be again."

Daniel glanced over his shoulder at the burnt stumps where his wings had been.

Lucas touched his face and got his full attention again. "Wings do not make an angel, Daniel. It's more than that, and you know it."

Daniel nodded. "I want to help."

"Then come with me. We have a king to usurp."

"You want to regain control of Hell?"

"It's the last thing I bloody want, but I need to take charge until I can figure something out. I need to get the place sealed up again. Hell's leaking like an old dear's bladder."

Daniel stopped walking and squinted at Lucas as if something suddenly occurred to him. "You kept me locked up for millennia, Lucifer. Why keep me prisoner if you turned back towards the light?"

Lucas sighed. "Because once you start opening cages in Hell, you never know what will get out. It was best your cage remained closed, but now that the patients are running the asylum, it doesn't matter. You are free. I can never give you back what I took, brother, but I hope to have eternity to make it up to you. Please, Daniel, forgive me."

Daniel flinched, as if the very notion was absurd. It was. Lucas had locked Daniel up for thousands of years.

Slowly, the Fallen angel nodded. "God would have me forgive you, Lucifer, so forgive you I will. I love you brother."

"And I you. Seriously though, it's Lucas now."

Footsteps.

A newcomer's voice. "What the...? Hey, man. I know you!"

Lucas turned to see the most unexpected thing. The young thug on which he'd bestowed Daniel's sword now stood in Hell's hallways, bumping into him as if they were old friends at a bar. "Jamal?"

"Vamps, man. Enough with the Jamal bullshit." He waved his flaming sword. "Thanks for this, by the way."

Daniel's eyes went wide. "Hey! Is that my sword?"

Lucas blushed. "Yeah, erm, about that... I kind of gave it to this fella."

Daniel glared at Lucas, and then at Vamps. Vamps pulled the sword closer to him like a child protecting his favourite toy. Then Daniel's eyes moved to one of Vamp's companions, of which there were two. "R-Rick, is that you?"

Rick beamed and went over to Daniel, giving him a hug even harder than the one Lucas had given him.

"Daniel, you're okay! What you gave to me... your gift..."

"Is gone," said Daniel. "If you are here in Hell, my power has left you."

"I know. As soon as I arrived, I could tell I was my old normal self again. It's made surviving in this place a little tougher, but luckily I had help."

"I have been here before," said Aymun. "The place has not gotten any nicer."

"We're going to change that," said Lucas. "Hey, who you got back there with you?"

Vamps yanked a chain he was holding. On his hands and knees, a naked, dirty man scurried towards them. "Prime Minister

Windsor," Vamps explained. "If you can believe it. He told us a
group of soldiers caught up to him and tossed him through a gate.
Lucky, we found him first."

"He's been helping the enemy," said Lucas.

"We know," said Rick. "We figure he'll learn his lesson eventually, but for now he gets to play doggie."

Windsor was broken but unharmed. Lucas could tell no one
had beaten the man. A little humiliation, however, was the least
the arrogant fool deserved.

"What are you doing here?" Lucas asked the three men.

"We came to end this," said Rick. "But we've been lost in Hell
for what feels like forever. This place is empty."

"Haven't eaten or drank anything in weeks," said
Vamps. "But…"

Lucas nodded. "You don't need those things here. The damned
are all back in their cages for now, and Hell is vast, which is why
you haven't seen anyone. As for being lost, it's because you are still
living. Only the damned may navigate the hallways. Luckily,
you're talking to the damnedest of them all."

Rick nodded. "You can lead us to the Red Lord?"

"Aye! It just so happens to be the very place I'm heading. You
fellas want to tag along?"

They all did.

So, Lucas strolled through Hell with a force far larger than he
expected, yet smaller than he needed. He re-joined Damien, who
waited sullenly for his return and gathered the dozen or so Fallen
Angels wishing to fight for mankind's future. Lucas knew each of
them ultimately hoped for God's forgiveness, but it was not something he could promise them. It was frightening to admit he
hoped the same thing for himself.

They gathered outside a giant set of gates, forged from the
thickest iron. They were so tall that one could barely see the top
while standing at the bottom. Lucas knew the gates well.

"I can't touch the iron," said Lucas. "Not since I gave up the
throne."

Damien stepped forward and placed his hands against the

doors. They began to open of their own volition. The throne room lay inside. Lucas led the way.

"Can't say I like what you've done with the place, Red," he said, walking down the centre aisle. Human skulls covering the walls and ceiling were part of the new refurb, but what worried Lucas more were the Creator's Crystals. In the centre of the throne room stood the Grand Repository. Inside were the ancient crystals. Each one represented a world. Each one allowed the reigning King of Hell to watch the lives of every man and woman on every world. Lucifer had spent millennia witnessing the acts of mankind, and it had been scenes of love, sacrifice, and devotion that had eventually led him to give up the throne and leave. A vast majority of the crystals were cloudy or black. The worlds were fading away, dying as the Red Lord laid siege to each one in turn. Only a handful still shone with their rightful vitality. One, he saw, was brightening by the second. A world the three humans by his side had recently departed. That world was healing. But the rest...

"Hey," said Vamps, moving up to take a look at the crystals. "I can see zombies in this glass ball. And this one... this one has a bunch of animals killing people. What the Hell?"

"These are all of God's creations," explained Lucas. "He had to make numerous worlds to contain his vast life force. As each one falls, the protection around Paradise weakens. Soon, Heaven will fall vulnerable to attack, and God's enemies will seek to depose him. That's what the Red Lord wants—to blacken all these crystals and take over Paradise. The human worlds are just a means to an end."

The throne room echoed with slow applause. Lucas looked towards the back of the room where a giant chair made of flame flickered.

The Infernal Throne.

Damn thing still had his butt imprint in it, he was certain. Strolling down the stairs in front of the throne, a dark-featured child gazed upon them.

He continued to clap slowly.

"A guided tour of Hell, how nice for you Lucifer Primus—to see you fall so low."

"Nothing wrong with menial labour," said Lucas. "Builds character. Good to meet you finally, son."

Rick frowned. "This kid is your son?"

Lucas blushed. "Yeah, it was a drunken night with his mum. Just the once, mind you. I should have worn protection. Turns out, I accidentally spawned the Anti-Christ. It wasn't my finest hour."

"My birth was pre-ordained before existence itself," said the boy. "On Earth, I was named Sam, but here, I am the prince of Hell, Wormwood."

"Didn't I already kill this kid once?" Damien muttered at the back.

"You're a brat," said Lucas. "You couldn't even destroy the one world you were on, let alone a thousand of them. What the Red Lord wants with you, I don't know."

"He wants me to gain my birth right, Father. Your death will complete the prophecies and endow me with the power of God's greatest adversary. I shall take your place at the vanguard of a new war on Heaven. I shall drag God's corpse before the Red—"

"Look," said Lucas. "Me and the man upstairs had a bit of a disagreement, but I wouldn't call us adversaries."

Sam snarled. "No matter. I shall end you, Father. And I shall become you. The new King of Hell."

Wormwood ran at them then—his childish grin melting into a monstrous, toothy leer. His arms lengthened into sinewy claws, and he grew twelve feet, towering above them.

Damien leapt in front of the beast, but was swatted aside like a bug.

The three humans scattered. The Fallen Angels raised their hands to use their powers.

Lucas exploded. In the blink of an eye, he grew thirty feet, and from his back leapt fiery wings. His eyes glowed like embers. He threw out a hand and engulfed Wormwood in a hot, white glow.

The beast screamed, twisted and lurched.

The white light grew brighter, filling the cavern and blinding all within. Then it began to shrink, the glow compressing like an imploding star. Within seconds, the glow was nothing but a tiny ball at Lucas's giant feet. Wormwood was nowhere to be seen.

A kitten meowed.

Vamps staggered. "Shit, yo! He turned that bitch into a pussy-cat. That's gangster!"

Lucas shrunk back to his normal height and tried to hide how knackered he was by brushing himself off briskly. Wormwood purred at his feet. He picked the animal up and petted it.

"I always say you should try keeping a pet before having a sprog. And cats pretty much look after themselves."

"The Lord still works through you," said Aymun. "You have his light."

Lucas put down the cat and looked away from his companions. "Any power I have is undeserved, but I hope to relinquish it one day and be forgiven."

"Is he… Will he stay like that?" asked Rick, nodding at the fluffy white kitten.

Lucas shrugged. His shoulders ached. "Unless someone changes him back. He may be a little sod, but he's still my son. Killing my offspring probably isn't the best way back into Heaven's good graces. He'll have to be someone else's problem if he ever comes back."

Damien rose from the ground, apparently unhurt by Wormwood steamrolling him. One of his ribs was sticking out, but he shoved it back into place with his palm. Then he went and stood at Lucas's side.

"The throne is empty," said Daniel. "Can you just take it back, Lucas?"

Lucas shook his head. "It's not empty."

As if proving the jig was up, the flames of the Infernal Throne began to rage, leaping higher and higher. Flesh and bone began to materialise in the fire—a figure taking shape. Lucas breathed heavy. He feared he would not be strong enough for the battle ahead. His brothers were with him, but their foe was almost as strong as God himself.

A being even more ancient.

"Get ready," said Lucas. "The Red Lord is about to grace us with his presence."

The Infernal Throne hissed and spat. Heat filled the chamber, and a million screams erupted from the flames. Something massive emerged and started down the steps towards them.

Something wicked.

"Holy shit!" said Vamps. "I'm gunna need a bigger sword."

39

TONY CROSS

Tony Cross was now a captain, which wasn't bad going for a former Staff Sergeant. Being an officer wasn't like the old days though. All the plummy, silver-spoon idiots were dead, and the only Sandhurst-trained officers alive were the ones with half a brain. Most officers today had been promoted in the field, and seven out of ten had been NCOs in an earlier life.

After the war in Turkey—won when a cancerous old Sergeant-Major jumped through the gate in Istanbul, allowing humanity's forces to take down two angels with bunker busters launched from the back of a lorry—forces in the area refocused on liberating the Middle-East. Tony had re-joined British Forces in Iraq, and he once again served side by side with his countrymen. Not that they worked in isolation though. Men and women from every nation fought together now, and for the first time in history, the Persian Gulf was unified. Arguments of religion and sovereignty had all been forgotten. All that mattered now was sending the demons back to Hell.

And they had been doing just that. The German Federation held Europe's centre with a vast Army made up of many nations. Britain had been liberated by a brave general with limited resources, and the United States seemed to be rallying slowly. The battle had turned. Tony witnessed it for himself—right here. The Middle East was fighting for peace—and winning.

But at what cost? Here in Iraq, the signs of war predated the demon's arrival, and there was now barely anything left. People lived in tents and caves because no buildings remained. The population was skinny and starving, unable to get supplies from either trade or carriage. The desert did not nurture.

The painful lack of children was the worst. It had been days since Tony heard their laughter. Were any children left? What of tomorrow? Who could continue mankind's future? Would people breed again? Or were the survivors of this devastating war too damaged to contemplate such a joyful act?

The last thing on Tony's mind was sex. For months, he'd done nothing but kill, so to enjoy a moment of tenderness… It sounded impossible.

Even now, blood stained his hands, and he had no idea if it was even his. He had lived so long in this dirt that his hands and feet calloused. He bled from them often. His feet were totally numb as he walked amongst the debris of some town whose name was probably lost forever. He did, however, feel it when his boot struck something in the dirt.

He reached down and found a Quran, its pages ripped and dirty. Delicately, he wiped the book, but could see nowhere suitable to place the Holy Scripture. He couldn't bring himself to toss it back in the dirt, so he wandered through the ruins until he found something that wasn't rubble.

It turned out to be something most unexpected.

The child's bicycle sat propped against the remnants of a wall. The building had disappeared, yet the bicycle had survived. Its pink basket was decorated with ribbons. What had become of the child it belonged to?

A question he didn't want answered.

Tony moved beside the bicycle and rang its little bell, smiling at the joyful sound it made. He gave the Quran another wipe and then placed it carefully inside the pink basket. The time for religion had ended, perhaps, but respect for the past was still important. If they had any chance of making it, they needed to do things differently. They had to do it together.

No nations, no religion. No more war.

No hate.

It was several days before he found what he was looking for. In the next village, his squad came upon a small community that had miraculously remained untouched by fighting. Only a few-hundred people occupied the village, but Tony found them all gathered together in a green garden outside the schoolhouse. There, an Imam gave lessons to a group of children—maybe a dozen in total. The adults listened too.

When he had one of his men translate what the Imam was teaching the enraptured children, he smiled.

Maybe this time would be different after all.

<<<<>>>>

40

DAMIEN BANKS 2

So apparently he was some sort of *Totem*. That was what the Irishman had told him several days ago, appearing from nowhere and disappearing just as fast. But the message he gave Damien had stuck in his mind.

You're a Totem, *lad.*

Demons walked the earth now, so tall-tales were suddenly far more believable. Damien was a totem, which made him special. His soul was a tether, split throughout a thousand worlds. Harry and Steph too, apparently, although Lucas had only shared the information with him. Obviously, at first, Damien had scoffed at the silly story. He was a mid-level bank employee, not a supernatural being.

But then Lucas had pressed his thumbs against Damien's eyes and made him see the truth. Made him see the countless versions of himself. All of him warriors in their own way. Many of him dead. What few of him knew, though, was that he had the power to travel between the many worlds of existence.

Damien Banks was not bound by the rules of space and time.

And he needed to believe that now more than ever.

Only he, Harry, and Steph were left alive.

They were surrounded.

The enemy had torn through a hundred soldiers like canines

piercing soft flesh. Now they beat at the doors of the abandoned fire station they three of them had holed up in after fleeing the centre of Birmingham. England's second city was in ruins.

The demons were about to get in.

Harry threw Damien a half empty magazine. He caught it and slammed it into the SA80 he had become disturbingly familiar with. "Make it last, lad."

Damien nodded. If what Lucas showed him worked, he wouldn't need to make the ammunition last. If what Lucas had said was true, he could save all three of them.

"We can't hold out much longer," said Steph, popping shots from her own combat rifle. The big weapon shook her entire body with its recoil, but she held on tightly. "It was nice meeting you both."

"We've met before," said Damien, remembering memories not his own. Memories belonging to the other Damiens. The three of them were connected, the three points of a node. When they were together, they could open up a gate. Harry and Steph had no idea.

But Damien knew how. Lucas had put the knowledge in his head.

"Wanna get out of here?" he asked.

Harry looked at him sideways and chuckled. "God, if that were an option."

"Let's make it one." Before the other two could question him as to what he was doing, Damien dropped his weapon and grabbed both Steph and Harry by the back of their necks. He closed his eyes, grit his teeth. Concentrated.

"The fuck are you doing?" asked Harry.

Damien opened his eyes and saw his companions staring at him in confusion. They both shrugged out of his grasp and rubbed their necks.

"Are you okay?" Steph asked, she looked out the window at the demon horde about to break in. "Stupid question, huh?"

Damien shook his head. "No, no, this is wrong. He showed me!"

Harry frowned. "Who showed you what?"

"The Irishman."

Steph shook her head. "Who?"

Damien sighed. After Lucas had left, Harry and Steph lost all memory of the strange man. Only Damien remembered him. Maybe he had imagined the whole meeting. Perhaps he was crazy. Who could blame him? He counted money for a living, not bullets.

"I just... I thought... It should have worked."

Steph's eyes had gone wide. She must think him mad.

But then he realised she was staring past him at something behind. He spun around, expecting the enemy to pour in and devour them. Instead he saw something amazing. And terrifying.

"It's one of those gates," said Harry, fear and awe spiking his voice in equal measure. "We're fucked."

The glass windows of the fire station cracked and shattered. The demons begun to climb inside. "We were fucked anyway," said Steph. She shoved the last magazine into her magazine.

Damien reached out and pushed her rifle downwards. "You can't take it where we're going."

She huffed. "I suppose you're right."

"No, I mean, we're heading inside there."

Harry swore. "You must be mad, lad. Those gates lead right to Hell, I can promise you."

"They lead everywhere. Hell included."

The demons screeched at their backs, tearing across the large, concrete parking bay. The fire trucks had all gone out on calls, never to return.

Steph swallowed. "I don't see we have any option that doesn't suck."

"Exactly!" Damien grabbed both of their arms and yanked them towards the gate. The fact that they were so obviously in shock helped him. They didn't resist.

"I wonder how many other Damiens have done this?"

Steph and Harry both frowned at him, their mouths open as they stood inches from the gate.

Damien grunted. "Nevermind. Let's hope this leads us back to Kansas."

He dragged the three of them into the gate just as a surge of demons crashed into their backs. Damien cried out as he felt a talon slice through the tender skin of his lower back.

But then the pain gave way to searing blindness and an emptiness in his chest that threatened to make him implode. He heard nothing. Felt nothing. There was nothing.

For a moment he feared—despaired—that he had been misled, and that he had just thrown himself willingly into Oblivion. But then something struck his face and body and knocked the wind from him. The searing blindness faded away and reality returned. He heard breathing either side of him. and when he reached out he felt warm bodies. Steph and Harry.

Sound returned too, but Damien's muddled brain could not decipher it. He clawed at the ground beneath him and felt mud. He pulled at clumps of grass and tested the parts of his body he needed. His legs worked, and he put them to use, climbing slowly to his feet.

Harry and Steph stood too, both of them pale and shocked. They could puke at any moment. He had to take responsibility for this. Only he knew what they had just done. They had leapt through existence. Grabbed onto God's life force itself via the gate and used it to travel across a great tapestry.

To here…

Where was here?

"Where the fuck did you just come from?"

Damien and his friends spun around in fright. An entire army met them—an equal mix of soldiers and civilians. An aging woman, not without good looks, stood at the front of the pack. Rifles and shotguns pricked up behind her like porcupine quills. She spoke with an American accent.

Damien stammered. "We… I… It would take a long time to explain. Is… is this Kansas?"

The woman frowned. "No, this is Indiana. We are the Hoosier Resistance."

Damien rubbed at his aching jaw and wiped away mud. "Indiana, huh? Close enough, I suppose."

"You came out of a gate," said the woman, looking at all three of them. "Are you…"

"We're not demons," said Steph. "A gate appeared when we were about to be overwhelmed by the enemy. Jumping through it seemed like the only chance we had. We just popped out here. I... I actually can't believe it." She glanced at Damien, but he looked away.

No reason to explain that it was they who had opened the gate. Harry and Steph could learn that later. "We came from the United Kingdom," he said. "The gate spat us out here, but we don't know how it works. We're good guys, I promise."

"I'll be the judge of that." The woman looked at them a few moments longer, then thrust out a hand. "My name is Nancy Granger. My children are in England. Don't suppose you saw them, Alice and Kyle?"

Damien shook his head. "I'm sorry. Everything is a mess."

A lump moved through the woman's throat, betraying the fragility she was trying so hard to hide. "I know. I keep trying to reach someone in charge in London, but the place is a ruin by what I have pieced together. The demons are trying to exterminate us, but that's why were are here, together. If you want to join the Hoosiers, there are only two rules."

"What are those?" Harry asked, slowly gaining a hold of his confusion.

"Rule one is that you kill any demons on sight."

"Doable. And rule two?"

The woman grinned. "Misbehave and I'll cut your nutsacks off." She glanced at Steph. "Or your tits."

The three of them looked at each other with a chill running down their spines, but they wasted no time in agreeing to the woman's terms. Harry even saluted her.

"I'm not a soldier, sir, so no need for that. I'm just a woman who decided to stop sitting back and letting idiots make bad decisions. My husband, Clark, and I were being corralled at a school like cattle, until a riot broke out and the soldiers left us to kill one another. Those who stayed to help are among us now. After the fight died down, I managed to talk some sense into people. Didn't take long for them to realise that there is only one good place to direct their anger."

Damien nodded. "The demons?"

"Yes. Just wish they could have realised it before my husband was killed in the murderous chaos. God bless his soul. But those days are behind us. We move forward. No one is in charge here. We work together as fellow human beings. We fight for one another against an enemy that wants us all dead. America was built on the defiance of it's people. We will not be ruled. We will not bend or break. This is the crossroads of America, and what we do here will determine our future. Do you have any idea how important we all are? Every one of us left?"

Damien thought about what Lucas had told him about being a totem. A walker of worlds. "Yes, I agree. We are important. Let's fight for the future."

"Can you do that as a Brit? Can your fight for the American flag?"

Harry and Steph nodded, but Damien shook his head. "No."

The woman bristled.

Damien explained. "But I can fight for humanity's flag. Will that do?"

Nancy exhaled slowly, her jaws locked together. Eventually she nodded. "I suppose that will do just fine. Welcome to the Resistance, friends."

"Glad to be here," said Harry, looking at Damien with a hint of suspicion. It wouldn't be long before they would all need to sit down and have a big long talk about the nature of the universe. And all the worlds in it.

WANT FREE BOOKS?

Don't miss out on your FREE Iain Rob Wright horror starter pack. Five free bestselling horror novels sent straight to your inbox. No strings attached.

For more information just visit this page:
www.iainrobwright.com/free-starter-pack/

In addition, you can also save money by purchasing my books in extra-value box sets. Grab yours now.

Boxset 1
Sam, ASBO, The Final Winter, The Housemates, Sea Sick

Boxset 2
Ravage, Savage, Animal Kingdom, The Picture Frame, 2389, The Peeling Omnibus, Slasher, Soft Target, A-Z of Horror Vol 1

PLEA FROM THE AUTHOR

Hey, Reader. So you got to the end of my book. I hope that means you enjoyed it. Whether or not you did, I would just like to thank you for giving me your valuable time to try and entertain you. I am truly blessed to have such a fulfilling job, but I only have that job because of people like you; people kind enough to give my books a chance and spend their hard-earned money buying them. For that I am eternally grateful.

If you would like to find out more about my other books then please visit my website for full details. You can find it at:

www.iainrobwright.com.

Also feel free to contact me on Facebook, Twitter, or email (all details on the website), as I would love to hear from you.

If you enjoyed this book and would like to help, then you could think about leaving a review on Amazon, Goodreads, or anywhere else that readers visit. The most important part of how well a book sells is how many positive reviews it has, so if you leave me one then you are directly helping me to continue on this journey as a fulltime writer. Thanks in advance to anyone who does. It means a lot.

Iain Rob Wright is one of the UK's most successful horror and suspense writers, with novels including the critically acclaimed, THE FINAL WINTER; the disturbing bestseller, ASBO; and the wicked screamfest, THE HOUSEMATES.

His work is currently being adapted for graphic novels, audio books, and foreign audiences. He is an active member of the Horror Writer Association and a massive animal lover.

www.iainrobwright.com
FEAR ON EVERY PAGE

For more information

www.iainrobwright.com
iain.robert.wright@hotmail.co.uk

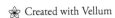

Made in the USA
Lexington, KY
23 November 2018